Wicked Words 10
The Best of Wicked Words

Other Black Lace short story collections:

Wicked Words
More Wicked Words
Wicked Words 3
Wicked Words 4
Wicked Words 5
Wicked Words 6
Wicked Words 7
Wicked Words 8
Wicked Words 9

Wicked Words 10
The Best of Wicked Words
Edited by Kerri Sharp

BLACK LACE

Black Lace books contain sexual fantasies.
In real life, always practise safe sex.

This collection first published in 2004 by
Black Lace
Thames Wharf Studios
Rainville Road
London W6 9HA

Reprinted 2005, 2006, 2007

Typeset by SetSystems Limited, Saffron Walden, Essex
Printed and bound by Mackays of Chatham PLC

ISBN 97 8 0 352 33893 8

Contents

Introduction and Newsletter

I always knew that compiling *The Best of Wicked Words* was going to be tricky, but I didn't realise how tricky until I was faced with the daunting task of choosing 17 stories from almost 200. We think the series has got better with each anthology – but we didn't want to limit the selection to stories from the past couple of books. Instead, we went for the imperative of there being something intrinsically, naughtily wicked about each of the stories, or that we were unable to exclude them because they were just so darned well-written. Either way, there sure is a whole bunch of bad girls in this book! They're either seducing their doctors, brewing their own booze and attracting the attention of the law – as in *The Bad Girl*, or they're disarming their tax auditor with expenses claims for sex toys – as in *The Last Deduction* – and using them to best effect.

There's some very horny behaviour going on down in the woods during army exercises in *Outmanoeuvred*, and some sizzling-hot repressed passions in Bible-belt America in *Saving Julie*. One very respectable lady plays games of exhibitionism and voyeurism in the shopping mall toilets in *Public Washrooms, Private Pleasures*, while a young witch sticks to her pagan roots in *Wytch-finder*. This eclectic compilation includes the inner-city feistiness of LaToya Thomas's *Bad Gal* but gives equal space to Astrid Fox's *Scratch* – which transports us back to the days of the Vikings, and the seduction of a young monk by a Scandinavian heathen priestess.

Special mention goes to Mathilde Madden, whose

stunning stories *You Spoil Me* and *Wheels on Fire* go bravely into the darker areas of the erotic imagination than most people are comfortable with but, with a writing style that is this eloquent, understated and mature, we are privileged to include two of this author's stories. Her first full-length Black Lace novel – *Peep Show* – is published in January 2005.

* * *

In this genre, style matters. Erotic characters should walk the talk, grab your attention from the first line of the story, and draw you in to their personality and their world. I'm proud to say that not one of these stories begins with a description of the weather or of someone waking up – a certain kiss of death for short stories as far this editor is concerned.

Erotica is the perfect genre in which to play with ideas about the dominant popular culture, overturning the expected behaviour with a sense of the sexy and unexpected. In this way, we are always looking for stories which are about more than just 'characters having sex'. The subtext of an erotic story should cleverly make comment about the modern power dynamics between men and women, as in Anna Clare's *Peaches* or the sexual tension between colleagues ... as in *Sex in the Office* – which will be our first themed collection of Wicked Words stories that will be appearing in February 2005. This is an exciting development to this amazingly successful series, so look out for that. Another piece of good news is that the first 8 books in the series are being reprinted with fabulous colourful new covers from August to November of 2004 so, if you are new to the series, you will be able to collect the set. I am sure that in years to come these will be collectors' items.

* * *

That's all for now. There is never space to mention all the stories but I'd like to say a big thanks to everyone whose story is included in this collection, and thanks to everyone who has contributed to all our volumes.

Salute!
Kerri Sharp
April 2004

We are always looking for talented new writers who know how to entertain and arouse their readers. If you think you could write for Black Lace please get hold of our guidelines by sending a large SAE to

Black Lace Guidelines
Virgin Books
Thames Wharf Studios
Rainville Road
London W6 9HA

If you are sending mail from the United States please bear in mind that only British stamps can be used for return postage. Alternatively you can read the guidelines at www.blacklace-books.co.uk

Bad Girl Mini Lee

He was middle-aged and had a crew-cut. I noticed him as he was passing through the neighbour's yard. Suspicious. He could be undercover. I watched him and saw him looking for a reason to be there and finally he walked towards the front street. He gazed intently at me, saying hello as he passed. He got into a white car. Had I seen him before?

In the empty lot behind the house was a police cruiser car. I noticed this when I went to my back yard. It gave me sudden shakes. I wouldn't be in touch with John today. Was it because of John, who regularly bought huge quantities of my home-made wine? The heat was on.

Before I reached the back door, I heard a car start up and drive off. I didn't dare look over. After a moment, when I did, the cruiser wasn't there any more.

I had two reasons for being nervous. I sold wine, which was against the law. Another concern was my penchant for masturbating in my private yard. Paranoid now, I went into my house and felt the place a testimony to my vices. I roamed nervously through the rooms, which seemed liked cages as my anxiety grew. Two rooms in particular possessed the all-too-hot fire of guilt, inhabited by liquor shelves and the sheer curtains where I've stood before, nude, at night. Touching myself.

Was it the fuzzola? Who was that man? My neighbour's boyfriend? I was unsettled all around. In my pit, I was already naked facing authority.

Who was that man today? He was ugly, in a way. Real crew-cut cop. White-haired, with a middle-aged paunch. He wasn't shy about his presence in the yard. The way he looked at me made me feel like he had something on me. I felt he knew everything about me. That I was a bad girl. That he would be back. Was he there right now, outside the house?

Poor naughty girl, had I no purer thoughts to contemplate? What was I to do? I had to do the deal with John, for bloody sakes. I was heavy in wine stock, I wanted to get it out of the house and I was waiting for him to pick it up and lighten his pocketbook.

Yes, I was a bad girl, and I knew it.

Nervous and titillated, I started to fantasise about showing my bare pussy to this man I'd seen, who'd so unsettled me and already possessed me; my cunt was his, the crew-cut man may have it. Just as my doctor did – he who knew all about my bad ways and habits.

Oh, I was a bad girl. Oh, what I've let my doctor do to me, what I'd like to let this bad man do to me. He could walk through the neighbour's yard and right into my garage, where he'd pinch my tits and finger me underneath my wet underwear. And it would hurt; it would feel marvellous. It would not be seen by anyone, but it would happen again and again, wetter and wetter, for I would feel him doing it to me when he wasn't even there. I wanted him to expose my bare breasts, squeeze my nipples, touch the bad girl.

My doctor touched my bare breasts every month. I liked a regular examination. He wanted to bring in a specialist sometime. I would co-operate. Just as I always did for him when we were alone. I remember my last appointment...

The doctor told me to undress and left the room. I put on the gown. I tried to tie the back, but it remained open like the curtains of the proscenium of my bare cheeks. Poor soft ass. I didn't want to think about my own nakedness right there. I couldn't let the doctor think I liked it, but ... What if I was wet for the examination? Oh God. I didn't want him to look at me. Because I fantasised about him, I felt dirty even though I washed and sprayed perfume earlier and everything.

He entered the room. He didn't look at me but told me to sit on the edge of the examination table. He wanted my feet up and tapped the heel rests on his examination table with his finger. As I got into position he pulled up my gown and reached under to guide my bare ass into place at the edge of the table. All the while, he stared relentlessly at my open pussy, not in the way a doctor properly should. He pushed my legs slowly apart and I felt my moist lips part, open, naked and waiting.

'Spread your legs apart as far as you can.'

I spread my thighs timidly and felt myself getting a little wet as I showed him more. He next lifted my gown all the way up my abdomen past my tits. I was fully naked up to my neck. He looked back down at my well-trimmed mound, my clit protruding. Then he eyed my breasts. He felt around the nipples. 'Any cysts?'

'No,' I said.

'How do you know?' he asked sternly.

'I don't, I guess.' There were butterflies in my stomach as he pinched my nipples.

'They can occur anywhere,' he said, squeezing hard. My nipples were erect and hard. 'Let's check under your arms.' He proceeded to do so, cupping both my breasts in his hands and fingering my armpits. He pressed down with his palms and moved his doctor's hands knowingly in a circle. He looked briefly for my reaction. I looked away and over again only to see his eyes travel down my torso to my opened legs.

'How's the wine-making?'

My pussy lips betrayed me as they swelled guiltily, and he moved away from my breasts, now intent on my lower nakedness. His eyes were fixed on my clit and I tried not to look at him. 'Spread more.' I could hardly part my legs any wider, but I tried, and my juices visibly oozed out of me. I caught a brief smile on his face.

'Are you drinking much of it?' he asked accusingly.

'Umm...' He slowly forced my legs further apart, so far that it hurt, and I groaned unwillingly.

'How much are you drinking?'

'Well, more than I should,' I answered, knowing his game, trying not to sound disturbed by what he was doing.

'You're selling most of it, aren't you?' His fingers rudely circled the wet lips of my pussy. I felt dirty and aroused. Suddenly he thrust a finger deep inside me. It hurt, his jabbing, but I deserved it and I loved it. I closed my legs on his hand and moaned in spite of myself.

'It's against the law, you know.'

I gasped and spread my legs again; he knew how to make me uneasy. I had once confided in him that I made a little extra money from homebrew. Since then, this irrationally made me feel sexually aroused, this confession of lawbreaking. Though I wished I'd never told him, he used it mercilessly against me. He pulled his finger out of my wet hole.

'It's all right.' He patted my clit. 'Did that hurt? I need you to relax now. Just tell the doctor everything.'

I remained silent and aroused as he slowly patted my sticky clit. The movement became a little more rapid. He looked at me, but I couldn't look back. He smiled and began to spank my pussy. Hard. It stung red hot. I tried to close my legs. He allowed me to at first but then pushed my knees to one side, exposing my bare ass, which he proceeded to spank several times, harder and harder. I turned to get away but was soon flat on my stomach.

'You are a dirty, bad girl. I could report you to the police.'

'I've stopped.'

'I don't believe you! You're going to make yourself sick with worry about getting caught. I'll take your temperature. Put your knees under you and raise your bum up for me, you bad, bad girl.'

I obeyed, shivering, my eyes wide with fear. He used my undammed pussy juices to moisten his thick thermometer. It was cold and smooth inside me.

'You're all wet.'

'I'm sorry.'

'No, you're not. Look at this.' He pulled on my cunt lips, separating them, elongating them. He fingered the wetness between the folds, moving the juices up to my asshole. Slowly, in and out, he worked the thermometer into my hole. I pulled away in shock, falling on to my belly whereupon I received many more sharp slaps to my naked ass. Following that indignity he made me tell him about how I was a bad girl, and what I did around my house. All the while he did many more shameful things to me, and he made me do things to him.

Perhaps my doctor had told the police all about me and they were watching my house now. Hence the crew-topped man. Was he a friend of the doctor's? All I knew was I'd best call off the deal with John tonight.

What kind of life was I leading? I was married, respectable . . . I needed to lie down. I was feeling shaky. I got into bed and lay still, feeling warmer, safer. Peter would be home shortly. I could rest for a moment and not think about anything.

But I did think. I fantasised about the man I saw in the neighbour's yard. I thought about him confronting me because he knew of my underground business affairs. Or perhaps he'd seen me touching myself in the yard. In my bed, I felt my heart beat fast and my clit fill so that it was fat with arousal.

I envisioned the scene from under my covers. I moved my hand down and inside my panties. I was already slick wet thinking of him coming through the back gate of my yard, looking for me wearing my short skirt on a hot summer's day. In my private yard, I have never minded that, when I leaned over, anyone could see I had no panties on. Perhaps the crew-cut man had already seen my pussy. I pushed off my bedcovers and felt my clit, erect as a small penis.

What if this man came back to punish the bad girl? What if he found me in my yard, when I had a short skirt on and no panties? I started to tell myself a bedtime story.

I could see myself bending over, exposing my naked pussy to the sun. But I heard the gate open and close around the corner. I nervously straightened up. I cast my eyes in the direction of the gate, but no one appeared. I continued my garden work, bending over again. My naked bush was in full view, out in the sunshine; I had an open, warm, wet pussy. With my ass, I reached up to the sun, moaning as loudly as a bad girl should. Like an echo, I heard the moan again. But it wasn't me.

The man with the crew-cut was standing a few feet away. He had seen what I was now attempting to hide, my naked pussy. I rose, embarrassed. He was looking at me without expression.

He said, 'Excuse me, miss.' He approached, looking me over.

'Can I help you?' I asked tersely.

'I have a search warrant,' he announced as he drew nearer.

'For what?'

'For bootlegging and for what I just saw you do, dirty, bad girl. Shall we go inside?' He roughly took my wrist and drew me close to him. 'Get in the house.' He held me with his hungry eyes. He looked at my breasts inside my flimsy shirt. My nipples were erect and I had no bra on to conceal them. He started to gently caress my ass under my skirt, feeling its shape. The doctor must have sent him. The policeman knew I might be in for trouble, in trouble with him, with the law.

'I have nothing to hide,' I said with a nervous voice.

'Where are your panties then?' He lifted my skirt slightly and poked my bare pussy with his finger. The bad girl was all wet. I pulled away, but he still held me by the wrist. 'Let's go inside and see.'

As he led me towards the house I was shaking like a leaf. What if he found my stash? The wind lifted my skirt to expose my naked ass cheeks, or was it him?

A long bursting orgasm moved me in my bed. Just then the door sounded below and Peter arrived home. I dried my soaking wet cunt with a tissue. After I washed my hands, I'd make dinner, I thought. I'd got him out of my system and I hoped I would never see or think about the white-haired, crew-cut man again.

Later that night, needing more release yet from my day, I had little sleep. I wondered if the crew-cut man was going to spank me sometime. My husband snored beside me.

I was tired the next morning. All when I had so much to do. I had put off tending the garden this spring and seedlings wanted to be planted. The sun was going to be hot on the south side of the house; I would wear shorts, or a short, wide skirt, perhaps with no underwear. I could feel the breeze already. It would be great. The prospect roused my energy for the chore when I was so weary. I dressed and I chose a shorter skirt than planned and went out into the garden. I lit a cigarette and let the feeling of my daring and vulnerability creep over me. My energy rose quickly. The bedding plants were over on the garden table and ready. Without hesitation, I set to the task. I was aroused by the way the breeze played with my skirt; it excited me. I remember how I had told the doctor what I sometimes did; it made me feel like I was a bad girl. I was faced with a feeling of concern for what I'd told the doctor and a yearning for redemption for being a bad girl. Like the things he'd done to me on the examination table. I was feeling wet. I was feeling the breeze up my skirt. How much could be seen of my naked pussy?

Bending over in the garden was easy, my wide skirt provided ample movement. I wondered if I should go in and put on some underwear, but when I felt the warm sun touch my pussy lips, I enjoyed it too much to stop. It felt so good, healing, intense, deeply penetrating. I could have picked the gauze skirt, which was somewhat safer. It went lower, but still provided ample exposure and it was practically like ether. But since my yard was relatively private, I felt I could freely enjoy this pleasant sensation of my fully naked sex exposed to the sun. I briefly wondered what the doctor would say if I had a tanned cunny. I felt myself getting wet at the thought of his discovering it – the spankings I would get. I liked being a bad girl. I heard the gate open and I straightened up. Then there was no noise at all. I rose and listened carefully for a while. Finally, I went around the corner to look and see. There was nothing and the gate was closed. My heart was beating hard. I thought of the crew-cut man and neared the fence to look over and see if there was a police cruiser car parked there again. Nothing. I hid by the fence momentarily, feeling completely culpable with bootleg wine in my house and the wind playing games with my skirt. Enough paranoia. I was simply leading my life. I had nothing to regret, I was smart, resourceful. I crept back over to where I was working, wanting to get back to the job. I leaned over; there were so many trees, no one could see, I thought, and the sun was so warm and so sensual. I spread my full cunt to the sun. Mmm.

I sighed.

Then I heard a sigh. I straightened up immediately. Someone was close by. I felt my sex release fluids, wetting me mercilessly. I looked around. The man with the crew-cut was standing over by the elm tree. He looked at me without expression. I knew he'd seen me with my skirt up, seen my naked pussy. I was a bad girl caught. As he started towards me, he smiled and said, 'Good day, miss. I have a search warrant for these premises. Do you own this property?'

'For what do you search?' I asked innocently.

'For bootleg products,' he replied as he pulled out his official documents from his chest pocket. I reached for them and with one hand he took me by the wrist. 'Take a look.' He held them out for me with the other hand. As I tried to look, I felt his eyes looking at the hem of my skirt, which was blowing up a little in the wind. He slid the papers down into my shirt, pulling it down-wards, exposing my hard, dark nipples and he said, 'It looks like you're in trouble, little girl.' He cooed, 'You can't go around dressed like that.' I felt his dry hand brush under my skirt, touching the skin of my sun-warmed ass. I tried to pull away, but he held my wrist tighter.

'I have nothing to hide.'

'Where are your panties then?' He guided me to the back door of the house. The wind picked up, lifting my skirt, exposing my bare ass to the crew-cut man. Per-haps it was he who pulled up my skirt. I heard him groan as I opened the back door.

Once inside, the crew-cut man pushed me up the stairs. I fell forward along the steps, whereupon my skirt went up. I tried to scramble up, my thighs and ass nude and trembling. Then I felt several sharp slaps on my bare bum. 'Get up. Show me where you stand all naked at night.' I turned to him angrily.

'I wasn't expecting company; let me get dressed.'

'Just get up the stairs.' Then he pinched the inside of my leg, close to my wetness. I sprang up with a frightened gasp. He lost his grip on my arm and so pulled me down by the ankle. Angry now, he pushed my skirt fully up and spanked my bare ass again, harder and several times. I moaned and squirmed, but this only made his spanking harder. Finally I lay still and he stopped slapping me. My ass was hot and red and he felt it with his huge hand. 'You're all hot and red,' he laughed. I was wet and, when he slid his hand between my legs, I felt his fingers slippery along my twat. He groaned. So did I, helplessly. 'Get up,' he ordered. I climbed the steps while he kept hold of my arm. I stood in the middle of the kitchen, trembling. 'Is it in front of this window?' He pinched my nipple; it was erect and jutting through my shirt. I tried to back away. 'I've seen you, bad girl.' He pinched my other nipple and I turned away. I was breathing hard and so was he. I knew he would be able to do whatever he wanted, incarcerate me perhaps.

'What I do in my own home is my business,' I pleaded.

'I know everything that you do, I know where everything is,' he said, lifting my skirt, looking at my naked display. 'The doctor told me; he told me many things.'

'Are you a friend of Dr Nuds?' I felt my face go red as I pulled away.

'Oh, you're in a great deal of trouble, you know. Do you like trouble?' he asked.

'You're my trouble right now, sir.'

'Don't you know it.'

'Please? Please don't report me.'

'The bad girl will tell me the whole indecent story. Would she like to take me down the basement to her wine cellars? Bootlegging bad girl!' His hand slowly brushed over my breasts, lingering, dragging the tip of his finger across my right nipple.

'There's nothing in the basement.'

'The basement is where I will see everything,' he said menacingly. He reached from behind and turned me, holding me by my tits, directing me back to the stairs. He slid one hand between my legs as we went down the stairs, his finger poking into my pussy and my asshole.

As we reached the bottom of the steps, the boxes of wine were lined up along the wall. 'What's that? How much do you sell?' He pushed me towards them. I regained my footing and turned to face him.

'None,' I said. I slowly lifted my skirt to show him my nakedness, neatly trimmed by the doctor. All my folds were showing and wet.

'Bad girl!'

I parted my lips for him and I pulled up my shirt to show him my erect nipples. I made my nipples wet with my juices.

'You dirty girl.' He unzipped his pants and slowly pulled out his large erect cock. 'Here, suck it with your dirty mouth.' He neared me, massaging his hard cock with his hand. 'Kneel down.' His penis was hot and sweaty as he pressed my face into it. I took him into my mouth. 'You going to break the law?' he asked, thrusting himself deep inside my mouth. 'Hmm? You bad girl. I could put you in jail, you know.' He pumped his cock in and out of my mouth a few times. Then he withdrew it quickly. 'Take off your top.'

I looked up at him. 'Will you keep my secrets?'

'I can do whatever I want to, can't I?'

I drew in a quick breath, feeling myself involuntarily releasing juices. I wanted to pee and my clit was burning. I began to pull off my top.

'I have to pee.'

'That's good. Hold it, little tits.'

He was right: I had small firm breasts, but I knew my nipples were beautiful – small, dark and true to the touch. He pinched them. 'Show me the rest of your basement,' he urged, his cock wet against my upper thigh. I felt I was dripping, such a bad girl that I was. I led the way into the nether regions of the basement. The light was crude and bright around the washer and dryer. He pushed me up against my dryer, from behind. 'What do I do with you? You deserve more than a spanking.' I leaned forward against the dryer and my nipples got harder against the cold metal. He spanked me several times. Then he felt me from behind, sliding his fingers into me. It made such a noise, my wetness ... He transferred his attention to my asshole. Then he poked with insistent moist fingers. I moaned, feeling his cock near the hole, pressing to get in. Wet enough, he squeezed his hard cock into my asshole, his fingers reaching to pinch my clit at the same time. He pushed himself deep into me and then guided it into my pussy. I peed a little into his hand.

'Don't pee. Does the doctor do this to you? He told me all about it; he's my brother, you know.' He pulled out suddenly and flipped me over, lifting me by the pussy on to the dryer, whereupon he had me spread my legs wide. He licked my wet opening and then his tongue circled my clit in slow, wet strokes. 'Do you need to pee? Go pee.' His lips sucked on my clit. I peed in spurts all over his face, laughing. When I was finished, he looked up at me. 'A urine test, eh? You should see the doctor soon. We'd like to meet with you together, you know. And a bad girl like you, you'd better come to see us. Discuss your illegal and dangerous lifestyle.' He leaned on my naked sex with his hard cock, his mouth pressed against mine. He rammed it into me and leaned back again so he could squeeze my nipples. He drove his large hot cock in and out of my wet, wet, orgasming cunt. He watched me rub my exploding, convulsing clit with my finger.

'I'm a bad girl,' I whispered.

Marilyn's Frock Julie Savage

You know the Marilyn Monroe frock – *that* one, the *Seven-Year Itch* white one with the cross-over bodice that outlined her breasts and the pleated skirt that blew up and showed her pants? Well...

Once upon a time, I ... er ... in it.

Once upon a time, before you and I knew each other, I was a curator in a movie museum. One particular year, we were doing an exhibition of key clothes from the movies, particularly Hollywood classics. We had Bogart's cool white jacket from *Casablanca*, Celia Johnson's I'm-just-an-ordinary-housewife coat from *Brief Encounter*, a Busby Berkeley feathery headdress two foot high: you know the score. The exhibition was a big-budget number, as you can imagine: megabucks to borrow the costumes from the film studios, US costume and private collectors; big dosh to courier it all across the Atlantic; a fortune and a half for the insurance and additional security.

The pièce de résistance, the thing that would draw all the crowds and Sunday supplement photographers, was Marilyn's White Frock. And it was my baby. I'd wanted it. I'd fought for it. I'd got it.

The day it was due to arrive, off an American Airlines jet from LA, with a courier from the Hollywood Museum of Historic Costume, I could hardly breathe. I dressed up to meet the plane at Terminal One as reverently as if I'd been going to meet Marilyn herself. It felt like an honour much greater than being blessed by the Pope or touched up by the President or knighted by the Queen.

I wore my best toffee-coloured leather jeans, a golden brown chenille cut-off sweater and Versace tortoiseshell shades, even though it was only April. It worked well with my sleek blonde hair, sweet complexion and fuck-you walk.

And I stood at Heathrow arrivals waiting for the courier to come through, feeling as if I should be sur-rounded by a posse of guards with machine-guns, maybe even armoured cars, in case anyone hijacked The Dress. I'd barely given the courier a thought: just scrawled

Tim Morgenstern
Hollywood MHC

on a placard for him. Art couriers are usually anal fusspots or nonentities. As this guy was in dress history, he was bound to be gay. My job would just be to allay his anxieties, take possession of It and get him on the next plane back, pronto. Out of my hair.

I couldn't wait to get the frock in my clutches, to handle it, put it on the model, pose it. You'd be the same, wouldn't you? The loaners had of course issued the strictest of instructions about where it should be displayed: air temperature, humidity, distance from the public, proximity to light. But I wanted just an hour – well, six – alone with this wonderful frock.

But then this tall, lean, more-saturnine-than-James-Dean-type comes pacing in from Customs. He's sexy, he's all in black, he's got more style than most movie stars, he's distinctly masculine and he's heading towards me. With a big flat box being wheeled on the trolley next to him, all straps and buckles and reinforced corners.

'Dr Crammond?' You know what Californian accents do to my belly.

'*Alexia* Crammond ... Tim.' I find myself smiling so widely that the grin pushes my shades up a little. 'I hope you had a ... non-tedious flight?'

'I would have done if you'd been sat next to me.'

His smile goes straight to between my legs, just nipping over my nipples on the way down. With such a sock-it-to-me start, how audacious is the end of our contact going to be? I can't wait – as usual.

'Perhaps some post-flight compensation, then?' I murmur. 'Let me ...' I'm going to say, 'buy you a drink before you go back', and am wondering if I am being precipitate in trying to work out if we could possibly shag in my Frontera in the grey concrete gloom of the car-park, bay J8, when he announces, 'I'm staying for a few days actually ... I have a couple of buddies in Holland Park.'

'Are they meeting you?' I try not to show my disappointment and anxiety. Surely he won't be snatched out of my hands so soon.

'Actually not.'

'Then may I drive you to ...?'

'Your place.'

I swallow. The nerve of him. Never before has someone who attracts me been so keen on me in return. They usually take months of fishing for, don't they? Yet here is a man who I fancy more than anyone in years – and he is going for me. I know I look good, despite pre-exhibition panic. But I wonder what I have done to deserve what is surely going to be nine inches of the most stunning cock to cross the Atlantic that day.

'Unless you're anxious to get the dress settled in?' he taunts.

'What dress?' All I can think of is 'but I'm not wearing a dress, and how quickly could I get a dress off if I was ...' and what's this 'settled'? ... Then ... 'Oh, *that* dress, well ...'

I gulp. He's used the excuse of crowds of new arrivals pressing through to edge closer to me. Somehow his hand is at the small of my back, pressing those tiny indentations in the sacrum that vibrate like piano keys, sending different pitches of reverberation through my entire body. Jeez – this is surely going to be a winner. The kind of guy you want to spend at least a week in bed with.

'Your car?' he prompts me, smilingly aware that my brain, as well as my legs, have just turned to jelly.

'Er, over here,' I motion.

You can imagine how crap my driving is, on that journey back home to Islington. It isn't just his presence, and the thought of what might be. It isn't just that Marilyn Monroe, by proxy, is in the back of my motor. It is his hand on my thigh. And worse, it is the teasing bastard's determination to not let those adept fingers go any higher than halfway up, no matter how much I hopefully slide my leg around to edge his hand higher, nearer to my cunt.

'I'm gonna make you beg, baby,' he says maliciously, bending to take a bite of my left nipple as we stop at a Shepherd's Bush roundabout jam. I pull his hair, hard, and want to get violent-ish with him, now. Instead we both seethe, lasciviously. It's delightful.

Throughout the journey home, which takes an infuriating two hours, I only occasionally give a thought to 'Is the bed linen clean-ish, when did I last Hoover, have the cats pooed anywhere horrible?'

Everything is focused on the effect on my whole body that his practised fingers are having. That, and the growing bulge in his black jeans that I can see out of the corner of my eye, as we head through central London.

By the time I let him in the flat door my whole body is screaming so much with lust that I think I'll have to yell or else go insane. He goes ahead of me, shrugs off his shoulder bag and puts the frock box down in the hall.

Marilyn's frock in my hall! For a minute the thought overwhelms me, then I turn back to look at him. I expect an embrace, our first kiss, to involve me being yanked towards him forcefully. No, there he is, Mr Cool-as-a-Cucumber man, looking round the flat. Looking at books, my bloody books, for God's sake! You can imagine how irrelevant that seems at this point.

'Tim . . . ?'

'Dr Crammond?' he smiles.

'Come and fuck me rotten.'

'Mmm . . . could do.'

'Hey!' I walk up to him and begin easing off his jacket. Should I play lady hostess and be concerned about his jet lag, offer him facilities for a nap, a hot drink? Nah, I want his dick, and fast.

He pulls me down on the couch and starts kissing me. His hair smells of a shampoo brand I don't know and his tongue is long and practised. It matches his fingers, which by now have got the measure of my bra-lessness, the buckle on my trousers, and the towering state of my nipples.

'Oh, let's fuck,' I groan.

'All in good time, lady.'

He stands up and starts to undress. First the soft slightly Angora black sweater. His chest is lean and the dark hair runs down it in a central line, waving out into two thin horizontals under his breasts. It looks like he works out a bit, and his golden skin is certainly a tribute to the California sun. He shimmies his crotch at me and I lean forward to breathe on it, grabbing his buttocks to pull him closer to my face. Then I ease up on the sofa arm, legs apart, and jam one of his legs between mine, up against my fanny.

'Bloody couriers. They should do as they're told,' I growl.

'Damned customers. They should be grateful for small mercies ... Except, I've only got a big mercy to give you.' He cradles his bump at me. I can't wait to find out the exact truth of this, but he breaks away.

'Oh no, what are you doing?' I gasp.

'I've got ... a little ... idea.'

'I thought we'd both got a big one,' I complain.

'The frock.' He walks over to the box with Marilyn's frock in it.

'You want her to watch us?' I ask, as he props the brown official-looking box upright on one of my yellow, much kissed-upon, armchairs.

'Better than that.'

'What then?' I'm mystified.

'You'll see. Get it out.'

'I can't. Not in my grubby little flat. It's Marilyn's, it's God's, it's sacrosanct,' I burble.

'Undo that box.'

'Christ!' But I get up – stiffly, because my sex is so sensitive, and go over to the box.

My clit is pressing so hard against all constraint that I have to take off my trousers. I do it so functionally that I forget that it might turn Tim on. And as I turn to address the box I sense him come up behind me. The heat of his hands is near to my thighs and on each side of my slender hips. As I bend over the box to undo the first of the many leather straps, he slides his hands up my jumper and presses his naked chest against my back as his fingers reach round to cup my breasts.

'Oh, those titties,' he sighs. They feel wonderful in his hands, like golden syrup puddings made of compressed hot buttercup petals, each one pulsating with life. I lean back against his chest and arch my spine, the better to stick out my breasts for him. The frock is forgotten even though the impress of the heavy steel buckles is still on my fingers.

'Ooh, baby!' He takes the weight of my breasts fully in his palms. And immediately I come. I come. Not with a shudder but just a gush. It's as sharp as if I've weed myself. And I feel wonderful.

'Oh baby,' he says again, moving a hand down to my wet fanny, cupping my mound through my saturated moss-green lace knickers.

I am helpless for a minute, and shocked at what has just happened. It has never, ever been like this before. I take in the smell of him, the remnants of a horse chestnutty kind of shower gel, some deodorant like the sea, aftershave a bit lemony.

He's tender, in the sunshine that comes in through the sitting-room window and lights us up. He understands that for a minute I am defenceless girl, not capable woman. He hums to me and rocks me a little, my back still to his front, as we gaze at the big brown still-trussed box.

'Think what it's going to be like later,' he murmurs, 'if we're like this together now.'

'How long can you stay?'

'As long as it takes, Alexia.'

'That could be a very long time.'

'So be it.'

I need to sit down, I am still so shaken by that unexpected coming. I totter to the sofa and he says, 'Shall I open the frock box?'

'Actually, I'd rather have a cup of tea,' I confess, 'before I cope with anything else.'

He smiles. 'The English. Well, it is tea-time I guess –' he looks at his watch – 'somewhere in the world.'

'Will you make it for me . . . us?'

'Sure.' He goes into the kitchen and finds his way

around competently, as I knew he would, while I just tremble on the sofa in my wet pants and rumpled sweater, gazing at the frock box.

'Ms Monroe, darlin', what have you brought me?' I breathe. If this is what it's like for starters what state am I going to end up in?

The container full of white folds that once encased her sits silently, of course.

I sprawl there, huge gusty sighs coming from me. God, this is likely to be a marathon – it could mean days off work. And I can't wait for it to re-start.

The mobile rings. Stuff it, it will be Evalinda, my secretary, wondering if I'd had any problems with Customs. Well, I am no more prepared to speak to anyone about duty than I am to take a slow boat to Alaska. What I have on hand – or rather, what I am going to have in my hands and between my legs – is far too important. Let them wait.

Tim, bouncy with pre-jet lag adrenalin, comes back in with a tray and turns my cup handle towards me.

'Ready for a bit more?' He grins.

'Getting there. Slowly...' and then he puts his hand on my right breast. Immediately it surges into his palm. 'Well, maybe faster than I thought,' I groan. 'Clear off, for a minute. I need my tea or I'm going to die.'

Smiling he takes his tea over to the window seat and begins crooning, 'The way she ... sips her tea ... can't take ... away from me.'

'It's a great frock, you know.'

'I know.' I sip my tea and think that 'gratefully' is actually a good way to describe the way I am drinking it. If sex with him is like this already then surely I am going to need gallons of brandy to help me recover from all Tim is going to do to me later.

'I guess we could say it's probably the greatest dress of all time,' he muses.

'I don't know. Maybe it wouldn't have been without the air blowing it up, and her holding it down. It was her in it, and the gush from the air vent, as well. The three factors make it great.'

'You know, it was her idea to stand over the air vent. She posed it herself. The photographer had been shooting for a while and not getting it quite right, when she started larking about and tried that pose.'

'Brilliant.'

'Did you fancy her in it?' he asks.

I hadn't thought. Maybe I'd wanted to *be* her, in that frock. But to *fuck* her ... no, it is more that I want to just join in that fun, of playing with our dresses blowing up.

'Maybe I'd have liked to be there with her, giggling, fighting the draught,' I reply.

'Don't you just want to put your hand inside those white panties?'

'Yes, a bit. But more to slide it inside the folds of that bodice and find her breasts all tight inside a white lace bra, and pinch her nipples and make her squeal ... And I suppose, yes, then I'd like to ease my hand into her knickers and see if it had made her wet.'

He begins unbuckling his trousers as he sprawls in the chair, rubbing the mound from left to right. 'I want you.'

I smile. 'You want me and Marilyn, both going down on you?' I smirk.

'Yeah, all right.'

'You want her to climb astride you, in that dress, only this time without any drawers on. To climb astride you, and pull that bodice down and stick those glorious tits in your face for you to suck and then ease down on your big long prick and say ...'

'"Fuck me baby, only me, fuck me like you'll never let me go."'

'You like clingy women?' I am shocked.

'It'd be an honour to be clung to by her.'

Talking him through it has made me horny. *I* long to climb on top of him, thrust *my* breasts into his mouth, have him groan as *I* ease *my* wet fanny down onto what I hope will be a long, thick, dark and eager dick.

He is watching me, and knows it.

'Can you take all I've got, baby?' he drawls.

'Come here and prove you've got it,' I tease. 'Unbundle that kit and let me take a look-see.' I lick my lips. I don't just want to look, I want to touch, and taste and bite and absorb every single bit of it.

He slouches over to me, unbuttoning his jeans slowly, the belt falling away. He draws his cock out of his jet black underpants and I can't help but groan with pleasure. It *is* big. It is dark. And it looks every bit as juicy as I had hoped. And I love the way his curly hair clusters round his balls, thinly enough so that I can see the skin on his groin. I reach out to touch.

'No, I'm going to do it in that frock.'

'What? Tim! You're mad. That's thousands of dollars' worth of frock. It's practically a holy relic!'

'You heard. I'm going to fuck you like there's no tomorrow, but in that frock.'

'You'll … we'll … ruin it.'

'No we won't. Anyway, Marilyn would like it. It's a good use. Better than having it lie mouldering in some upgraded Beverley Hills thrift shop.'

I look at him. He's right. And so adoring that I can hardly believe it.

'Can you get into it, Tim?'

'Yes, just about. I just don't have the right bits to fill it out.' He gestures towards his chest and begins putting it on. I sniff and wonder if there is any scent of Marilyn still left on it. If walls retain memories of what's happened within them, then do clothes too?

Suppose she fucked the President in this? Am I going to feel like JFK or Marilyn screwing JFK? Will I now start to sort-of know what it felt like to be Monica Lewinsky?

'Do you have an electric fan?' Tim asks.

'As a matter of fact, I do.' My eyes gleam. Jeez, this is going to be so saucy.

First I help him on with the frock, as carefully and thoroughly as if I was Marilyn's devoted theatre dresser, or a cardinal helping the Pope on with his most sacred vestments. Tim smoothes it over himself, turning and admiring his flat chest within that bodice, his hard buttocks beneath those skirts. While he is looking in the mirror I go and get the fan heater, hoping its airflow will be powerful enough.

'Put it on the floor, here,' he commands.

Switching the controls to 'warm' I lay it on the carpet near the fireplace, where there is lots of room. On it goes. The air whooshes out. I stand in the electric breeze, letting my hair blow awry, deliberately with my back to Tim to tantalise myself.

Then, on a whim, I lie down next to it. That way I can do what I and half the world have always wanted to do: look up Marilyn's frock.

The skirts billow out well in the air stream, just as in the photo. It's a turn-on, rather than ridiculous, to see that dark erect dick beneath the snowy, girly skirts. I groan as I see that nude powerful shaft that is going to be for me, in a minute, lurking there where Marilyn's clean white pants had been, covering a pussy that had been penetrated by a President.

Tim places his legs astride me. Dancing, crooning a Marilyn number about wanting to be loved by you alone, boo-boopey-doop, he lines his cock up with my eyeview.

I am overwhelmed. Marilyn's frock, in my living

room! And in a minute I am going to have it next to my skin. Her dress is going to be crushed against the sexiest man I've seen in years.

It is almost scary. I reach down to myself for consolation, slipping my fingers inside the sodden moss-green knickers. But instead of comforting myself I find that I am turning myself on, and so fast that I can barely see the frock or Tim's dick. It is a blur. Suddenly I feel the frock brushing my face.

'I wish you were wearing her white knickers,' I groan.

'I could wear yours,' he offers.

I yank mine off and hand them up to him. It almost feels like making an offering to a priest, to put on the plate and be offered up to God. My knickers where Marilyn's should have been. My green pants next to that white frock. My drawers over the place where her backside would have been. I just can't believe it.

'Tim, fuck me,' I beg.

'On the chair.'

He gathers up his frock. Then, sitting back in my ordinary chair, just off ordinary seedy-groovy Upper Street, he folds up the skirts of the most-fantasised over dress in the world so that I can sit astride him.

And slowly, as Marilyn might have done, I breathe 'Shaft me like there's no tomorrow,' and lower myself down till my hot wet frills are just touching the tip of his dick.

The famous frock brushes against my legs. He reaches up and strokes my lower back.

'Come to me, baby,' he croons.

And I come to him, and come all over him, many thousands of times, sometimes sliding my hand into Marilyn's bodice so I can feel his nipples, sometimes just stroking that frock, and his legs in it, so sinewy against its soft fabric.

'Oh, Marilyn, oh, Tim.'

'Oh, Alexia, oh, Marilyn,' he murmurs.

And that is the story of why, if you see that frock in the Hollywood Museum of Historic Costume today, you may well see a slight blemish on the left of the skirt. It's my come, where it shot out at some point during those manic hours. Try as we might, afterwards, we two museum professionals, we semi-experts in textile conservation techniques, couldn't get that stain out, in that kitchen in Islington.

Which is why there were insurance problems. And why Tim had to sweet-talk – or sweet-a-bit-more-than-just-talk – Lorna, his director in LA, into accepting that accidents do happen if you do – ah – this. Like – ah – ah – ah Tim – this – this!

And surely, Marilyn would quite understand that this is a frock to orgasm in. That this is the most comed-over frock in the world.

Scratch Astrid Fox

Imagine, if you will, a tree. A tree more enormous than the world itself; a tree which itself holds the earth within its scope. The green sweeps of the tree's branches arch out from its trunk like plumage, and the jade-blushed feathers of the leaves are impenetrable and thick, exposing little of the undergrowth. But among the depths of these same leaves, and along these same branches, stride various creatures, initially familiar but strangely equal in size: a stag nibbling at the foliage; a huge squirrel poised on a hidden limb; a vast glittering hawk whose wingspan takes in the breadth of a thousand villages. Beast and fowl alike might be colossal, but they are also dwarfed in the great emerald cloud of the mythic tree's foliage. Below its dense greenery the trunk curves down, a huge astral trunk of crumbling bark and layer upon layer of new growth, dead wood, new growth, dead wood ... The tree shifts, changes, retreats: the process is endless; the tree is eternal.

Down goes the trunk, down through the constellations and the firmaments, past the gods' abode, all the way down to the world itself, set high above the roots of this Yggdrasil Tree, roots whose base is still watered by the tears of three crones. Yes, the world itself is set high: a world of ice-bright seas and lands of blood and soil, of stench and sex, and a world bound tight by the coils of a great serpent, whose constricting hold squeezes and shakes the very seas on which the priestess's boat now topples, a hold that jars and shudders the invading Viking ship in a shower of foam and dirty brine. With salt water clogging her throat, the priestess prays to the Red Thor to stop the storm, to ease his hammer between the snake's tight spirals, spirals held fast by daggers of its own teeth. With her knife, she scratches a rune into the oak of the ship. At last, there is success. Her words and her carved invocation coax the worm's great fangs to loosen, and all is calm again.

The men are grateful, but no one speaks to the priestess for the next few days of the journey.

They sail for another three and a half days and when they reach the coast the stink from the vessel is terrible. But clear skies hasten the last leg of the journey into the island, and spirits are high. Adrenalin is in the air, too, as the sailors morph into warriors ready to pillage, rape and burn.

The men have avoided the priestess, as much as they have been able to in a cramped ship where a person can scarcely take a breath without inhaling someone's beard. Still, she has kept to herself down by the far end of the prow and, apart from making the usual enquiries as to weather and luck of the battle, the men too have tried their best to keep their distance.

She is a strange woman, and there is no denying that. She admits it herself. The priestess Veleda enjoys her reputation.

In this Year of Our Lord 793, the young monk Cuthbert guards over the incorrupt body of the Sainted Cuthbert, after whom he has been named. His hands riddle over a rosary made of the small white rocks the sea spews up. Each of these stones looks like a bone-hard tiny sea-creature. Each resembles the Holy Rood itself, each is a little crucifix bead spat out from the sea that surrounds the Holy Island. Already pilgrims take the stones away after they have visited the incorrupted body which young Cuthbert tends. Already the stones are known as Cuthbert's Beads, after the saint whose name this seventeen-year-old has the privilege of using.

In this summer month of June, there have been flashes across the heavens of Lindisfarne, great streaming lights across the sky, portents of fire and dragons and trauma. The other monks on the Holy Island are uneasy in the evenings as they whisper to each other after vespers, but throughout the early summer while the other brothers worry, young Cuthbert sneaks off to his cell and strokes himself with pleasure, the comets roaring outside the groove of his window while his fist is on his cock, and he strokes and pulls and gasps and thinks of evil flesh, of men and women, of the smell of his own juice in his hand. He licks his lips, eases his hand along himself and dreams of soft bodies and hard sinews. Then the pulse comes, and he shudders with a terrible enjoyment; he grunts in satisfaction then cries out as his sin shoots out into his fist, liquid and sexual. The comets still tear through the twilight heavens, and Cuthbert hopes then that the other monks have not overheard his efforts.

He knows these self-ministrations are wrong. He knows these thoughts and actions both are evil.

The fighting has quieted, and Cuthbert still waits in his hiding place in the cellar where he has been sobbing silently since darkness fell. He has heard the slaughter above, and he has caught just a glimpse of the yellow-bearded warriors who had landed their boats on the shore and then attacked with such force. The smell of smoke indicates that they might have set fire to the living quarters and they have taken all the holy icons and gold in the church where he is now hiding, but by some miracle have left the holiest item of the monastery untouched: the incorrupt body of the saint.

In his cellar, young Cuthbert spits. These pagans cannot see the true value of sanctity; they see only the glitter of silver and gold. They do not see God's worth. But then Cuthbert censures himself: of course, it is a blessing that the pagans did not take the abbey's most valuable treasure. There is Our Lord's hand in this, somehow.

Though not young Cuthbert's, because his hand had been elsewhere; he had done nothing to prevent the ransacking of the chapel. Instead he had watched through a crack in the cellar beneath the shrine as the filthy warriors had laughed at the saint's body when they had seen it was only a corpse, and one of them had even reached up and shoved it. Most had seemed hesitant to touch it further, however, and Cuthbert had seen through the crack how the blasphemers had busied themselves with the gathering of silver chalices and golden plates and pewter candlesticks instead, and his heart had boiled in wrath. And then, worst of all, Cuthbert had watched as he saw a female heathen come forth from amongst all the filthy savages, a sorceress of some sort, and saw how she marked the wooden base of the holy shrine itself with a knife, making some sort of devil's symbol, which Cuthbert, because of the angle of his hiding place, could not make out. A female, a most evil Eve, in God's own house, defiling the shrine of a saint!

And now Cuthbert shivers in the cellar in which he has hidden since the attack, for he had been attending to his own dirty lusts in his cell when he heard the first shouts, and had just spent himself in a profane orgasm when, in a surge of deep guilt, he had left his living chamber and had run to the chapel which held the saint's body over which he was supposed to be keeping watch; he had run like a coward, and then, as he had sneaked by the butchery, seeing how the other monks had been slain or raped and bound as slaves, he had crept below the church by an old tunnel he had once discovered, and there it was that he had witnessed the great plunder of God's own riches. Now Cuthbert closes his eyes and shudders. That someone could steal from God Himself! What particular penalties of Gehenna await these murderers, he cannot imagine. Surely a worse hell than the normal one, for the theft of God's possessions is far worse than the theft of those of mere mortals!

Still, Cuthbert can not at the moment fathom a hell worse than the situation in which he now finds himself. Brother Abelard was slain as well as Brother Joseph, and young Brother Jonas, whom Cuthbert had always secretly admired, had been bound up by rope with twenty or so of the other monks, heading towards some evil heathen slavery ...

But now Cuthbert's breath catches, because he sees the sorceress entering the chapel once more. Anger swills up in him as he watches her light the candles of the church – candles which have been discarded on the ground after their holders were stolen. The sorceress pays no attention to protocol, so she does not care that the wax will now drip and tarnish the holy floor; she rights the pale-blue candles and anoints them with fire anyway, so that soon the whole church is glowing with flame. But it is wrong, so wrong, Cuthbert thinks, because what wicked heathen ritual will now be performed?

There is some terrible devil's magic at work here, because though Cuthbert should hate the very sight of the Jezebel, instead he discovers that he does not – worse, the sight of her inflames him with the very passion that is his secret guilt every evening in his cell. Her flaxen hair seems air-light and sensuous, her lips seem to moisten even as he stares at them, and there is the evil flush of sorcery to her cheeks and her bosom, a flush that makes his chest grow tight. Beneath his robes, he is stiffening at the sight of her. And now, as she bends over to light another candle, a slim tapered candle blue as the sky itself, he can see the sway and jiggle of her unbound breasts, promising a Satan's lushness of silky skin, promising the satiny feel of carnal satisfaction with another human that Cuthbert himself has never yet experienced. Cuthbert's mouth has gone dry, and his heart is pounding.

With a stick dipped in God knows what substance, the sorceress marks a symbol on the floor of the chapel, and this time Cuthbert can make out the stick-like figure. It is no symbol with which he is familiar. He begins to shake. She has lit what seems like a hundred candles, and there is a hellish glow in the chapel now. Cuthbert has never been more frightened in his life.

Yet also his blood is rushing through his veins, making him rigid and urgent with need. He runs his fingers over the white beads of the rosary strung round his neck, but his hands are shaking – he wants to touch himself, but to do so in this profane way, under these profane circumstances, under the very shrine of St Cuthbert, is surely a mortal sin. Perhaps it would be justified if in some way he could match the profanity of the spell the northern whore now was weaving. He could desecrate her religion, and by his action then redeem his own.

Candlelight floods in through the crack in the floor of the chapel and quietly, quietly, Cuthbert scratches out a replication of the sorceress's symbol in the dirt with his index finger, upturning the rich dark loam of the cellar so that the rune stands out in relief like a brand. He moves feverishly, his hand cramping, desperate now to fulfil the invocation, to tarnish the sorceress's own spell. But now he is too full of his own need; he grips his hand round his cock and pushes his fist up and down on himself, as desperate to come as he is desperate to finish this spell of desecration. It is the Jezebel's fault; it is this sun-haired Jezebel who has tempted him like a succubus, tempted him in her whorish manner with her heathen magic.

He feels dirty and unclean, as dirty as a woman, as a shameful daughter of Eve, and it makes him masturbate harder, poison and lust swilling up to the tip of his stalk. He has to rid himself of sin. He has to force it out. He looks through the crack at her wet, sly lips and her long white throat and he screws his eyes shut. He wants to come all over that throat, spew over it in a rain of sinful, hot seed. He can feel lust rushing through him now, tight and urgent, like an itch. The whore. The – sluttish – vixen. How – dare – she – tempt – him – like – that. In his mind, he sees her neck and chest covered with his emissions and this makes him even harder, and he jerks more forcefully at himself.

'Deliver me, O my Lord,' he prays, as the evidence of his temptation bursts out onto the ground in a cool white spurt, over the devil's rune that he had torn into the ground with his own fingernails. And what did it matter? Let sin lie with sin. He feels better now. Clean. Purified. Deep in the cellar, under the altar, young Cuthbert sighs and kicks dirt over the rune, as if he'd never drawn it at all.

The warriors have done their work, and now it is up to Veleda the priestess to ensure the continued success of the raid, for these warriors have never come across such easy pickings before. Not only was the settlement rich beyond dreams, with treasures to be melted down in a molten sea of silver and gold that would shame a dwarf but, amazingly, the defenders of the settlement, though all male, had put up no resistance at all – had not even been trained, apparently, in the simplest art of self-defence. Really, they had only themselves to blame. And now, while her countrymen drink their toasts to a future of many similar raids, it is Veleda's task to purify this stinking church of stone and twigs where the islanders conduct their primitive religious ceremonies, for her countrymen have insisted that the exposed body is in itself a *draugr*, the most unholy of all undead spirits in the form of a living corpse, and it is up to the resident priestess to render the curse of a *draugr* unable to affect the luck of the invaders.

So Veleda puts on her robes, tries to block out the events of the evening – the killing, violence and enslavement were necessary, of course, but not to her own taste – and begins to light the candles that are littered round the dank chapel.

It is good that she does this, because as soon as the chapel is illuminated it becomes a far less fearful place, and Veleda is able to see quite clearly that the body that lies on the shrine is not that of a *draugr* at all, but only a dead man, albeit a well-preserved dead man. She wonders for a moment why he has been attended to with such ceremony, but then dismisses her musings: who knows how the minds of such people work – with their odd little all-male cult on an island off the coast of this foreign land. They no doubt worship death itself, not life, if she is to judge by the decorated walls of the building in which she finds herself – for many of these illustrations depict a pale man hoisted up by his wrists on some type of a frame, with his feet nailed fast, and if he is not meant to be dead, then he is certainly meant to be seriously ill. To Veleda, this is distasteful: she worships life itself, however short or long it might be, and she knows she is only capable of understanding a cosmology such as her own people's – a sacredness of living things like the Great Tree itself. Anything else seems pointless – even abhorrent. Perhaps the men of this settlement all deserve to be killed, after all, so that they do not spread their death-worship even further. As she lights the last of the candles, Veleda thinks of the White Christ missionaries who had visited her country so unsuccessfully, and a frown crosses her brow. The men of this island are of the same type, she thinks.

But now she stands, holy in the middle of the building, and feels herself surrounded by light, by fire itself, and it clears her thoughts. She feels calm for the first time since the long sea journey – she often wishes it were not necessary for there to be a priestess aboard each raiding party, but the raiding sailors insist on it, for luck – and she closes her eyes and lets the candle-light flicker behind the shutters of her eyelids. Her body too relaxes, and her heart slows, and she knows that even if it is not a *draugr* that sleeps there on that platform of wood that she had marked earlier, well, it will soothe her mind and flesh to let herself go once more into the peace of meditation.

So she stands there for a while, eyes closed, and feels the whole power of the Tree flow through her, feels life itself pour out into the church through the channel that is her body, feels the excitement of life-force flicker through veins, out through her fingertips, out through the soles of her bare feet, and then she knows it is now time for the final step of the ritual: it is time to mark the environment with a rune.

Her heart is beating quickly once again as she brings forth the charcoaled stick from her robes; she feels strangely light, excited, aroused. The marking of the rune is always a moment of anticipation, and her body reacts accordingly. She slides her fingers beneath her robe and over her breasts, pinching at her nipples, then removes her hands so that she can write the rune.

She still has no idea which rune shall be revealed to her.

She stands there in the middle of the foreign cult-place, candles flickering around her like many stars, and feels something like a wind rush through her: again she feels full of the life-force; she is driven to write down the rune the Tree has given her. She scratches it out on the stone floor of the church with the charcoaled tip of the stick.

It is a surprise to her: the lines she has drawn spell out the N-rune – *naudr*, need. But I have no present needs, thinks Veleda, I am at the moment quite content, except perhaps for the pleasurable ache in my groin, but that is the usual result of the ceremony.

She stares at the symbol *naudr*, her breath coming quickly.

Then she hears what sounds like a sigh from where the corpse is lying, and at first her blood chills, but then there is another sound underneath it – a scurrying, like that of mice or rats. She knows she is hearing another human, and for some inexplicable reason she now feels *naudr* throughout her body – she needs to fuck, and she will fuck whoever is there, be it a spying countryman – who should know better than to peer in on one of her rites – or a withered male inhabitant of this defenceless but rich settlement.

'Come out!' she commands, but there is silence. The need of the rune courses through her, its magic and its desires, and she repeats herself. Then she takes out her knife and catches the candlelight on it, so that any spy might see that she is indeed a threat and would do well to obey. She has no fear of her countryman warriors, strong though they are, for they are too frightened of her power and they need her services and advice for the sea-voyage home.

But again there is no response.

Veleda walks closer to the altar. There, she sees a crack in the raised floor, and a pale eye staring up at her. She puts her knife down to the crack and shows the eye its blade. 'Come up now,' she says, 'come out from your hiding place.' She knows that even if her tongue is not understood, her meaning is implicit.

Now there is a stirring, and it sounds like a movement below the very stone floor she stands on, and then out from behind one of the pillars there creeps a young man.

In fact he is a very young man, a boy of sixteen or seventeen, perhaps. He has rust-coloured hair and a freckled complexion, though his hair is shaved round his skull. He wears a long brown robe of simple woven material, and around his neck is a string of white beads, which he is clutching in both hands. Compared to her countrymen, he looks effeminate and weak, as if the blood he spilled would be as pale as milk. He looks pious.

And, amazingly, he smells of sex. And Veleda, who is well versed at reading faces, can discern that, through the terror evidenced upon his visage, there is also a trace of guilt. She glances down, and sees a dampness evident groin-high on his robes. And she realises that he might have been hiding in terror, and his hands have not been idle, not at all. And as she stares at his crotch, she watches as the swelling there once again begins to emerge.

Ah, the resilience of the young.

Immediately, she wants to bed him. Veleda wants to train those adolescent hands of his to stroke her body; she wants his lips pressed to her anus hot and tight, licking her until she squirms. Already she can see how his breath quickens when he looks at her; how his gaze falters, but then how he tries to sneak a look at her breasts under half-closed lids, for her robe had fallen open earlier when she herself stroked at her cherry-red nipples. Veleda wonders whether this young man has ever seen a naked woman.

Yes, her own land had had the missionaries of this man's ineffectual White Christ before, and Veleda had heard tell of the White Christ's hatred of flesh and pleasure, but this young man seemed to be no stranger to self-pleasuring, even in the midst of a raid.

Veleda feels *naudr* run through her body and she grabs the necklace of the young man and with it pulls him towards her, though in doing so the string breaks, and the beads fall to the floor. The boy doesn't flinch, however, though it is plain that he is aroused, and he stares Veleda in the eye with something like hate. This irritates her. She is a priestess of life, after all, not a stripling of some order that worships death. She stares him back in the eye, perhaps only a hand's breadth between their two faces, and says, 'I am Veleda. I am a priestess – you are merely an acolyte of some effeminate cult that can't even bring itself to bear arms. I am Veleda,' she repeats, pointing to herself.

The boy glares back at her, and then he mutters something that sounds like 'Cuthbert', a hideously harsh sound of a name, and he points to himself, before glancing quickly up at the corpse above them with something that looks like shame. But Veleda doesn't care about the boy's motives – he has disturbed her ritual, and now he is going to help her complete it.

She points to the charcoal rune. '*Naudr*,' she says.

The boy – Cuthbert? – looks at the rune and spits on it.

Veleda strides up to him and grabs his jaw. He is still

glaring at her, but he has also positioned himself so that he is surreptitiously running his fingers against the side of her bosom, as if he thinks she will not notice. She slaps his hand away, and then pushes him down to the floor. He leers at her – has he no shame? – and then, worse, strokes the bulge of his erection through the cloth. He mutters something at her and, for Veleda, this is the final insult.

She tears off her robe, and watches the boy's eyes grow wide at the sight of her breasts, her tapered waist and the fine, full blonde bush of her sex. She motions for him to remove his clothing and, to her surprise, he does so, with no mutterings and with more respect than he has exhibited only moments before. Veleda shoves her hand between her legs until it is wet with fluid and then holds the result a finger away from the boy's nose. His anger seems to have dissipated, as is surely typical with men of his weak stock. He sighs, and closes his eyes. Veleda takes the occasion to pause and run her gaze over his body, and she finds it entirely to her liking. Then he sticks out his tongue and licks her juices away from her proffered hand, inhaling her scent with obvious relish, and Veleda understands from his eagerness and clumsiness that he is, indeed, a virgin, and that somehow this was why the Tree had offered forth the N-rune of Need, for it is her need too that fills her with desire and makes her thighs sticky with want, even now. For most of her countrypeople are too frightened of her power to approach her with sexual intention.

The young man who calls himself Cuthbert lies back on the floor, passive in his inexperience but still eager as a puppy, lapping and kissing her hand and wrist like a true sensualist, not like a flesh-hater at all. Veleda first resolves to be gentler, but then she kisses him hard, and soon his tongue and mouth are as ardent and even as violent as hers, biting and nipping and probing her lips like a man dying for water, such is the young man's thirst for erotic sensation. Veleda indulges herself in the sensation, and her nails scratch his back in pleasure. Then she raises herself and steps back for a moment to observe him. He is an avid student, despite his initial anger for her, which she supposes was understandable under the terms of the raid.

The candlelight laps around the two of them on the stone floor, the sticks of blue wax shining across the entire church. Then Veleda sees the white beads, spilled onto the floor from the force of her initial tug on the string round Cuthbert's neck. She gathers up several in her palm, six or seven of them.

Cuthbert is leaning back on his palms, watching with interest. He also looks fearful, as if she were doing something quite forbidden.

Veleda does not break his gaze and she pushes one after another of the beads up inside herself, beads which have no particular importance to her but beads which no doubt are filled with some terribly important meaning for young Cuthbert. Her fingers grow sticky with the task, and once more she allows Cuthbert to lick at her hand, a favour for which he seems very grateful.

Then she stretches her naked body down on the cold stone beside him, and guides his mouth to her sex, so that he can continue his licking there, and she feels soft tremors start to flow, and she swivels so that her own bright lips are fastened tight on his cock, which is so urgent that already a drop of moistness appears at its tip. She sucks that moistness away, and is rewarded with a soft whimper from Cuthbert himself.

Veleda can feel him licking out each of the little beads, and she thinks of the blasphemy he must feel as his tongue curls into her heady juice. With his mouth, he strokes out each little marked bauble. Veleda's mouth goes dry, then she feels herself relax into the slow eroticism of the act, and finds herself enjoying the thought of his young pink tongue moving slowly over the slippery lips of her sex, drinking her. His prick in her mouth becomes harder and more urgent as he licks and licks at her, slurping and swallowing and she slides into pleasure even as she sucks yet more violently on his stiff cock. Then young Cuthbert draws his penis away from her lips, his penis with its musky animal scent that inflames her, the scent and flavour that makes her just want to suck and suck and suck.

Cuthbert's fingers enter her cunt, and seek out the last of the little beads. He speaks now, pointing to each X-mark on each bead, beads which he seems to consider sacred, but the words he says – 'crucifix', 'rood', 'cross' – are words which Veleda has never heard before. He draws back so that Veleda can watch him put each into his mouth, her juices mixing with his saliva, her juices corrupting his flesh-hating religion, and this thought makes her burn with even more desire. Her nipples are tight as rocks themselves, her thighs are quivering, her powerful sticky come is in his mouth.

She stretches her arms out towards him, wants to feel those tender ribs, his delicate, cloud-pale buttocks, the hot yet tender flesh of his prick. Cuthbert sighs, and puts his hands on her waist, and pulls her on top of him with the confidence of movement from a more experienced man than he is, so that Veleda straddles him and he groans with pleasure. And Veleda, well, Veleda feels the thickness of his cock impale her, as she slides down on him, her cunt tight and moist, for she is dripping liquid, she is so wet she feels as if she were melting into a lake. But here in the lake's middle is a source, his cock, that plunges up inside her and fills her with an itching lust, a need to push down further and further on him.

He moans with her movements.

It fills Veleda with a thrill that she is fucking this boy for the first time, that he is moaning from the pure pleasure of sensation, not the removed fantasies of sex that fill the heads of those more experienced. He wants her, not an idea of her. And he wants the gritty satisfaction she is giving him, as she grinds her hips down. She can see it on his face when she looks down through half-drawn lids, can see the wonder in his eyes and his slack, open mouth. Now she shoves herself down on him with force, and he gives a soft groan and a whimper and stiffens even more inside her. Veleda falls down on him, whilst still moving her hips, so that the pressure on them both is not alleviated. She feels wanton as she nips at his tiny nipples, pale as his lips, and bites the taut young skin on his upper arms. She smells his underarms and sticks her tongue into these crevices and licks at his downy fur that she finds, and this sends a pulse all the way down to her cunt, a long string of desire from her wet mouth to the pounding drumbeat of the bead of her sex. As she inhales the scent of his excitement and sweat, he begins a long drawn-out moan and starts to thrust his hips upwards rhythmically, pulsing with a climax he can't long restrain.

Veleda is so aroused by his lack of control, his unconscious moaning, his inability to do anything else but rock his hips towards his own pleasure, that she too begins to moan and flush and rock back and forth, so conscious of his stiffness rock-hard inside her, and her hand rubs out a complementary rhythm, sticky and frantic over her own small stiffness. His cock. Her fingers. His innocent face. His tongue snaking out to lick at his lips still smeared with her own juices.

After their pleasure they lie there for a while on the stone on the warm June night, Cuthbert's fingers playing idly with Veleda's sex, and she lets him insert and remove his fingers in her wetness until she grows a bit bored with the game. When their breath has returned to them, Veleda gets up and walks to the entrance of the church. She looks outside and sees that her countrymen have congregated down on the beach, where they are drinking. From where the church stands, Veleda can see all the way down to the other side of the island as well, where there are several abandoned boats, and so she beckons Cuthbert towards her and motions to him that he might at this moment make a clean escape while the backs of the Viking men are turned.

As Veleda quickly helps him don his robes again, she smiles. For there, scratched in red relief onto Cuthbert's back in the course of their passion, is a large invocation of the *naudr* rune. May he never forget or dismiss the pleasures of the need of flesh again, despite the teachings of his faith. She hopes it will be a lesson he remembers. It is the least she could do for the sake of his life-force, for the sake of the eternal green sap of the Tree that runs through us all.

Cuthbert is full of wonderment and fear as he rows his way swiftly to the mainland. And once there, he will seek out those who will help him recover the Saint's body. It has been a night of both delight and trauma. When he looks up across the lap of the waters, he sees his own abbey, full of flickering light, and he mourns for those slain and for the future of the souls of those brothers of his who have been spared, at the heathen hands of such strange monsters as these invaders. And yet there is still a resonance in his groin when he thinks of the pleasure the sorceress has just shown him. Surely these must be the delights of Eve against which he has been warned, and rightly so, it seems, for surely the taste of the sorceress's sex is like the fruit of Eden itself, the one forbidden fruit. His arms ache and yet it is his whole body that is flooded with the memory of her flesh. Though perhaps there is hope for her? She was not unkind to him; perhaps Our Lord will see fit to save her soul. Was not Magdalene herself spared? Cuthbert sighs and feels himself hardening again, even as his arms pull the last stretch towards the mainland. He has himself made a small attempt, in any case – he left one of the crucifix-marked rosary beads behind in the wicked flower of her sex, so that the message of Christ might flourish even there, even there in the very source of tempting sin itself. He thinks of the small white bead lavished with her juices, and his groin tightens. Though he concentrates on his rowing, instead. He tells himself it was a selfless act. It was the least he could do for the good of her soul.

You Spoil Me Mathilde Madden

It's early evening, already starting to get dark, and you are on your way back from buying tobacco from the corner shop at the end of our street. Coming out of the shop and heading back down the road, you're not looking where you're going, rolling a cigarette, and nor is he. You bump into him and send him sprawling, head first, into the wall.

'Sorry,' you say, looking up, and, as he wipes his messy hair out of his face, you see who it is.

It's him, the beautiful young man from over the road. The one I have a little crush on. The one I've been going on about. Neither of us knows his name, so we refer to him using the number of his house: we call him Number Eight. And it's Number Eight you've just collided with.

And it's such a coincidence, because only last night I'd persuaded you that Number Eight should be the star of one of your particularly dirty stories. Your beautiful stories: the whispered filth that you breathe into my ear in the dark. It's one of my favourite things about you, darling, the way you bring my fantasies to life in every way you can, even when all I want is the words. The way you happily talk about whoever I want and in whatever scenario I want. You're never jealous. Why would you be? You know that some little cutie I spy in the street or on television could never be any real competition. Of course not! You're the one, and you know it.

After a little probing last night, checking out what I

was in the mood for, you had invented a fantasy for me.

Your story featured me as an evil seductress and kidnapper – one of my favourite roles. I had pulled up in my car next to Number Eight as he walked home. You had described in exquisite detail his dark fuzzy hair, thin little student body, cute squashy nose and dark heavy brows. He had been wearing tight, faded denim, tight on his arse, one of the first things that had attracted me to the beautiful Number Eight.

Under the pretext of asking him for directions I had persuaded him into my car and whisked him away to a deserted and mysterious cabin in the woods.

Oh, that I had such a den in real life!

In your version of my fantasy I was ruthless; far more ruthless than I could ever be in reality. Perhaps, I'd wondered, this was a little of your own fantasy too. I had noticed how as I had got crueller in the tale, you had become harder, pushing yourself against me in the dark as you breathlessly recounted the endless torments I had inflicted on poor abused Number Eight.

For over a week I'd kept him prisoner in that cabin, blindfolded and helpless, tormented by a tight gag. You'd thrown it all in, from bondage (chains, collars and handcuffs) to torture and humiliation (beatings and starvation, and at one point I'd hosed him down with cold water, just to make him even more uncomfortable). As you'd described me laughing as Number Eight squirmed in his chains trying to escape the dousing, and how his begging for mercy was muffled by the cruel gag, I was fighting to hold off my orgasm, desperate to hear the end of the story. Finally, of course, he'd capitulated and agreed to become my sex slave, kneeling naked before me, bowing his head and vowing eternal devotion. I love a happy ending. As your tale had reached its climax, so had I, panting and crying out in the dark next to you as you pulled me tightly into your arms.

I'd recovered and found you were squirming, rubbing yourself against my body, demonstrating that you had enjoyed the fantasy, too, but were left hanging. And I'd reached over and found your hard cock. You had come, too, within a few moments of my well-practised manipulations and I had rolled over to sleep, exhausted, leaving you to feel under the bed for your tissues and clean up before following me to dreamland.

And now, with the memory of last night still fresh in your mind, you feel a little ashamed to be looking the poor victim right in the face less than 24 hours later.

'Er,' mutters Number Eight. He seems a little bit confused, bashful, even. He raises a hand to the back of his head and rubs it.

'Did you hit your head?' you say. 'Let me have a look.'

Reaching up, you brush his hair aside and feel the spot he was nursing on the back of his head. It seems fine. Not even a bump. You smile and your eyes meet his.

It's the first time either you or I have seen Number Eight at close quarters. Up until now he's only ever been a glimpsed figure hurrying in and out of the tatty shared house across the road, where he lives with a group of what we assume to be fellow students. Now, as you look at Number Eight, you realise a couple of things.

First, I'd always said I thought that Number Eight was about nineteen, maybe twenty, but close up you can see he's a little bit older than that; more like twenty-five.

Secondly, and rather more significantly, you realise

something else about him. I'd always assumed Number Eight was straight, but looking at him now, so close to, in those too-tight jeans and with that devastating little pouty mouth, and looking at the way he is looking at you, you're not so sure.

And, if that look in his eyes is what you think it is, who could blame Number Eight for being attracted to you? You are, as I am always telling you, a fantastically attractive man. In fact, one of the things I first noticed about Number Eight was the fact he looked rather like a younger version of you. Truth be told, it was that above all that attracted me to him. My type is so clear-cut: I've always been attracted to men who look the way you do. You share his dark brows and thin elegant frame, although your nose is bigger and sharper and your similarly dark hair is close-cropped, the way I like it, not shaggy and overlong like his. In fact, as the two of you stand there, facing each other in the darkening street, your hand cradling the back of Number Eight's head, you could almost be brothers.

So perhaps it is noble fraternal concern for your surrogate brother that drives you to invite him back to our flat for a while, so you can observe him and ensure he has suffered no serious damage. Perhaps.

'I live just across the street,' you say, pointing to our front door.

'I know,' Number Eight whispers rather shyly. 'I've seen you around.'

Interesting.

In the flat you make some tea and small talk and then lead Number Eight into your small study.

It's a bit of a mess as usual and you have to move a pile of papers and books off the battered sofa so he can sit down. You sit at your desk, balancing your cup of tea on top of a pile of books about film and filmmaking, swivelling the chair so you are facing him.

Now, with a plan forming in your mind, you look at Number Eight. He is not particularly attractive as far as you're concerned (I guess you're no narcissist), but you know how I feel about him and you know what I would like you to do. Yes, making my fantasies come to life has always been your speciality. And, as well as in verbal form, you've often taken things a step further and role-played for me. You can be a wonderful actor with the right motivation and an appreciative audience, playing everything from a slutty street-walking rent boy to a nervous *ingénue*.

I'm so lucky to have you, I know that. I never thought I'd find a man who understood me so well, who indulged me so completely and found pleasure in the things I did – who found pleasure in my pleasure. When I told you how much I fancied a certain television presenter, or some bloke in my office, or, of course, the young man who lived at number eight, you revelled in the knowledge, turning it to your advantage. You loved to encourage me to tell you exactly what I'd like to do with my latest object of desire, giving you plenty of material to draw on when, late at night, you'd recount the stories back to me, delighting in my obvious arousal.

You never blanched when the fantasies I shared featured you, either. Frequently you were the kidnap victim, the object of my dominating desires.

Together we'd always experimented. I loved to tie you up and watch you struggle for me. I bought leather straps to bind you comfortably and safely for hours. One day you had come home with a short black crop and that was when I discovered how much you loved pain. A true masochist! The pain got you hard and I loved to see that. Our toy collection had grown from there.

Tying you up will always remain one of my greatest pleasures. I love to see men helpless and struggling, especially when their helplessness turns them on. When they're hard and moaning with frustrated desire. There's something beautiful about the way a submissive man is more enslaved by his own sexuality than by my control. And there is no doubt that you are a submissive, my darling. Pleasing me takes precedence over everything.

Truly nothing shocked you when it came to my darkest secrets. So I hadn't thought twice when I'd told you how much it excited me to think of two men together, taking each other roughly, making nasty love, bondage, beating, everything I enjoyed but darker and nastier because it was between men. And I'd told you how I liked to think of you as one of those men. Sometimes the top, sometimes the bottom.

I would tell you how I'd like to hire one of the studs who advertise in the back of gay free sheets. Pick out one of those adverts that consisted of nothing more than a name, a number and a photo of a torso – and an erection. Rent a stud and watch him take you. You'd be tied down, gagged and blindfolded with no idea, no escape, but knowing I was watching. You'd enjoy submitting to this strange man whose face you'd never see.

I'd tell you these things and you'd just smile and ask for more details, revelling in being party to the darkest parts of my sexuality.

I suppose you've probably wondered if I'd ever really go through with it. Of course I'd ask for your consent. Of course you'd give it.

Often, too, of course, I would fantasise about you and my latest crush together. You knew this. And so here you are and it falls into place. You're in your study in an empty flat, with exactly such a crush object, Number

Eight, who's clearly pretty keen on you. Of course you hit upon a plan to make one of your stories, not the one from last night but another favourite of mine, come true. In the most intense way you can. Your priority is to please me, so you can hardly do anything else. You spoil me, darling, you really do.

So, after chatting for a while about your job and his, the area, the other people in the street, the poor range of stock in the corner shop, you drain your cup and move from your armchair on to the sofa next to him, smiling softly as he gives you a questioning look. A moment or two after that you place your hand softly on his leg, just above the knee. He stops what he's saying and looks up at you when you do this, then glances down, biting his lip shyly for a moment before trying to continue his sentence. After a few words, though, he falters and tails off, staring at your hand on his leg.

To break the silence you say something, asking him lightly about the others who live in his house, and he, relieved by the distraction, starts to tell you something about his eccentric landlady and her three overindulged cats.

All the while your hand still rests on his leg. In your mind you are carefully planning your next move, meaning that when he pauses you haven't been listening. So, instead of replying to his question, you pretend to check where he hit his head again, and, as you reach up and stroke his hair, he responds with a sigh of unmistakable desire, and that's all the sanction you need.

This is the moment when you decide to go for it. You take hold of a handful of his hair to keep his head still, lean forward and kiss him very slowly. You are quite shocked when he struggles a little, pulling his mouth away and whispering, 'No', but then gasping with pleasure as you yank at his hair to pull his mouth back to yours. You slide your other hand up his leg and grasp his crotch. Through his jeans you can feel he is slightly hard and you force your tongue roughly into his mouth. He gets harder. But, despite his obvious enjoyment, he is still squirming around as if he's putting up a fight. You pull away from his mouth and look at him, confused.

'Make me,' he says very gently. 'Force me, please. I need it this way.' He shivers a little, clearly turned on by asking for what he wants.

You smile. Even better.

Grabbing his whole jaw in one hand, with the other still tangled in his hair, you pull his mouth back on to your own, roughly. He struggles and murmurs, 'Please, don't.' But he doesn't try to fight you at all.

You pin him right where you want him, pushing him back against the sofa. Then you swing one leg over his lap and straddle him. Crashing your mouth against his, you kiss him so hard he can barely breathe. You relish the taste of him.

As you force your tongue in deep, your own cock begins to stir as you grind it against his own desperate erection.

Sitting back a little, but keeping one hand firmly in his hair and sliding the other between his legs to grip his cock, you look at him. You can tell he is turned on, although trying to stay in control. His lips are slightly parted and he is breathing hard. His cheeks are flushed red and you can feel his cock growing harder all the time under your fingers.

'You dirty little bitch,' you hiss at him, making him flinch and squirm. 'You want it, don't you?'

'I . . .'

You tighten your fingers painfully in his hair and, raising your hand from his crotch, slap him hard round the face. 'Don't you?' you snap.

He lowers his head submissively and looks up shyly at you. 'Yes,' he says, very softly, 'yes I do. Use me, please. Please, sir.'

You smile and feel your own cock growing harder at his submissive posturing. It's quite strange, you wonder to yourself: you really didn't expect to enjoy this so much.

After a short moment you let go of him and snarl softly, 'Strip, now, and make me want to give it to you.'

You slide off Number Eight's lap and he stands, turning to face you, only a few feet away in the tiny room. He keeps his head lowered in deference, but holds eye contact with you all the time.

Slowly, carefully, and rather seductively, he pulls his loose-fitting top over his head. His chest is thin and pale, with a little dark hair on it, and his smallish nipples are bright pink and tightly erect. He looks vulnerable and scared standing there topless, and it turns you on. You can't help but start to tease your own cock through your trousers, getting it hard, getting it ready. Ready for him.

The boy pauses, his hands on the waistband of his jeans. He is staring at you as you rub your cock and seems to be frozen. You wait a moment or two. He still doesn't move.

'Come on,' you say, keeping your voice low, but still sounding threatening. 'Get them off, slut!'

'Please,' he says, 'please, don't make me do it myself. I can't.'

'Do I have to come and tear them off you myself?'

The boy doesn't answer, but he still doesn't move, except to tremble slightly. He looks so scared and it's so beautiful. You are sure he's done this before. He knows just how to play little boy lost. It's a role you've played for me so many times and he, like you, has got it down beautifully. He even knows just how to tilt his head and look shyly through his hair at you, just to look all the more vulnerable and helpless. The only thing that gives him away is the unmistakable bulge of his straining penis. You realise how much this boy needs to be put in bondage and punished. You realise how much you want to do it.

'OK,' you say, suddenly softer, 'come here.'

The boy walks towards you and you urge him closer and closer until he is standing between your knees.

'Put your hands on your head,' you say, and he does so, instantly appearing more vulnerable once his hands are out of the way.

Reaching out and placing your hands on his hips, you can feel now that he is still shaking slightly. He really is amazing, you muse to yourself. I really do know how to pick them.

Slowly, savouring the moment, you slide your hands along his waistband to the fly of his jeans and undo the button and then the zip. Holding your breath, you slide the unfastened trousers and then his underpants down to the floor.

Still with his hands on his head, Number Eight glances down at his own, now very erect, cock. He's so turned on that the head is adorned with little flecks of glistening wetness. He flashes you a shy grin before lowering his head again in submission. Reaching out, you grasp his cock and stroke it firmly from top to bottom. Then you scoop up a little of his wetness in your fingers and bring it to his lips. Pushing your fingers into his mouth, you force him to taste himself. He closes his eyes and sucks eagerly on your fingers, almost as if he were sucking a little cock, cleaning off every last trace.

Withdrawing suddenly, you fix him with a stern look. 'Get on your knees, you bitch.'

He suppresses a little moan and lowers himself down

on to his knees between your legs. His face is now a little lower than yours and you touch his cheek, smiling.

'Turn around,' you whisper.

The naked Number Eight shuffles around on his knees until he has his back to you, and then you use your hands on both his shoulders to push him down on to the floor. His arse is right in front of you now. It's pale and rounded, flawless. You remember how much I love your arse, how I love to touch and caress it, and you reach out. He moans as you begin to stroke him, gently at first and then more and more roughly. You slowly run your fingers up and down, occasionally giving him a twisting little pinch or a light slap. You run a finger along the crevice and find the little warm bud of his arsehole. Still with just one finger, you start to tease that soft little mouth until it opens up greedily and you push inside him.

You can hear him panting hard. You slide your free hand between his legs and find his cock, which you stroke lightly, while you continue fucking him with one finger.

You continue this teasing until both of you are very hard. You'd love to fuck him right now, but it's too soon – there's so much you want to do to him before you come. He gasps and whimpers when you let go of his cock and pull out of him.

'Get over that table,' you say, in a low, matter-of-fact tone.

He looks at you with a timid expression for a moment, but obeys quickly, spreading himself face down across the low coffee table and reaching down to hold on to the legs.

Most of my bondage toys are kept in the bedroom, but not all of them. Luckily for you, because you'd hate to have to leave the room now to get equipment, there is a small bag of spare ropes and less favourite toys stashed out of the way on one of your study shelves. You stand up and pull the bag down from the shelf. A quick inspection of its contents reveals some rope, a small paddle shaped like a table-tennis bat, condoms and lubricant, and a pair of rather nasty silver nipple clamps. To begin with, you pull out four lengths of rope.

He catches his breath as you begin to tie his wrists in place. Once you are satisfied that they are secure, you move round and tie his knees to the other two legs, fixing him in place kneeling on the floor. To your delight, he squirms a little in his bondage, testing the restraints, but you know your business and he's held fast.

He seems to enjoy his new predicament. Along with his struggling, he is grinding his hips, pushing himself into the table. Well, you'll soon put a stop to that.

You pull your belt from its loops. He hears the sound and quivers. Doubling up the belt, you draw it through your fingers and pause, making him wait.

The first time you hit him gently, checking your aim, but soon you build up some force and begin to lash his arse, hard, panting as you see bright marks come up. He squeals and makes to try to move away, but the ropes keep him in place. As the beating goes on and he struggles and yells, you find yourself wishing there'd been a gag in that bag.

You continue the lashing until you are desperate to come and he is yelling in earnest on each stroke. He starts to beg for mercy through his screams of pain.

'Please, please, sir, no more, please.'

That piece of begging turns you on more than anything. You have to have him right now. Kneeling behind him, you slide on a condom and push a finger into him again. He's even more open and ready than before. Clearly he has enjoyed his bondage and beating.

You remove your finger briefly and squeeze some lubricant into him, replacing the finger to work it inside him. He knows what's coming and begins to writhe eagerly, bucking against your hand. When you replace your finger with your hard cock he moans out loud.

'Oh, yes, master, please! Fuck me, please!' You glide in and out, already close to climax from watching the arse you are now taking turn pink under your belt. Spurred on by his begging, you come quickly, thrusting hard and deep into him.

You slump back on to the sofa, exhausted. He turns his head to look at you, still tied in position, now covered in red lash marks and splashes of your come. You smile at him and spend a long moment enjoying the view. You are aware, though, of Number Eight's own frustrated arousal and after a brief respite you stand up and free him from his bonds. He stays where he is, waiting for permission to move, as you settle back down.

'Come here,' you whisper.

The naked young man stands up and makes his way over to the sofa. Again he stands between your legs, head down submissively. His cock is bright red and desperately hard. You pull him on to your lap and cradle him in your arms. 'We'd better sort this out, hadn't we?' you purr in his ear. You grasp his cock and slowly begin to move your hand up and down, starting with soft teasing strokes and then building up a firm rhythm that has him wriggling and gasping.

'Please, sir,' he gasps desperately. 'Please may I have permission to come, sir?'

'Wait for it, bitch!' you hiss, and in response he moans. A sound both of frustration and desire.

You continue teasing him, keeping him right on the brink of orgasm, while he squirms and writhes.

Eventually you say, 'OK, slut, come, now.'

He comes, that very instant, into your hands, thanking you breathlessly.

When he opens his eyes you hold your fingers up to his mouth for him to lick clean.

Later, after he has shyly thanked you and left, you check the camera. By the time I arrive home you are in bed, fast asleep. I am disappointed until I see the Post-it note on the video recorder, which says 'PLAY'.

You really do know how to spoil me.

Peaches Anna Clare

If a person watched carefully enough they might have
noticed that Alex always smiled when presented with
a peach. It was an almost Pavlovian response: pass the
man a peach after supper, or offer one from the fruit
dish, and the smile would be there without fail. I'd tried
it with various fruits, but only peaches seemed to elicit
the response.

He'd sunk his teeth into an apple with matter-of-fact
abandon, emasculated a banana with a savage bite that
would have given a Freudian a field day, and cursed
the impenetrable nature of orange peel in a perfectly
normal fashion.

Watch him with a peach, and it would be an entirely
different performance. The Mona Lisa smile made its
inevitable appearance. If you caught him completely off
guard you might catch him out with his lips very close to
the fuzzy skin of the fruit, breath lightly beading the tiny
hairs, as though he were trying to inhale the smell of it.

Eventually, I had to ask.

We were in his rooms that night, drinking (of all
things) peach schnapps, when I asked him. We drank
such a lot of crap in those days – cheap cider that had
never so much as seen an apple, repellent bottled beers
– whatever wasn't too hard on the wallet. The schnapps
was sticky and burned on the way down, but alcohol is
a recreational drug and gets used as such when you're
young.

'Oh ... it's kind of a Proust thing ...' he said, when I
asked him.

'Proust?' Proust and peaches? I gave him a warning look, like we were not heading for a trip to pretentious-student-burblings-land tonight, no matter how pissed we were. No way, peaches. Ain't never gonna happen.

He picked up on it and curled up cross-legged on the other end of his bed. 'Yeah. Like madeleines – you know, *A la Recherche du Temps Perdu*.'

'That's the only bit of Proust anyone remembers, and you know it,' I accused.

'Yeah yeah ... we pick out the pseudo-brainy stuff and the rest kind of gets *perdu* along the way ...'

'So ... madeleines? Peaches?'

'You know how a taste or smell can send you sort of barrelling back into the past?'

'Picked up the pseudo-brainy stuff, yeah.'

'Well, it's like that with me and peaches.' He leaned back, head against the wall, mouth sticky with schnapps, a smug smile all over his face.

'Must have been a happy memory.'

'Oh, it was ...'

It was the peach smile, I swear. It lit him up from the inside. You can't spark a person's curiosity like that and hold back. So I told him to tell me.

'Kiss me and I'll tell.'

So I kissed him – a sort of sticky, burned-peaches kiss, the taste of fake fruit synthetically sweet over the burn of the alcohol. He didn't tell, so I kissed him again, hoping to get a secret out of him, but men tend to be freer with sex than secrets, so it took a lot more to get him to tell me his story. Not the kiss-and-tell type after all.

He was right about the Proust thing, though. Seven years later and I can't taste peach schnapps without being catapulted back in time to my night with Alex – the babyish softness of his skin, the astonishing tensile strength in muscles that didn't seem to have any business flexing under such girlish skin. He was so perfectly smooth all over. Even his cock felt smooth and sleek inside me, and I can still remember every silky stroke of it, punctuated by the hard butts of bony boyish hips and the prickle of his small tangle of pubic hair.

After the first round, we huddled together on his narrow plywood-and-foam student bed, trying to drive away the ugly reality of a Hall of Residence loft room with incense and lighted candles, and succeeded for a short time, while we were lying spooned up in the bed, feeling sated and depraved, sharing a joint.

'So tell me . . .' I had to prompt him again.

He laughed. 'Oh yeah, that. I was seduced.'

'What's that got to do with peaches?'

A whole lot, as it happened. I can't remember the conversation now, so I'll tell Alex's story to the best of my memory. He was seduced by his next-door neighbour, a woman he swore was a witch. Sweet seventeen – innocent as you can be at that age in a small seaside town where there's very little to do other than grope under the pier at night. That was our hero – Alex.

He lived at the time in a Victorian semi-detached on the corner of the street. I know because he pointed it out in a photo on the bedroom wall – one of those little bits of home you cling to when you're away from the security of your family for the first time. I could imagine myself in the photo, in the house – a rather beautiful whimsy of a place with a glass porch and an upstairs room with a five-sided bay window that looked almost like an observatory.

'She moved in there.' He pointed out the bay window to me. 'Lene. That's where she lived. She moved in one summer with her cat – Pyewacket, he was called. Weird fucking thing.'

He told me about the day she moved in, his harassed, divorced, eternally busy mother determined that she'd be a good neighbour and give the new arrival a hot meal on her first day in a new town. Lene ate with Alex and his mother that night. Her name was Lene Lane – a child's storybook sort of a name, and she had this fey quality that went with it.

Alex described her in sensual terms – floating dark curls, a snubby, witchy, mischievous face over rounded breasts that were barely covered by a cheesecloth blouse. He'd been trying not to stare at her tits all through dinner, he said, but it's impossible not to look at nipples exposed through clothing like that. The outline of them was clear under the thin cloth and he could tell his mother disapproved and thought she ought to put a bra on, but he was too busy trying to grab furtive glances to care about her opinion. You could see the shadows beneath her breasts, the upturned jut of her nipples, the hang and shift of them when she folded her arms or reached for more bread or salad.

Her boobs had a symmetry that her eyes lacked – one eye brown, the other blue. He later noticed that the cat was odd-eyed, too – one amber eye, one blue, peering balefully from the patch of white fur that surrounded the blue eye. He was named after a minor demon, she said, because since he had been a kitten he had behaved like an animated hairball coughed up by Satan himself.

She talked about angels and demons a lot – late at night in that observatory of a living room of hers, which she'd hung with throws patterned with mandalas and filled with burning incense and candles. She sounded to me like the quintessential hippie chick, all daisies in her hair and black eyeliner, avowing she was a witch and reading tarot cards to finance her hash and cider cravings. I'd disliked the spectre of Lene at first, being a dumb nineteen-year-old working very hard at being cynical and jaded. I was rebelling against the warmth and tolerance that my own hippie parents had taught me by sneering at everything. Sex in those days was a transaction, a necessity, and oh so very sad.

You grow out of these things, fortunately. You learn to believe in angels and demons and witches once more, and get back to the wisdom you had as a child, in the days before your own pose of faux intellectualism cut off your imagination. I think she was probably like that – Lene Lane. Innocent as a child, pure as an angel, lecherous as a demon.

She was sloppy, Alex said – so lazy he never figured out whether it was because she had mountains of cash tucked away or was on the social-security fiddle like so many others. He'd call round in the afternoons and she'd come to the door wrapped in a throw-over, some glittery Indian thing, then trail back to what she was doing before – lounging in bed reading and eating chocolates.

He'd sit on the end of her bed until she coaxed him to join her on the pillows and share her chocolates and read over her naked shoulder about palmistry, her exotic drapery hoisted over her tits with uncharacteristic modesty. She told him he had a long life line, a deep heart line and a fame line – a rare gift – and let him kiss the smooth skin of her neck behind the frothy dark sweep of her hair, as casually accepting of caresses as her nasty little familiar, Pyewacket.

'What's a fame line?' he asked her.

'Here...' She held his hand out, tracing a little line that ran from the base of what would one day be his wedding-ring finger and connected with the curve of the heart line that ran between his middle and index fingers. 'It ends on the Mount of Mercury at the base of your little finger here ... means you'll be famous by virtue of your natural eloquence one day.'

I could picture Alex – a wide-eyed, dark-eyed boy, raised in all the nice conventions of suburbia, before he grew the bleached blond dreadlocks he wore when I knew him, buying this hook, line and sinker. Spellbound. He loved the smell of incense, candlewax, the allure of a world of such gorgeous laziness, where you could lie in bed until four in the afternoon eating chocolates if you wanted to. I could see him snuggling closer in the bed, taking such pleasure in the touch of her fingers on the pads of his palm.

'Mount of Mercury? There?'

Their fingers would have touched on the pad of flesh at the base of his little finger, a game of tiny touches, the smallest of brushes of skin; then, with daring, she would press her thumb into the thickest pad at the base of his thumb, leaving the crescent-moon print of her nail in the flesh.

'That's the Mount of Venus. It means that you have a sensual nature.'

He was so excited he could have screamed out loud. Her thumbnail had left a mark in his skin, in the middle of the mount, which she'd squeezed and pressed and caressed as though she were trying to feel the very sensuality it described according to her crumpled books on palmistry, which lay scattered all over her bed. She took hold of his wrist and kissed the mark her nail had made, then laughed and teased him by pushing another cappuccino truffle into his mouth when he tried to move in for an inexpert kiss.

Her presence was constant, even when he was away from her in his sullen, teenage sanctuary of a bedroom. There would always be a whiff of incense in the hall, the tinkle of hot, sweet New Orleans jazz from her open kitchen window downstairs, and sometimes she'd be heard singing along in a cracked, husky but melodious voice. Old songs – 'These Foolish Things', 'A Fine

Romance', 'Summertime'. He'd see the crescent moon
swinging above the peach tree in the back garden and
look for the faded mark of her fingernail in the pad of
his palm, sometimes impressing it anew with his own
thumbnail so he knew it was there whenever he got
himself off to the memory of her nail pressing the
crescent moon into his flesh.

The most awkward moments, he told me, were when
he was with his mother, Ruth, watching her sniff with
disapproval around Lene's ramshackle kitchen, noting
things to pick on later – the cat's presence on the
kitchen table, the stew sitting in a pan on the stove and
not hygienically stashed away in a Tupperware
container.

'I think that peach tree is dying,' Ruth remarked,
peering out of the kitchen window. I met Ruth once at
the end of term, a pinched, nervous-looking woman
with fair hair and narrow lips. Alex, she told me bit-
terly, took after his father, which I figured was a bad
thing in Ruth's eyes.

Lene looked out at the peach tree, tired, withered, a
depressed-looking specimen if ever there was one. She
took a big, unladylike gulp of hot tea and nudged Alex's
foot under the table. 'Nah – I don't think it's dying. It's
just lacking something.'

'Needs root space?' Ruth speculated. 'Maybe if you
were to dig up that forsythia bush next to it – provided
you didn't cut into the roots of the tree of course.'

Alex sketched the next scene in a handful of phrases
and I relished the images – Lene, sloppy, scruffy, wet-
lipped, odd-eyed little witch, swinging her bare foot and
talking in hot, erotic metaphors while Ruth sipped her
tea with tight lips and Alex sat there with an erection
up to his navel and a permablush on his hairless cheeks.

'The gardener can't have done his job right when he
planted that tree,' Lene said, swatting the cat on the

arse and perching on the chair he'd forcibly vacated. Her elbows, dimpled and pale like something painted by Romney, rested on scarred, old wood, her white hands, those naughty, pinching nails painted glittery blue, supporting her chin. She licked her lips a lot when she talked, I'm told, and I can see her sitting impishly poised over the table, breasts squeezed like ripe fruit in one of her untidy, indecent shirts, her mouth wet and wicked as she spoke.

'The thing when you're planting something – you see, you gotta realise what, or rather *who*, you're putting it into.'

Alex nearly choked on his Brooke Bond at the double entendre, thinking of all the times he'd thought long and hard about putting it into a certain *who*.

Lene carried on unabashed. 'You see, you gotta treat Mother Nature like a lover, 'cause she's a cold old bitch really. She hates it when she gets woken up in the spring after doing her Ice Queen thing all winter. Flirts a bit, shows you her spring greens, but won't give you too many signs of enjoyment during the summer. She lies back and takes it, lazy, like she can't be arsed, sort of drowsy, you know? Autumn, that's when she comes, fruit, flesh, fowl, fish – all ripe and ready, kind of exploding out of her as she gives up the act and admits that she *loves* it.'

While she spoke she swung her foot under the table, bare toes nuzzling the top of Alex's Doc Martens, making him gulp and gasp and flush crimson with lust. Ruth smiled politely and said that that was certainly an interesting way of looking at it.

'The person who planted that tree had no juice in them,' Lene said, dreamily. 'They were all dried up. No potency. No passion. It shows.'

Soon after that, Ruth went away one weekend, to a duty family funeral, and Alex hoped he might be able to make a move on the object of his desire. His mother had given him the usual parental injunctions: telephone numbers to call, don't you dare have any wild parties – that sort of thing. There wasn't much chance of wild parties. Alex had isolated most of his peers over the summer, the company of fellow teens seeming somewhat vanilla next to the spicy, intoxicating Lene Lane. The girls he'd groped before – immaculate as per the instructions of fashion magazines for which they were surely too young – seemed sanitised, all nicely encased in glitter and PVC, neat strips of perfectly shaved pubic hair and eyebrows plucked to nothing.

Not like Lene, who'd sometimes rush to the corner shop to get milk for her cat dressed in nothing but a raincoat and heels, whose disregard for electrolysis and the pursuit of well-scrubbed perfection meant that she had this nice fuzzy quality to her smooth cheeks, like peach fuzz.

'I mean, it was like she was a real woman, you know? She reeked of sex the whole time. Didn't shave, preen or pluck every hair out of her body – kinda sexy, the *nerve* she had to be all woman like that.'

I was warming to the image Alex was painting as he told me this story. She sounded like a free-spirited, cheerful slut with a whole load of healthy contempt for everything that mothers told you was nice behaviour.

'So what happened?' I asked, hoping we were finally getting to the seduction part of the tale.

He was never sure who'd seduced whom, he said. She was so innocent in all her overblown sexuality that it was impossible to imagine her doing anything as manipulative as seduction, but personally I reckon it was Alex's ego talking there. He wanted to imagine that he'd seduced the witch next door – a seventeen-year-old Don Juan. Not bloody likely, in my humble opinion.

'She called me.'

'A siren song, huh?'

'No. On the *phone*.'

'Oh.'

She rang him up and asked what he was up to that evening, since she had a bottle of Southern Comfort and a nice chunk of Moroccan and was a girl who liked to share. Any invitation like that is honey to the bee to any seventeen-year-old in their right mind – alcohol, drugs and the chance to lose his cherry. You bet. He'd be on her kitchen doorstep faster than you could say testosterone.

They got shit-faced – stoned and pissed beyond even the worst sins that Ruth could imagine. Lene peeled peaches and dropped chunks of their skinned flesh into glasses of Southern Comfort, where they infused the liquor with the taste of bittersweet fruit. She rolled joints and they lolled around on her scatter-cushion-infested floor, cackling and flirting and fishing the booze-sodden peach slices out of their drinks to assuage their munchies.

'Wouldn't it be great if we could get the peach tree to wake up?' Alex remarked. 'Then we could lie under it and get smashed and let the fruit just drop off the tree and into our mouths.'

'Make ourselves sick on 'em.' Her voice was hot and dreamy, as it had been when she was equating garden-ing with fucking Mother Earth to bright, blooming orgasm in the dusty, spice-scented surroundings of her kitchen.

'I have an idea.'

'You do?'

'Yuh-huh. Needs both of us, though.' She rolled over on the cushions and one of her breasts almost spilled out of her top. Emboldened and tanked, Alex looked, letting her know he was staring.

She took his hand and the movement of her arm made the cloth slip further, and one pale-rose nipple was exposed. His eyes were nearly popping out of his head, his dick so hard he thought it might burst, but Lene was lingering over the pad of his thumb again, pressing the crescent back into his flesh.

'There – Venus, the crescent moon, me, and you. Especially you.'

Her thumb rubbed across his palm and her mouth came down on his wrist, her tongue flickering over the pulse point like a wet snake. She kissed the crescent mark she'd left there like before, holding his hand like a prize in her palm, her weird eyes wicked, her hair floating like dark smoke over her shoulders and bared breast.

'So young, so full of juice. Potent. Powerful. I *must* show you.'

'Yes. Show me. Please.'

As you can imagine, our young hero didn't take much persuading. He was standing barefoot under the peach tree in Lene's garden in the middle of a summer night, horny, infatuated, and eager to be relieved of his virginity one way or the other. Lene, in the dark, was transformed – by booze, hash or something older – into a dancing sprite, a maenad tangled in the ivy, slipping out of her clothes. Her breasts and buttocks were like round white moons, her pubic hair a dark, untended tangle between her rounded white thighs.

He laughed awkwardly and too loudly as he took his own clothes off.

'So this is what you think this tree needs?' he asked, giggling out of nervous excitement as they wrapped their arms around one another, chilled despite the humidity of the summer night.

'Totally. Needs some potency. A little youth. A little passion. The right moon.'

He followed her gaze upwards. It was the new moon, swinging like a sickle in the sky – the moon you weren't supposed to look at through glass lest it bring you bad luck.

'Is this witchcraft?'

'Course it is. The oldest sort. Now let's get to it. This poor tree's desperate.'

Her mouth tasted of peaches, hash and Southern Comfort, her tongue rough and broad, licking slow, smooth swirls around his own. He moaned into the kiss, even more desperate than the tree, and nearly exploded with his own surprise and pleasure when she knelt down and took him in her mouth under the tree. He didn't take long, being seventeen and all that, and she emphatically spat his come into the roots of the tree.

She stood and rested her hand on his head, playfully pushing him down. 'Down you go.'

Oh. *Oh.*

He had no idea how to do this, but she'd taught him well, clearly. He demonstrated his skill to me, sinking down with a sparkle in his eyes as he looked up at me from between my legs. I was grateful to Lene Lane that night when we were nineteen, because she'd taught the boy the meaning of oral fixation and made a man of him. I was already wet from hearing his hot little story and I could feel the moisture leaking out on to the tops of my thighs, pubic hair all sticky, bristly and musky from last time.

He licked the wet dabs off my inner thighs and opened me up with one smooth lick, and I felt like a peach, like a fruit he was holding open with his tongue and thumbs to devour the sweet flesh inside. I was thinking of a peach while he ate – the image of a crescent-shaped slice taken out of the side of the fruit, exposing the wrinkled, red-brown core, the flesh in graduating sunset shades radiating outwards from the creased heart of it towards the silken, furred skin at the edges. Mother Nature at her teasing, naughtiest best. He found the core, the wrinkled centre, and licked it smooth, pushing it up between his thumbs so he could iron out the creases all the better.

I think he restored my faith in magic, in the flesh, that night. I owe Alex a debt – and Lene, for teaching him so well. The way he pushed his fingers inside – as if he were trying to dig out the pit, coring me with his finger as he found the circle of my arse and pushed inside. Never have I felt so completely penetrated as I did with his fingers and mouth, hands filling both holes, tongue working relentlessly over my clit with small spirals, then deep, hard licks that made me howl out loud – not giving a shit about what that cloying confection of a student nurse who slept in the next room thought.

I never found out the end of his story, either. We didn't talk much for the remainder of the night and for one reason or another we never did it again. He dropped his medical degree shortly after – said the smell of formaldehyde and the pathology classes gave him the horrors – and the next thing I knew he'd gone home to Falmouth, dropping out entirely to get a 'real job', as he put it, pissed off with dissection, academia and Proust.

It was seven years before I saw him again. I met up with him at a breast-cancer charity function. He was working as a journalist for a national newspaper, making a hack like me simultaneously green with envy and congratulating him vigorously. Hating him for making it, and loving him for proving that it could be done.

'You're still living in Falmouth?' I asked.

'Yeah. Same house, actually. Mum's place.'

'How is she?'

'Oh ... uh ... she died. Five years ago. Breast cancer.'

'*Shit!* Oh, God. I'm sorry.'

'No, no. Not your fault after all. Turned my wife kind of evangelical, though. She knocks herself out for these charity dos.'

'You got married!'

'Yup!' He grinned and held up his left hand, a band of white gold around the third finger, the Apollo finger, just above the fame line. 'She's here somewhere.'

I tried to imagine what kind of woman he'd marry since he'd cut off all that matted blond hair and ditched the skateboard gear he'd habitually worn when he was a down-at-heel med. student.

'Oh, there she is! Hey! Peaches!'

Peaches? Holy fuck! I thought. Trophy-wife kind of name or what? Then I found myself looking into a pair of bright, unmatched eyes. One blue, one brown.

'Lene, this is Anna. We were at King's together. Anna, Lene.'

'Hi.' She gave me a quick smile and grabbed Alex's arse. 'Nice to meet you.'

'Lene's a chef,' Alex announced, proudly.

'Wow. That's quite an art.'

'Nah ...' She shook her head – a big Jimi Hendrix explosion of dark hair. 'It's a doddle. It's just *food.*'

'Perhaps you'd like to explain the concept of that to the caterers,' Alex said, menacing her with a piece of withered broccoli quiche. She laughed.

'Yeah, OK. So it's not that easy. The food here's *shit.* You shoulda seen those tragic-looking peaches on the so-called tarte tatin. Poor things were on the *brink*, I swear. Not like the ones we get off the tree at home ...'

Alex winked at me and I knew the end of the story at last. It *had* worked, after all.

One of the Boys Robyn Russell

He promised me she wouldn't be back that afternoon. And we made love, unabashed and hard, as if we were making up for all those lost years. All those years ago she'd taken him from me. Now I was taking him back where he belonged. Inside me, between my thighs, beneath my body, still slim, but now the body of a full-grown woman.

After sating ourselves fully, we slept. I woke first and, while Jamie dozed, I thought back ten years to the time our innocence suddenly evaporated. I looked down at his face, at his body, and remembered.

We'd grown up together, me and the three Johnson boys: Ben, Jack and Jamie. They were cousins, but so alike that folks mistook them for brothers. I wasn't related to them but it used to seem like I was. Our parents were friends from way back and I wanted to be one of the boys. But I was a girl.

Ben, Jack and Jamie Johnson pretty much accepted me as part of their group until one summer in the middle of our teens. That year was different from the start. We were swimming in the lake when Jamie, who was my secret but undisputed favourite of the troupe of cousins, commented casually on my developing body. As usual, we were nude, stretched out on the wharf to dry in the sun after our swim.

In recent years I'd watched the boys' bodies change with dispassionate interest, and that summer I'd caught them glancing expectantly at my slender, underdeveloped figure. When Jamie's comment came, it was unexpected. 'Sam!' His shout bounced across the lake that hot afternoon. 'Sam, you have titties!' He seemed to be accusing me of something.

I was so embarrassed, I plunged back into the water and swam frantically to shore, my face burning. The blush seemed to travel all over my wet, naked body. I didn't swim nude with them any more.

That afternoon I rode to town and bought a bra. I resolved to wear it all the time, even while sleeping.

The boys continued swimming naked, of course, and only occasionally did they tease me about wearing the concealing, black bathing suit I'd found in my mother's closet. They were totally unembarrassed about their nakedness, and romped and splashed across the lake like spirited colts, even when they knew I was looking at them.

Watching them, I began to feel a serious stirring between my legs, especially when regarding Jamie, the youngest of the boys and only a few weeks older than I was. That feeling was hard to ignore but was stifled by my new-found shyness. One afternoon, I was trying to take my mind off the boys by reading a novel, reclining in the old treehouse we'd used to play in as kids. Despite the heat, I was wearing my bra beneath my dress.

'Sam?' It was Jamie's voice.

'Up here. Climb on up.'

His tousled head appeared in the rudimentary doorway, followed by his body, tanned and naked except for faded khaki shorts.

'Mind some company?' he asked. I gestured to the spare cushion and went back to reading.

We lay in companionable silence until his voice broke in on my thoughts, hesitant yet urgent.

'Sam? Sam, can I show you my dick?'

I shot up to a seated position, and there was Jamie's short, thick penis, out of his pants and longer than I had ever seen it.

'Touch it, Sam. Hold it in your hand.'

I reached tentatively, then grasped the warm, firm flesh. He stiffened under my touch. One pump, then two and three, and he shuddered, jetting a stream of semen over the floorboards. Much to Jamie's chagrin, I giggled, and he fled down the tree trunk, embarrassed by his boldness and my laughter. But soon this afternoon meeting became a regular ritual. Jamie's hands often sought my body in return for his, but I stubbornly allowed his hands only to caress me through my thin summer clothes.

We knew we were playing with fire.

We were all sixteen that summer. Except for Ben. He was seventeen already. And I didn't actually turn sixteen till after the middle of July. But we were all about the same age, all four of us. Me and the boys. Just me, skinny Sam and the guys. Until Margaret arrived. Then there were five of us, all teeming with lust, unwatched by our elders, running wild.

It was two days before my sixteenth birthday, and I was especially eager to be with Jamie in our treehouse retreat. I was ready for him to take off my bra this time; I thought I was ready to go all the way.

But that very afternoon Margaret came into our lives and, with one fell swoop of her sexy young hand, all Jamie's and my innocent exploration into our blossoming sexuality came suddenly crashing down. She arrived by car with her mother, an old college pal of Mama's and a real-life floozy-looking lady. The minute Margaret got out of the car, she and I were enemies. She preened artfully in front of the three Johnson boys. 'Hi, guys,' she said. 'I see we're going to have fun this summer!' But she ignored me.

Margaret was as curvy and blonde as I was dark and slim. If I was one of the boys, she was all girl.

The boys were all lined up, hair brushed just so, like a row of *Masterpiece Theatre* servants, there to greet her. I was leaning casually against the fender of her mother's car. 'Y'all look like you're standing in a police line-up,' I told them.

When she heard my voice, which was high and sweet, Margaret turned at last to me and smiled. Pretence colouring her words, she said, 'Oh, she's a girl! I thought she was a boy, too.'

I was mortified when Margaret said this, of course. And my usually sharp tongue was silent. All the time I'd wanted to be a boy, but now I desperately wanted to be a girl. I could think of nothing to say, especially when I heard Ben snort with casual derision at her comment.

'Oh, this is Sam,' he said easily.

'She thinks she's a boy. Always has,' Jack added with a cackle.

I was glad that Jamie didn't say anything.

Margaret laughed softly. 'Oh how cute! Ben, Jack, Jamie and Sam!' Giggling, she let her big, blue eyes rest on my chest where my renowned 'titties' were held firmly in place by the bra. By now it was two sizes too small. Up until Margaret's statement that day, I'd had no real desire to advertise my anatomical differences, but now I'd get a new bra. I stuck out my chest. I'd show her.

But nobody noticed. I blushed furiously. I looked at Jamie. Even he was grinning at the blonde interloper. Suddenly I hated them all, especially Jack and Ben, but also Margaret and even Jamie. I turned hotly towards the boys, venting my frustration their way. 'Shut up, you dopes!' I shouted, angrily spewing my teenaged venom. 'This will spoil it all! You idiots don't know anything!'

'My goodness,' Margaret said with a toss of her golden curls. 'She's quite a little spitfire, isn't she?'

The boys, at last, were silent. I couldn't tell if they were loyal or merely embarrassed. As my anger subsided, I felt Jamie staring at me and I looked back. His stupid grin was gone, like he was afraid something bad was going to happen. But I said nothing more; instead I tried tossing my hair (much too short), turned on my heel, and stormed inside to the cool kitchen for a tall glass of lemonade to quench my anger.

All that summer Margaret continued to speak of me in the third person, as if I weren't present. She spoke directly to the boys, of course, plying and practising her seductive charms on them, as if preparing for a contest. Margaret wasn't content with mesmerising Ben and Jack; that she did quickly. She was interested in Jamie, too, and, to my alarm, started working her ways on little Jamie. My Jamie.

Despite her attentiveness to all three, Ben and Jack were lusty enough to keep Margaret busy most of the time. Even a *femme fatale* like Margaret couldn't always control two fellows the likes of blue-eyed Ben and long tall Jack. Both were blond and athletic, with muscular torsos and powerful legs. 'Jocks' in any other American setting, here on the farm these two big, handsome young men were in their earthy element: a lush fertile land with lots of trees, a lake and a few crops to tend. They lived for the summers on the estate. What would they do when Jamie and I went away to school in the Fall? Stay here?

For Ben and Jack, the farm was paradise. And Margaret was their Eve. They hadn't yet realised that two

Adams might be a problem. While she teased and taunted them with her sexual games, Jamie and I would slip away to be alone in the treehouse.

By now I was greedy for Jamie's hands and we made a lot of progress in the treehouse that summer, where we both learned a lot about masturbation and speciality kissing, and came close to 'doing it' several times. Yet I was reluctant to 'go all the way', being naïve enough to think that if we started having 'real' sex, we'd be trapped.

Between my reluctance to 'go all the way' and my pressure on Jamie to be like me and go to college – along with normal erratic teenaged lust – we broke up frequently. But we always got back together the same day, or later that evening, usually by making love in our virginal way.

As the long August afternoons stretched towards Fall, I knew I had to decide whether to do two things: whether to have sex with Jamie and consummate our love affair; and whether to take a job off the farm, one that paid the money necessary for college. I drove into town to think about it.

I thought these two questions over for a long time. When I got home, confused as ever, it was dark. I looked for Jamie. We'd 'broken up' that morning and I was eager to make up. But when I walked into the woods behind the big farmhouse, looking for him, I found Ben and Jack building another treehouse by the light of big lanterns. This one was Margaret's. Jamie was helping, and lapping up the blonde's attention as she skipped around the working boys in her normal revealing tank-top and shorts, pretending to help, and stroking their muscles. I couldn't help notice the bulge in Jamie's pants and was jealous. It was only me who could tease his beautiful cock!

* * *

Margaret quickly installed herself in the new treehouse. As soon as the simple structure – no more than a wood palette with some walls – was completed, she was up there like a little bird feathering her nest. Soon Ben and Jack began going up there, too.

As the days and nights went by I didn't know exactly what was going on in Margaret's enclave, but I could guess. I clung to Jamie, using my hands and the promise of my body to keep him with me, but it was clear that he was getting mighty curious about what Margaret and the other two boys were up to. Ben and Jack didn't talk much in my presence, but they must have regaled Jamie with their sexual exploits. Jealously, I grew hot to think about what they were doing.

Jamie and I had another argument – our worse to date – the morning I was to take my first round of college entrance exams. I'd wanted Jamie to go, too. But I went to town alone.

It was full dusk when I returned, and I saw Margaret sitting in the little window of her roughhewn treehouse shack, illuminated by the new-risen moon, and radiant as any Juliet or Rapunzel. Nude to the waist, her eyes were closed and she was smiling, like it felt good to sit naked in the moonlight.

Looking at her pretty, upturned, pink-nippled breasts, I swallowed hard, and watched her stand to reveal her complete nakedness. Confused and oddly heated, I turned away and ran into the house. In the past, Jamie and I had always made up the moment I returned from town. But this time it was different: on that sticky August day, we'd had our most intense lovers' quarrel to date and, instead of looking for him, I went to bed thinking of Margaret, how much I hated her, and how lovely her naked body was.

I slept fitfully that night, dreaming about a confused vision of Margaret smiling, unclothed, in her treehouse window, and when I woke up late the next day, my hand was nestled between my legs.

Everybody was out working but me, so I spent most of the morning upstairs in my bedroom. Staring out of my window over the apple orchard, and reading fitfully, I finished a rather melancholy and romantic novel. Feeling a little sad and more than a little horny, I opened the window and picked a ripened apple from a tree-limb just outside. Chewing on the fruit, I looked at the pleasant view of treetops. Through gaps in the branches I could see Margaret's treehouse from my attic window; it seemed empty. I was all alone.

Leaning over the sill, I unbuttoned the top of my simple, cotton shirtwaist dress. It was unusual for me to wear a dress and today I wore no bra or panties. I'd thought of wearing no clothes at all, advertising my nakedness to myself. But residual shyness kept me loosely covered. The breeze entered the top of the dress to tease my naked breasts. I finished my apple and tossed the core outside.

Recalling Margaret's flagrant nudity in the moonlight, I pulled my dress over my shoulders and down to my waist, leaving my breasts bare. Feeling hedonistic, I cupped my small breasts in my hands. Shuddering deliciously as the warm air brushed them, I kneeled at the window and leaned forward, admiring my bare flesh in the dappled summer sun.

I was leaning further over the sill, breasts out, when I heard the distant voices of my three erstwhile male companions.

Instinctively I pulled back inside but, unable to resist the urge to eavesdrop, I redraped my torso across the windowsill, listening. When I heard the voices again, closer now in the orchard below my high-up window, I felt my bare nipples tighten.

I heard footsteps rustle in the dry grass, and muffled giggles, almost childish in their glee.

I stared down, squinting through the leaves, and saw, just below me, the most incredible sight. I felt my naked skin prickle deliciously and held my breath to keep from gasping. Below me in the apple orchard, the three boys – led by Ben, of course – stood in a semicircle, all with their pants down! Beneath their worn, denim shorts, none wore underwear. The flesh of their buttocks and thighs was camouflaged by the patterned shadow of the leaves, but there was no mistaking Ben when he turned around to reveal his large penis. I gasped. It was much larger than Jamie's!

Had they heard me gasp? Clearly they were sexually charged and the sight charged me too. I watched them with fascination, growing yet more excited to think they might see me sitting in the window, as I had seen Margaret the night before.

But they didn't look up.

Aroused by their activities, when I saw Jack's equally large erection, I gasped again. Of course, I'd seen the boys naked before, but that was just playing around at the lake. And naturally I knew Jamie's handsome little dick quite intimately. But this was different. This was really hot.

'Look at me, boys!' I wanted to shout out loud. I wanted them to see the freckles popping out cinnamon colour upon my pretty, creamy breasts. Busy as they were, comparing their cocks' lengths and thicknesses, and starting to masturbate beneath my tree, they didn't know I was there.

Instead of shouting, I listened and watched as, in the late afternoon heat, the murmuring trio of boys played with themselves. The sight of those stalks of eager young flesh highlighted in the afternoon sun ignited a voyeur's passion in me, especially since I, too, was almost naked. I quivered with the eroticism of it all, and the palpable excitement hanging in the still summer air incited me to pull off my dress and reach between my legs.

Vicariously voracious, I stared at those three lovely, erect penises, and imagined their flesh rubbing against my flesh. Vibrating with desire, I stroked the insides of my thighs. I shivered deliciously. When I touched my clitoris, I was shocked at how good it felt to rub myself. Surprised by my sexual arousal, I closed my eyes and felt my pulse gather. Arching my back, feeling my inner lips moisten, I could hear the boys' voices clearly.

I was starting to play with myself when I heard Jack besmirch my name by calling me a 'cock-tease', and by asking Jamie if I'd let him fuck me yet. Opening my eyes wide, I saw both older boys point their cocks at Jamie, miming the act, rutting with their hips.

'She just isn't ready yet,' I heard Jamie say valiantly, his penis drooping slightly.

The other two boys laughed, and Jack said, 'Well, Margaret licks me off. I bet she'd do that to you, too, Jamie. She really likes you.'

I was sprialling my index finger delicately between my pulsing labia when Jack continued coolly, 'Yeah, I bet Sam hasn't even sucked you off yet, has she?'

Jamie was silent.

I rose to my knees. Part of me wanted to swing down in the branches, land naked in front of them, and suck the come from Jamie's cock right there on the spot, in view of his taunting cousins. But, coward that I was, I merely leaned forward to peer down again through the boughs from my bower window. The boys were tantalisingly close beneath me.

Ben commented, 'Well, Margaret will suck you off. She might even fuck you. Tonight she's going to do Jack and me. Are you game? We'll make her wet and ready for you.'

Laughing, Jack masturbated blatantly close to Jamie.

Jamie's own erection was painfully hard and straight.

Jack said, 'Margaret's ready, ain't she, Ben?'

Authoritatively extending his own prick, Ben said, 'Yeah, man, Margaret's ready and willing!'

Jamie was still quiet. But he was gripping his erection like he wanted to pump it.

'One time,' Jack continued teasing, 'she let me come on her face. Another time she let me come all over her tits.'

'Wow!' Jamie gasped in spite of himself. All pretence to coolness evaporated. He was obviously very aroused.

'Let's see you pump that slick little dick of yours, Jamie!' continued Jack.

Ben watched, chuckling. 'Margaret wants to fuck you, too. She likes you,' he added sagely.

Jack chimed in. 'That's it, Jamie. Pump it. Think of Margaret. She likes you better than Sam does.'

Through the leaves, I saw Jamie pump his dick faster. He was going to come. Stimulated by the confusion of desires, I almost wept. Riding my passion, I masturbated fast.

Jack spoke again. 'Think of it, Jamie. Margaret is ready and willing, stretched out naked on that treehouse floor. She wants to fuck us all.'

Heart pounding, I panted with anticipation for something, some resolution to my lust for them, wanting sex, wanting Jamie, wanting to be like Margaret and have the boys at my beck and call. Still kneeling, I nestled my fingers deeper inside my vagina, and arched my back high and rubbed myself sensuously, feeling fresh pulses of excitement ripple across my belly and groin. For a virgin, I was really feeling it! Suddenly, a delicious decadent shudder travelled up my body. Was it a shudder of fear or an orgasm?

Closing my eyes, I relished the luxuriously erotic feeling. When I opened them again, I saw Jack reach out his hand and grasp Jamie's dick, pumping it hard. Jamie cried out suddenly and I saw him come in a streak of semen. Again, I came, and fell forward, my fingers soaked with my juices. I closed my eyes and shuddered a last, long frisson.

In those seconds, Jack had pumped Jamie dry. As for me, I was wet, wet, wet, and wiped and patted myself dry with my discarded dress.

My heartbeat was slowly returning to normal as Jack's enthusiastic voice surfaced.

'Jesus, man,' I heard him say to Jamie. 'You were horny as hell.'

I looked down. Jack held his own penis, still engorged and red, and pumped himself with renewed vigour. Taking a deep breath, I watched as Ben masturbated, too. Within seconds, both older boys came, their arcs of semen competing for range and trajectory.

All three were breathing hard.

'God, I feel like I ran the marathon,' said Jack.

Ben said, 'That's good. Now we won't come too fast with Margaret.'

'Yeah man,' drawled Jack. 'Let's draw straws to see who gets to fuck her first.' Ardour restored, he was already playing with himself again. I wondered: Did they do this often?

'No, you guys go,' said Jamie, caressing his own spent dick. 'I can wait.'

'Now you've used up your come for the hour?'

Jamie grinned sheepishly.

'OK, cuz,' said Ben. 'But you'll feel different about it when you see her, and you get hard, hard, hard!'

Feeling desolate, I watched from my perch above as

they all laughed and clapped each other on the back, penises still hanging out. It was odd. They took off their shirts and dried themselves. Their shorts were still down around their ankles.

'Let's draw straws,' shouted Jack, as he tore up a few strands of dry grass.

Quite suddenly my three lifetime companions were again tumescent at thoughts of having sex with Margaret. They drew straws before they even fastened up their shorts. Ben got to go first, of course. Jack was miffed to be second. Jamie was last.

'Come on, guys. Button up. We've got to get ready for Margaret!' Ben exclaimed.

I was paralysed and watched through a sheet of tears as they tucked their dicks in their shorts and fastened their belts, all three very jolly in their partially erect partnership to relinquish their virginity, all together. Like it was a fishing trip or something, Jamie went along with Jack and Ben.

Just one of the boys.

I watched as all three walked through the small orchard single file – Ben first, then Jack and Jamie – towards Margaret's treehouse. I was sure Margaret would fuck them all. Each and everyone of them. I was only surprised that she hadn't already had Ben and Jack. And now Jamie. As usual he would be last. Unless I could get to him first.

I often wonder what would have been the consequences if Jamie and I hadn't had the last little lovers' quarrel. Or if we had made up like we always did before. He didn't even know how ready I was to give up my virginity to him.

I pulled on my wrinkled dress and buttoned it all the way up as I watched them cross the shallow creek to where Margaret's lair hung in the trees. As I shimmied down the tree trunk, again I felt that exciting tingling down between my legs. Standing below, I dried my eyes. Slowly, I walked to the edge of the creek and looked through the scrim of trees, only to see Jack and Jamie, shirtless and standing at the base of Margaret's treehouse. Their suntanned and well-muscled torsos were dappled with sun and shade. I stared at such masculine beauty.

I thought it was funny that Margaret could keep someone like Jack, the wildest, the tallest, perhaps the most handsome, waiting. That said a lot about her 'goddess power'. As I watched, both young men craned their necks to look up into the branches like a pair of eager young bucks sniffing for the female. There was no sign of Ben, so I assumed Jack and Jamie were waiting their turns while Margaret finished 'doing' Ben. Neither boy beneath the tree had noticed me yet.

From his taller height, I saw Jack smile down at Jamie and clap him on the shoulder companionably. Then, much to my surprise, Jack again unzipped his pants and withdrew his cock, stroking it, pointing it at his younger companion. Jamie ignored him.

Unfazed, Jack shifted his weight from foot to foot, caressing the mighty, pink length of his erect penis. Quite oblivious to everything but his beautiful cock, Jack still didn't see me standing across the creek bed, but Jamie finally did, and the way he ducked his head made me realise that he wanted to fuck the blonde whore as much as the other two did. And he was probably hard, hard, hard again. I thought I could make out a distinctive bulge in his shorts.

Then Jamie lifted his head and looked right into my eyes and straightened his shoulders. Hot, aroused, and ready to give up the hymen, I stared back at him. But did he leave his position as last in line to come to me? No. He continued standing there, waiting to climb up the tree and get laid by that interloping slut Margaret. I'd lost my chance to be the one to get him first. I felt sad but too proud to do anything about it. Burning with desire, I was too haughty to make the move to take him back.

Jack said something to him, and I saw Jamie shrug. We didn't even break eye contact.

Following Jamie's gaze, Jack snapped around to face me, his eyes blazing. When he saw me standing there, he got all cocky. Strutting, he displayed his enormous erection for me to see.

'Want to join us, baby doll? Little Sammy girl?' Jack called across the creek in a mocking voice.

Jamie said angrily, 'Stop it, Jack! Shut up!'

But Jack, pumping himself furiously, just laughed. 'Sammy girl,' he sang.

'Leave her alone, Jack, or I'll hit you,' Jamie said angrily and made a fist.

Jack ignored him and, leering at me, said, 'Want to suck my dick?'

'Shut up, Jack,' Jamie said and swung his fist. He swung wide and hit the air instead of Jack's jaw, but by the time they stopped scuffling and looked my way again, I was gone.

In bed alone that night, I burned with shame and frustration.

Very early the next morning, I packed a few things and prepared to go out. Anywhere. Just to get away. But to my surprise, Margaret, the only other person awake, stopped me in the kitchen. I turned away, scowling. She put her hand on my arm, but I shrugged it off.

'Oh Sam,' she said. 'Don't be mad.'

I blinked with surprise at her sweet, dimpled smile. Her touch persisted. I stood there sullenly.

'I saw you yesterday, Sam. I could see everything

with my binoculars. The boys in the orchard playing with their cute little dicks, and you in the window playing with your little clit. I was masturbating too, watching you, thinking of sucking those lovely little tits of yours. I came thinking of you, Sam.'

Her hands strayed across my shoulder, down my arm and, ever so softly, brushed over my breast. I was transfixed by fear and a lust I didn't know I had, but when she gently led me towards the stairs, I followed without a word. Taking me by the hand, she led me upstairs to her bedroom. 'A place the boys can't come,' she giggled softly.

I followed her hips and buttocks as they sashayed and swayed beneath the hot-pink dressing gown she wore, to her room. She closed the door and took off the gown, revealing see-through baby doll pyjamas in matching bright pink.

She asked casually, 'Why don't you get undressed, too, Sam? You certainly don't need your outdoor clothes on here.'

Spellbound by the sight of her body, so different to mine, I couldn't move.

'Here,' she said and, with typical Margaret impatience, proceeded to pull off my T-shirt and unfasten my bra. After flinging the offending garments aside, she cupped my 'cute little tits' briefly in the soft palms of her hands and repeated, 'Get undressed, for gosh sake!'

My nipples were excited from her fleeting touch. Trembling with arousal, I managed to slide out of my shorts, revealing my own panties, utilitarian by Margaret's standards.

I was staring back at our reflections. Standing behind me, Margaret slipped her hand into the band of my grey jockey bikini briefs and said, 'You should try wearing a thong panty, Sam.' She paused caressingly. 'You

have nice cheeks. You should bare your bottom more.'
She reached all the way inside my panties and cupped
my buttocks. 'Nice and firm,' she said.

'Dance classes,' I replied, without thinking.

I watched in the mirror as the blonde – who, yesterday, was my arch-rival – turned her back to the mirror
and lifted the edge of her shortie pyjama top, revealing
a pink thong.

'See how sexy?' she said with a quick wiggle of her
hips. The band of the thong crept up the crack between
the two fleshy globes of her buttocks.

'Oh,' I said, my voice cracking.

She laughed. 'Here, lie down,' she ordered, and
swiftly slid my briefs from my legs. In a dream, I
watched her get naked and enfold my body with hers.

She licked me; she rubbed me; she finger-fucked me
and made me come. What can I say? I had my virginity
taken by a woman, just like one of the boys. I didn't
complain. If this was lesbian love, I was a recruit. I was
in lust.

The next day she was gone, without a word. Our
summer fell apart after that. We all had our own
memories but were not prepared to share them, at least
not me. Maybe we all felt we were just notches on
Margaret's bedpost.

I got a job in town and didn't go back there for the
rest of the summer. In fact I didn't go back to the farm
for many summers. I stayed in the city and worked two
jobs and saved money for college. News from home was
fleeting. One letter said Margaret was engaged to Ben.
There was no news of Jamie.

Once I enrolled in college, I took readily to having
sex with men, too, and in a big way. I had several lovers
my Freshman year. I took to college, too, and didn't let
the casual fornication that was part of the social scene
keep me from performing well academically. I enjoyed

the panoply of lovers, and didn't miss 'the boys' – or Margaret – back on the farm for quite a while. In fact, it was ten years before I went back.

When I did return, Ben wasn't there any more. Thinking he would inherit, Margaret had married him first. They'd had two children, two blonde girl brats, as handsome and tall as Ben, and as golden blonde and pouty as Margaret. When Ben didn't get rich, Margaret discarded him and married Jack. No more kids, but a liaison that lasted another few years. Now Jack was long gone, too. But Jamie was here now. Right here beside me.

I must have dozed again myself because I was startled out of a dream. Beside me, Jamie still slept. I reached for his penis. It was slightly hard. Jamie stirred. I slid across the bed and straddled him, gripping his strong body firmly between my knees. When I heard the step on the stairs, I grasped his thickening rod in both hands and directed it towards me. The steps grew nearer. Had Jamie's wife returned early? Though not fully awake, Jamie was hard, and the bulbous tip of his erection pressed against me. He groaned and his hands gripped my hips urgently. There was a knock on the door. Jamie's eyes flew open. I smiled down at him. He stared back, panic in his eyes. But I held him insistently, smoothly pulling his penis between the moist lips of my vagina. My breasts bounced with the motion as I rocked back and forth on his pelvis, his penis held tightly inside. I placed my hand over his mouth to stifle his exclamation.

The knock was repeated and a voice called, 'James? Are you there?'

Savouring ten years of waiting, I said sweetly, 'Come in, Margaret.'

Playing With Fire
Kimberly Dean

The fifth letter showed up at work.

Erin's hands shook as she slit open the envelope. By now she recognised the typewriter face. There was no return address, but she didn't need one to know what the vile contents of the letter would be. Somehow, she couldn't stop herself from unfolding the paper and reading.

You're so beautiful. I can't wait to fuck you. I watch you every night on the ten o'clock news. You act so serious, but I don't hear the words you're saying. All I see is that luscious mouth. If I concentrate real hard, I can feel it on my cock.

Her hands shook so badly that the letter slipped from her grip. It fluttered to her desk, but landed face up. Like a magnet, her gaze was drawn back to the filthy words.

And your hands. I look at those long fingers wrapped around your microphone, and I imagine them on my balls. Your hands kneading my balls and your mouth sucking the life out of my cock – that's what I want, Erin. That's what I'm going to get.

Blindly, she reached for the phone and dialled her boyfriend's number. 'Mark?'

He heard the tremor in her voice. 'You got another one?'

'Yes.'

'Son of a bitch!' There was a slam in the background and then a long silence. When his voice finally returned, it was under control. 'Is it the same as the others? Is the "f" lifted?'

Her gaze skimmed the words and landed on 'fuck'. She squirmed in her chair but tried to be analytical. 'Yes,' she said. 'It's raised slightly higher than the rest of the lower-case letters.'

'Get over here. Now!'

The drive across town was nerve-racking. With every turn, Erin checked her mirror to make sure she wasn't being followed. By the time she parked and rushed up the front sidewalk to Mark's house, she was a mess. The door was pulled open for her and she fell forward into her boyfriend's arms.

'Are you OK?' he demanded.

She nodded against his chest. Now that she was with him, she felt better.

'Did you bring the letter?'

She shuddered. 'It's in my purse.'

'Let me see it.'

After pulling out of his grip, she rummaged around and found the envelope. Mark carefully took it by the corners and stuffed it into his jacket pocket. It was only then that Erin realised he was dressed to go to the office. Panicking, she grabbed him by the lapels. 'You're not going down to the station now, are you?'

'I have to, baby.' His hands settled on her shoulders and he massaged them gently. 'I need to get this to the lab as soon as possible. I'm sick of this asshole running around terrifying you.'

'But Mark!'

His touch ran down her arms and he gripped her hands tightly. 'Don't worry, baby. Chris is here.'

Chris.

Erin looked sharply over Mark's shoulder. As always, his room-mate was hovering in the background.

'Did you get another sicko letter?'

The cool drawl of his voice sent a shiver of energy down her spine. His blue eyes were watching her so carefully. Her throat tightened and she nodded.

'Can you watch over her tonight, Chris?' Mark asked. 'I want to go down to the station and see if I can get any leads as to who's doing this.'

'I'll take care of her,' he agreed.

Mark softly kissed her forehead. 'You'll be fine here. I'll get this pervert, baby. I swear I will.'

She tightened her grip on him until he lowered his head. His lips covered hers possessively and he gave her a long kiss. She clung to him, not wanting him to go. He gave her a tight squeeze before pulling away.

'Try to relax,' he whispered.

Erin watched him turn and leave. Feeling abandoned, she wrapped her arms about her waist and stared at the door. Chris finally walked over and flipped the deadbolt. She flinched when he turned to face her. His blue eyes were so intense, so piercing.

'He's right,' he said in that quiet voice of his. 'You need to relax. You're about ready to jump out of your skin.'

She rubbed her arms, suddenly feeling cold. She couldn't relax. There was simply no way. 'I hate what this guy is doing to me.'

Chris settled back against the door. His pose was casual, but his eyes were alert. 'Are the letters really that bad?'

'They're horrible.' A shiver trickled down Erin's spine. Nervously, she ran a hand through her hair. 'Some of the things he's suggesting are just outrageous. I can't imagine letting anyone touch me that way.'

'Outrageous.'

There was a wealth of meaning behind his one word, but she didn't quite understand his point. 'Yes, they're outrageous.'

'Not "sick". Not "repulsive".'

She opened her mouth to respond, but she found that she didn't have an answer. 'What are you trying to say?' she asked slowly.

'Nothing,' he said as he pushed himself away from the door. 'It was just an observation.'

Stunned, Erin just let Chris walk from the room. When she realised what he'd implied, her jaw dropped. Fuming, she stomped into the kitchen after him. 'I don't know who you think you are! I'm being stalked. Don't even try to say that I'm enjoying it. The guy is sick. He's got some very strange ideas, and they scare me.'

Chris filled a cup with coffee and turned round to face her. 'That's what surprises me so much.'

Erin realised that she'd got closer to him than she'd thought. Awareness made the little hairs on the back of her neck stand on end, but she refused to back away. Chris had always affected her that way. He was the strong, silent type. She could never tell what he was thinking, and that unsettled her. 'Explain,' she demanded.

He shrugged. 'I don't know, I always thought you were braver than this. You never seem to take much caution when you're pursuing a story. When you were investigating that prostitution racket last month, you went at it head first.'

She cocked her head and tried to understand. 'This is different. I'm not pursuing a story. A freak is pursuing me.'

'Right – and you're reacting by cowering in the corner.'

'What else am I supposed to do?'

'Fight back.'

'I can't. I don't know who he is. Mark's a detective and even he hasn't been able to track this guy down.'

'So you can't do anything about your little stalker; do something about your fears.'

Erin finally took that step backwards. She didn't know where the conversation was going, but it made her nervous. 'How?'

Chris took another sip of his coffee, but his eyes never left hers. 'How do you conquer any fear? If you're afraid of flying, you get your ass on an aeroplane. If you're afraid of heights, you go to the top of the nearest skyscraper.'

Erin's cheeks turned pink, but he didn't stop.

'If you're afraid of sex . . .'

Her blush went right up to the roots of her hair. She was mortified to be having this discussion with Chris of all people. Most of their previous conversations had centred on the weather. She couldn't believe she was hearing this, much less considering his idea.

Sexual therapy. Was that the way to ease her mind? The ideas in those letters had been haunting her for weeks. They filled her thoughts night and day. If she could somehow manage to associate pleasure with the kinky threats, would her terror go away? She chewed her lower lip as she thought about it. Finally, she shook her head. 'I can't. Mark wouldn't go for it.'

He took another drink of his coffee, but his gaze pierced her to the core. 'Who said anything about Mark?'

Erin's heart stutter-stepped, but then exploded at a frantic pace. She took another step back, but butted up against the breakfast bar. 'You?'

He set the coffee cup on the counter. 'Why not?'

'Because Mark is my boyfriend.'

Chris pushed himself away from the counter and trapped her. 'This would have nothing to do with that.'

'I . . . I can't.'

'You can. I know you've thought about it.'

The blood rushed out of her face. 'You self-centred bastard.'

'I've seen you looking at me.'

She couldn't deny it. He wasn't the type of man she was normally drawn to, but there was something about him. Mark was more the dark, handsome type. Chris? Chris had closely cropped strawberry-blond hair, and blue eyes that made her nipples harden every time he glanced her way. And his body. He was built like a brick house. As a fireman, he worked out regularly. The results were enough to make her mouth water. Any time he took his shirt off, she couldn't stop looking at him.

'You know I want to fuck you,' he said.

Her toes curled in her shoes. 'I won't let you.'

'Fine. Walk around like a scared little girl. See if I care.'

Instead of moving back, though, he leaned forward and braced his hands on the bar on either side of her. Erin felt overwhelmed by his presence. He was much taller than she was and probably twice as wide. She felt dominated, and the twinge between her legs shocked her.

'Mark would be crushed,' she whispered.

'It would be our dirty little secret,' he whispered back.

'Do you really think it would work?'

'Take off that suit and we'll find out.'

The order stunned her. Tilting her head back, she looked at him. He was dead serious. He was waiting, though, for her consent. Her breaths shortened as she considered what would happen if she said yes. She couldn't think, though. Her pulse was pounding too frantically. She stared at him with fascination and saw the pulse thudding in his neck.

His suggestion was too bizarre. She shouldn't even be considering it.

'I don't know...'

'Take off the damn suit.'

Erin's insides clenched. She didn't know why she did it, but she reached for the top button. Chris didn't move, but his gaze focused on her actions. His rapt attention made her hands begin to shake. She was taking off her clothes for a man she hardly knew. By the time she got her jacket off, she was excited beyond any previous experience and her pulse was pounding at twice its normal speed.

His gaze took in her lacy black bra. 'Now the skirt.'

Her arousal pulsed between her legs. She couldn't rationally understand why, but she reached for the back zip. His gaze nearly singed her breasts. The position had thrust them forward until they nearly brushed against his chest. He was looking straight down into her cleavage.

The rasp of the zipper was uncommonly loud. Erin felt like a wanton as she swirled her hips and let the skirt slide to the floor. She still wore her bra, her panties and her practical journalist shoes, but she'd never felt so naked.

'Now, tell me,' he ordered in a voice that had dropped even lower, 'what does your stalker want to do to you that scares you so much?'

Her stomach clenched. 'I can't...'

'Tell me.'

Her breath hissed out of her lungs. The tell-tale sign of stickiness appeared between her legs, and she closed her eyes. God, what was wrong with her? 'He wants to tie me up,' she said finally.

'And?'

Her face flushed. She knew he would stand there all night staring at her semi-nude form until she told him.

Her voice dropped very low – so low she could hardly hear it herself. 'He's got a thing for fire. He wants to drip hot candle wax on my body as he ... as he screws me.'

The silence in the room was deafening.

'All right,' Chris said, just as softly. 'Then it's on to the table with you.'

Erin's knees nearly buckled. Her sex began to ache when he took her hand and turned her towards the kitchen table. It loomed in the centre of the room. With a tug on her wrist, he walked her to it. His hands settled on her waist as he made her look at it. The touch burned against her skin.

'Don't move,' he ordered.

She couldn't. Her breaths shortened as she stared at the table. He was going to do exactly what the pervert had threatened yet she was excited to the point of breathlessness just thinking about it. Her panties were wet and her nipples were hard peaks under the cups of her bra. What kind of a woman was she to want this to happen?

Chris wasn't gone long. When he returned, he had a pile of supplies in his hands, including a long length of rope. She shivered uncontrollably when he set them on the table.

'Turn around and sit,' he ordered.

Her heart jumped up into her throat, but she did as she was told. The surface felt cold against the back of her thighs and, with embarrassment, Erin realised she was smudging the table's surface with her juices.

Chris gave her a hard look. As he held her gaze, he reached for the front clasp of her bra. It was almost a relief when the confining garment loosened. Still looking at her, he reached for her breasts and caught one soft globe in each hand.

It had been so long since anyone besides Mark had

touched her that Erin gasped. The action pressed her breasts harder against his palms, and he squeezed gently. Her breath went ragged and her eyelids drifted shut.

'Look at me,' he said.

Her eyes popped open. When he saw he had her attention, he began working her breasts in his palms. His touch was so different – almost rough. His occupation was physical, and his hands reflected it. He had a grip that could hurt her if he wanted, and the knowledge further aroused her. She loved the calluses on his fingers. They scraped against the delicate skin, causing jolts of sexual energy to rush to her core.

'Have you ever been tied up, love?'

Love. The affectionate term made something bloom inside Erin's chest. He'd started calling her that not long after she'd started dating Mark. She'd always thought it odd, but right now she liked it. It made her feel sexy. 'No,' she said softly.

He pinched her nipples hard and she inhaled sharply. 'Good,' he said. 'I'll make sure you like it.'

He let go of her breasts and swept the bra off her shoulders. His hand ran down her body until it rested on her stomach. 'Lie back.'

Hesitantly, she relaxed on to the hard tabletop. She was a little uncertain. Once he had her tied up, he could do absolutely anything he wanted to her. Her stomach tightened, but she couldn't tell if it was from fear or anticipation.

'Lift your arms overhead.'

She slid her arms upwards and Chris measured out a length of rope. He pulled a handkerchief out of his back pocket and wrapped it around her skin to protect it from burns. Soon, she felt him twist the rope around her delicate wrist. Panic flared inside her, but with it was an overwhelming sense of arousal.

She'd never played these types of games before. Still, she couldn't help but notice that the little smudge of dampness under her buttocks had spread. She felt like an ancient sacrifice with her arms spread wide and her breasts thrust into the air.

'Oh, that's a pretty sight,' he whispered.

She shut her eyes as his hand settled on her breast again. This time when he pinched her she was halfway expecting it. Knowing it was coming didn't lessen its effects, though. If anything, her reaction was magnified by the fact that she was bound to the table and couldn't get away. When she finally cried out, he turned her loose.

'That's a good girl,' he said as he moved away.

'Now we're set,' he said as he came to stand at the base of the table.

Uncertainty gripped her one last time. 'Chris, I'm not sure . . .'

'Let's get those panties off of you,' he said in a low voice. His hands settled at her hips. 'Lift.'

Erin's stomach clenched, but she obeyed. The silk was pulled off her hips, down her legs and over her shoes. Chris's strong hands settled on her thighs, and he pushed them open. She could feel the blue heat of his gaze on her most secret place. His fingers bit into her inner thighs, and her sex spasmed uncontrollably. He bit out a curse when he saw her muscles working.

'Look at you.' His voice was almost a groan.

He swallowed hard, and Erin could almost see the determination cross his face. He pulled back from her suddenly and reached for the back of his T-shirt then whipped it over his head. Before it even hit the ground, he was reaching for the zipper of his jeans. He stripped in about half the time it had taken her.

He turned from her for a second and doused the lights in the room. Soon, there was the rasp of a match and the hiss of a flame. Erin's fingers bit into her bindings as one of the candles was lit. The fire danced on its perch and her supine body was bathed in soft light. Shadows emphasised the valleys, while the peaks basked in the glow.

Chris slowly moved the candle down her body. The light flickered across her torso until the flame was right above the triangle of her pubic hair. Erin squirmed as he lovingly petted the light brown curls with his free hand.

'Aren't you a pretty pussy?' he said softly as his fingers delved deeper.

She closed her eyes, unable to watch, then felt his fingers part her lower lips. The sensation of heat had her eyelids popping right back open. Her head came off the table as she frantically looked downwards.

The candle was still inches away from her, but he'd moved the flame closer so he could examine her more intimately. His fingers spread her wide. Her reaction seemed to fascinate him, so he tried it again. He got the same response.

'Careful!' she cried. The candle's flame danced too close for comfort. Sweat broke out on her brow and she locked the muscles of her spine and buttocks. She couldn't afford any more harsh movements.

He pushed her resolve, though, when his fingers moved upwards. With a practised flick, he pushed back the hood of her clit. Erin shrieked and tried to shimmy away. There was nowhere to go. The heat from the candle pulsed around the sensitive bundle of nerve endings. Chris applied direct pressure with his thumb, and her back arched off the table.

'Is the pussy hungry, love?'

'Yes,' she moaned. She wanted him inside her so badly, she could cry.

'All right. Patience.' He reached for another candle

and held it up in the flickering light. 'Let's see if it likes this.'

Erin's pulse exploded. 'No!'

Her protest was too late. She felt him placing the hard wax taper at her sensitive opening.

'Yes,' he crooned to her.

He rubbed the candle against her, making her accustomed to its feel. She couldn't relax. She couldn't fight. When he finally gave up teasing and began easing the candle into her, she groaned in delight. She felt so dirty. The taper was long – oh so long – and smooth. He'd put the base in first and the thickened knob pushed deep into her.

'Oh, my God!' she shrieked. 'God!'

Her body went taut and her neck arched as sensations pummelled her. He pumped the candle in and out, watching her hips lift to receive it. When he sensed she was coming close to peaking, though, he pushed the taper in deep and left it there.

'Not yet,' he cautioned. 'I want to be inside you when you come.'

Erin squirmed on the table, so aroused she was almost in pain. 'Oh, please. Chris, please!'

Then she saw it. He'd moved the lit candle over her stomach. Ever so carefully, he tipped it sideways. A droplet of wax poured over the edge. It seemed to fall in slow motion. Her eyes widened, but there was absolutely nothing she could do.

She'd been thinking about this for weeks. Ever since her stalker had painted the scenario in her mind, she'd been able to think of nothing else. The drop fell down, down, down. When it hit her skin, the heat was explosive.

Erin screamed.

The wax wasn't hot enough to burn, but it stung. Another drop hit her skin, lower on the abdomen. Her tummy clenched and, in turn, her cunt muscles clamped down on the candle that was still buried deep in her. She twisted her body, trying to roll away, but Chris firmly pressed her hips flat on to the table.

'God, you're a little firecracker!' Reaching between her legs, he gave the candle a twist.

She responded like a flashpoint. Her entire body became suffused in heat and her hips began thrusting uncontrollably.

Suddenly, hot wax was being dropped everywhere. The splashes hit her so quickly that she couldn't prepare for them. Every one of them edged a little closer to the juncture of her legs. Finally, one plopped on to the edge of her pubic hair.

Everything in the room suddenly went still.

Erin's heart pounded so hard that she was sure Chris could hear it. He wasn't interested in it, though. All his attention was on the puddle of wax oozing about the fine hairs low on her pubic bone.

He reached a curious hand out to touch the cooling wax. Helplessly, she looked up at him. His gaze was so intense, she forgot to breathe.

Without warning, he gave a yank.

Her pubic hair was pulled out at its root. The hot sting shot straight to Erin's core. Her scream lodged in her throat, but her body went wild. She began tugging at the ropes. Her legs wrapped around Chris's waist and her hips twisted in agony. Her breasts shuddered as she took deep, gasping breaths of air.

'Fuck!' Chris exclaimed. Her volcanic reaction sent him into overdrive. He tugged on the candle. It popped out of her with a slurp and he tossed it on to the floor.

Erin cried at the loss. 'Put it back in!'

'I've got something better,' he said with a ragged breath. He quickly doused the other candle and the room plunged back into darkness.

'Oh, please!' she begged. 'I need something inside me.'

He hooked his arms under her legs and settled his hands under her buttocks. The position stretched her obscenely, but she greedily lifted her hips. She heard the sound of his zipper, then his cock poked at her, searching for her opening. He found it in the darkness and, with a hard thrust, plunged into her as far as he could go.

'Chris!' she screamed.

He was much thicker than the candle and she had to stretch to accommodate him. With her hands tied and her legs pulled open wide, there was nothing she could do but accept his thrusts. He pulled out, leaving her almost empty before pushing in deep again.

'Yes,' she whimpered.

With a growl, he dragged her right to the edge of the table and began pounding into her. Erin felt the strain in her arms as the ropes pulled tight. He was fucking her mercilessly, and her blood pounded harder in her veins as it rushed to her core. He thrust one more time, and colours exploded inside her head. Her muscles clamped down hard and squeezed his cock, trying to capture it deep inside her.

'Erin,' he groaned as his own climax overtook him. His fingers bit into her buttocks and he ground her on his spurting cock. He came for a long, long time before that big cock went limp.

When it was done, his knees buckled slightly. With another groan, he leaned forward and let his weight settle on top of hers. He buried his face in her breasts and closed his eyes.

'Are you all right?' he asked.

Erin's heart pounded in her chest. She didn't know. She'd never been so thoroughly seen to in her life.

He lifted his head and his gaze settled on her like a laser beam.

'I'm fine,' she breathed.

He gave her a strange look. Then he did something totally unexpected.

He kissed her.

His lips settled across hers and her fingers bit into the rough rope. This wasn't a soft, questioning, first kiss. This was the kiss of a man who wasn't finished fucking his woman.

His hard lips moulded against hers. His tongue sought entrance and Erin opened her mouth. It darted inside and swirled across hers in an intimate mating dance. As just a kiss, it was powerful and overwhelming. She made a soft sound at the back of her throat and he pulled back to read the reaction in her eyes.

'Love,' he sighed. He gently laid a kiss on her forehead. 'Let's get you out of these ropes.'

With infinite care, he untied her. He looked over her wrists carefully, searching for any marks. Convinced he hadn't hurt her, he set about removing the wax from her skin. It had cooled and set. It cracked under his fingers as he applied gentle pressure. He dusted her off before his hand settled against her pubic hair.

'Did it hurt too badly?' he asked. His fingers rubbed the reddened bare spot.

Erin bit her lower lip with embarrassment. 'It was the best bikini wax I've ever had.'

That made him smile. She'd never seen him smile and her heart tripped in response. When his arms swept around her, she went into them willingly. He sat down on one of the kitchen chairs and pulled her into his lap.

Erin felt some of her arousal return. God, he was just so hard. She pressed her finger against his pectoral muscle, but his skin had hardly no give to it at all.

Giving in to the temptation, she explored the tattoo on his biceps. It had intrigued her forever. As she looked at it more closely, she realised it was a ring of fire circling his arm. She kissed his hard muscle and felt his hand come up to cup the back of her head.

'Scared any more?'

For a moment, she didn't understand the question. Then, with a rush, it all came back. They'd had sex for a very specific purpose – to rid her of her fears about her stalker.

Oh God, how could she have forgotten? Her spine stiffened and she pulled away from him. This wasn't her lover. This was her lover's room-mate!

'I think...' She cleared her throat and searched for the detachment she relied upon so heavily as a reporter. 'I think it helped.'

The look in Chris's eyes chilled. For some reason, her response seemed to anger him. Suddenly, the hand at the back of her head tightened. His head swooped down and he held her still for another kiss. The pressure of his lips was hard and Erin felt a thrill pulse in her veins. He filled her senses until she could hardly breathe. Only when he had her limp and writhing on his lap did he let her go.

'Good,' he said in a gruff voice. 'What's next?'

An hour later, Erin found herself bent over a hot gas grill with her ass sticking up in the air. Her heart was pounding, but she was afraid to move. Chris had made it safe for her by covering the lid with towels, but she knew she was, literally, playing with fire.

'Lean over a little further, love, so you can grab the legs.'

She followed his instructions, but the move pressed her breasts against the towel. She'd been afraid to let her skin touch the grill at all, but there was no way to avoid it. Heat radiated up through the thick cotton terrycloth and her body was suffused with a dangerous warmth. Her stomach clenched, but the heat on her breasts felt good.

'How's that?' he asked. He parted the curtain of her light brown hair so he could see her face.

'Good,' she sighed.

'How's this?' he asked, pointing his dick at her mouth.

'Better,' she groaned. She opened her mouth and found it soon filled with his cock. She twirled her tongue the way she'd learned he liked. He grunted and thrust. She nearly gagged, but relaxed the muscles in her throat to take him.

His hand ran up and down her spine as she sucked on him. Erin shivered at the picture they must be making. Just as she found her rhythm, though, he pulled his dick out of her mouth. Her lips were left wet and wanting.

He circled around behind her, and her hips wiggled. She felt like a woman who'd been stripped naked and put into the stockade. He hadn't bound her, but he'd ordered her to stay in position. He might as well have used the ropes.

'Chris, please,' she begged. She'd lost all her pride hours ago. He'd reduced her to a quivering mass of need with that big cock and those strong hands.

'All right. I'll give you the fucking you need.'

He leaned down to turn up the heat and Erin shifted with some discomfort. She was protected from the hot metal, but her internal temperature was rising quickly. Sweat beaded on her skin and her nipples felt raw from the heat. She gripped the legs of the grill hard and waited for the relief of his penetration.

It didn't come. Instead, she heard him moving around on the deck. 'Chris?'

The slap of water was so unexpected that she went right up on to her toes. Turning her head quickly, she saw that he'd picked up the garden hose and was aiming it straight at her backside. 'That wasn't in the letter,' she gasped.

'I'm improvising,' he said with a grin.

Another zing of water streaked against her and she groaned. The icy stream lashed repeatedly across her sensitive flesh. It felt almost as if he were whipping her with water. As a fireman, he knew exactly how to control the spray.

He walked closer, and the impact of the water increased. Erin screeched when he stopped its random motion and centred it on her clit. Tormented by the cold spray, she shifted her hips wildly. His hand touched her lower back and she settled into place.

It was too soon, but she felt her orgasm approaching. The heat against her breasts was making her sweat, but the water between her legs was giving her chills. The contrast was overwhelming. 'Oh God! It's too much!' she yelped.

'No,' he said in that low voice that still made her melt inside. 'This would be too much.'

Her spine went stiff when she felt that icy stream of water become harder and more concentrated on her core. This time, she really did try to get away, but he wrapped his arm about her waist and held her in place. With his other hand, he guided the hose to her numbed opening.

'It will be good,' he promised.

'No,' Erin groaned.

It was too late to deny the pleasure. He pushed the cold metal end of the hose into her. The water gushed deep inside her, chilling her from the inside out. Her hips bucked and swayed as she cried out in pleasure.

She thought she saw a neighbour's light turn on, but

she didn't give a damn. All she cared about was the icy douche. Excess water was spilling out of her, but the internal pressure was enormous. She might as well be fucking the Abominable Snowman, as cold and hard as the icy water was inside her.

Then Chris did it; he sent her over the edge. He pushed her hips forward against the towel. The heat from the grill seeped through the material and caught her directly on her clit. It was the only stimulation she needed.

She yelled as her body convulsed in pleasure. She hardly noticed when Chris pulled the hose out and plunged his thick cock into her instead. She sagged over the hot grill as he hammered into her from behind. When he came, he spurted into her almost as hard as the garden hose had.

Erin welcomed the feeling. When he pulled out and turned her around into his arms, she was nearly weeping.

'That's enough for tonight,' he said. He pushed her hair back from her face and dried the tears from her eyes.

'Chris,' she said in a tiny voice. There was so much she wanted to say to him, but she just couldn't get out the words. Instead, she buried her face against his chest and wrapped her arms tightly around his waist. 'Promise me there's going to be more than just tonight.'

Chris's body went stock-still. After a moment, he threaded his fingers through her hair and pulled back so he could see her face. He liked whatever he saw there, because he smiled. It was the second smile she'd got out of him and Erin felt blessed. She felt even more special when he leaned down to give her a soft kiss.

'I promise,' he said against her lips. 'Let's go to bed.'

Quickly, he turned off the grill and used the towels to dry the water from her body. With a laugh, he tossed her over his shoulder in a fireman's carry. Erin howled and demanded he put her down. He ignored her as he carried her through the house to his room, stopping only to close the door to Mark's bedroom.

The blood rushed to Erin's head as she hung upside down, but the position gave her a great vantage point of his ass. Tempted into an action she never would have tried with him before tonight, she reached down and gave the tight little globes a squeeze.

'Hey!' he said.

With a whoosh, her world spun again. When her head cleared, she found herself lying in his bed. Smiling, she opened her arms. He lowered his body heavily on top of hers.

'Did our therapy work?' he asked. He brushed a rough kiss across her lips. 'Any more fears I need to address?'

'Stalker? What stalker?' Her hands whisked down his back and settled again on his butt.

He kissed her, and their playful mood turned serious as their ardour heated. It had been that way the entire night.

'Chris, what about Mark?' Erin finally asked. She pulled away from his seeking lips and gave him a serious look. 'I don't want to hurt him.'

'I know,' Chris said. His hand came up to her breast and he squeezed it possessively. 'I'll talk to him.'

'What will you say?' She arched when his thumbnail flicked across her nipple. Panting hard, she tried to concentrate. 'I still love him, but I want to be with you too.'

He soothed the turgid peak with a long lick. 'Maybe we could work out a three-way deal.'

Three-way? Erin knew she should be appalled, but a thrill sizzled down her spine. 'But Mark's so conservative.'

'I think he'll surprise you.'

She couldn't imagine her straight-laced boyfriend sharing her with anybody. Still, Chris had an assured look on his face. 'You really think he'd go for it?'

Chris lifted his head from Erin's breast and looked down at the beautiful woman in his arms. If anybody had been holding back on this deal, it had been her. His thoughts were immediately drawn back to Mark's bedroom and the old typewriter that his room-mate had forgotten to hide. Laughing, he said, 'Oh yeah, love. He'll go for it like his ass was on fire.'

Size, and Other Matters
Stella Black

Dr Benito Bacardi was the world's acknowledged leader in the field of penile augmentation. He had started in urology before transferring to plastic surgery and, while working in Hollywood, he had become famous when he created a fourteen-inch-long organ for a porn star named Jeffrey Strong. The actor's momentous groin initiated record-breaking box-office returns and inspired a line of merchandise whose most popular item was an awe-inspiring flesh-toned appurtenance that arrived in a plastic cannister bearing the label: STRONG DONG.

Taste, greed, gender and sexual persuasion are only a few of the factors that influence an individual to judge whether fourteen inches is an average portion, a harmful defect, or a phallo-god to be worshipped by all who look upon it. Rational discourse does not enjoy encouragement in an area where emotions, opinions and perspectives are as volatile as the haphazard neural processes that precipitate that lucky engorgement of blood to the vascular muscle.

America's manhood rose as one to avail itself of Jeffrey Strong's cosmetic advantage because America's manhood had been brought down by testicular cancer, hormone disrupters, toxic action on the gonads, urethral abnormalities, epididymal cysts, hypoplasia, teratogens and oestrogen. In these conditions, fourteen inches looked like a very generous offer.

Dr Bacardi gave many interviews in which he noted that his work was becoming more and more valuable in a climate where the feminisation of nature was a well-documented fact of environmental health science. He often referred to the perverse mid-life sex change of the common periwinkle and to the plight of the Florida panther, blighted with undescended testicles and poor sperm quality thanks to the hormones that it ingested from eating racoons. The racoons carried these emasculatory chemicals because they fed on fish that swam in polluted rivers.

Supporting his arguments with these sad phenomena, Dr Bacardi would then go on to boast about the adventurousness of his techniques and proclaim that, as no woman can be too rich or too thin, so no dong can be too thick or too long. This opinion did not shock the inhabitants of Los Angeles because it was widely shared, but various 'aesthetic surgeons' said his attitude was irresponsible.

Dr Bacardi was reported and several medical authorities began to investigate him.

These difficulties arrived at the same time as a legal action initiated by a patient whose operation had resulted in the condition known as 'scrotal dog ears', so Dr Bacardi decided to transfer his clinic from Beverly Hills to Brazil, where the law was more understanding.

Having perfected dermal fat-wrap grafting, penile girth enhancement, degloving, and circumferential incision, Dr Bacardi now offered a revolutionary full organ transplant. This was an expensive operation, and risky, but it offered hope to the macrophallics who crowded his waiting room.

He had developed his unique procedure by searching out meritocrats (athletes, pop stars, poet laureates, and so on) then persuading them to leave him their genitalia when they died. This was easier than one would at first think; many of the donors were flattered that their manhood should be preserved for the benefit of posterity and if they were uncertain, they were usually persuaded to comply by any heir who stood to benefit from the huge sums of money offered by Dr Bacardi.

He earned a reputation for discretion (the posthumous castration was performed in the morgue) and his scheme of offering 'Golden Replacement' gift certificates proved to be very popular, particularly at Christmas.

It was not long before word of mouth exalted Dr Bacardi and volunteers began to approach him, hoping to reap remuneration for the virility of which they were proud but which would be of no use to them in the afterlife.

Dr Bacardi's team of highly trained clinical technicians froze the amputated organ and then used it to make a mould. This mould was filled with a poly-latex mixture that Dr Bacardi had developed in Tokyo and patented under the tradename Mandex. The warm fleshy material was the secret of his success and set him apart from the multitudinous institutions that competed in this field.

The only problems arose when clients made unrealistic demands. Everyone seemed to want a Johnny Weissmuller or a John Wayne, neither of which graced Dr Bacardi's 'collection'.

There were also difficulties when the richer patients demanded exclusivity. As their wives did not expect to turn up at premières wearing the same Dolce & Gabbana evening gown as anyone else, so the high-profile Hollywood nabob did not wish to take his clothes off in a gym, or anywhere else, to find himself faced with a groin that was the same as his own because some other man had purchased one of Dr Bacardi's 'best sellers'.

Dr Bacardi's patients did not tend to be aware of the full panorama of medical misfortune that this revolutionary procedure had the potential to initiate. The physician did not tell them about the possibility of chronic oedema, for instance, nor did he mention that the upwardly nubile 'actress' Belize von Belize had had to receive emergency treatment when her boyfriend's newly acquired transplant had detached itself during the act of love. The discarnate member had become stuck inside the starlet's cervix causing much distress to Ms von Belize, who felt that all her orifices needed to remain free of obstacles if she was to advance her career in Hollywood.

Dr Bacardi did not tell his patient these things. If the new penis did not 'take' and the shaft dissolved into a pulpy mess, or if green pus started to ooze from underneath a discoloured foreskin, or if purple abscesses started to blister the skin around the pubic bone, Dr Bacardi would calmly attach an intravenous morphine drip to the client's right arm and assure him that some set-backs were 'perfectly normal'. These symptoms were simply the body's reaction to a heavier design. The muscles had to adjust to the new weight and this set up temporary stress in the tissues.

The various infections could be cured with antibiotics and were nothing to worry about. The situation was soluble. Once the swelling had disappeared they could make the necessary repairs before the organ dropped off altogether.

In 1991 Dr Bacardi bought a job-lot of African-American donations (fourteen medical students had died in a bus crash in Atlanta) and proceeeded to sew the Mandex replicas on to needy Caucasians. This spearheaded a two-tone trend in gay discos and then spread further afield, causing a rash of publicity in which certain cultural and philosophical questions were raised but which posed no genuine threat to the clinic's popularity.

Dirk Mannerheim had long lived with smallness, unpleasing shape, and a warty condition, and he decided he had had enough. He was a bantam moving in a field where only size mattered. He wanted to be able to cause a sensation in Ravage and Rage and all the other thumping, sweating clubs in West Hollywood. He wanted to have his pick of the buffed-up gym-bob beauties. He wanted to bathe in expressions of awe and supplication. He wanted to wear a gold lamé posing pouch. He wanted oral sex. He wanted a life.

And Dr Bacardi could give these things to him.

Pearl sat on a plastic patio chair in front of the open fridge, cotton vest, breasts, thighs spread. She was a huge woman. She leaned in, felt the chill on her face, loved the crush of food and loved Los Angeles for supplying it. Food bought in supermarkets such as a girl had never seen, where the aisles were monstrous and the trolleys motorised and the choice was without end.

She spent many hours here, in front of the fridge, cooling herself from the summer sun, fingering, licking and staring; many hours with Betty Crocker, Paul Newman and Little Debbie.

There were ten shelves, a deep freeze with the capacity to hold gallon tubs, an ice-making machine, a dairy cabinet, easi-tilt deli cabinets, bottle chillers, canned beverage racks and five slide-out freezer baskets.

The fridge was big enough to live in and, according to Dirk, a man named Manuel once had. Pearl had found his power drill in a salad drawer, but now there were Swiss Miss Swirls and Rainforest Smoothies and

Healthy Choice chocolate chocolate double chocolate-chip cookies.

She studied a syrup by Mrs Butterworth whose manufacturer described her as 'thick and rich'. Next to Mrs Butterworth, the label on a meatloaf portrayed the boxer George Foreman. He was wearing a pair of silk shorts.

Pearl ate twelve peanut power balls and, without moving from either the chair or the fridge, she rang Dirk on the mobile telephone. He was lying in the Hospital of Santa Maria Concepcion.

'What is it?' he snapped. 'I'm in quite a lot of pain, you know.'

'Oh dear,' said Pearl. 'Was the operation successful?'

'Well, they've managed to cut the original one off, if that's what you mean. Now there's bandages and tubes –'

'What do they do with the old one?' she asked.

'Put it in the garbage, if they've got any sense. It's hardly a recycling opportunity.'

There was the sound of clanking trolley wheels in the background. An unremitting scream rose and fell.

'Oh, shut up!' Dirk shrieked. 'No, not you, Pearl. Some guy is having a haemorrhage.'

There was a short pause. The scream peaked and then died away into the sanitary distance.

'I must say, though,' Dirk went on, levering himself gingerly on to the pillows and closing the copy of *Vogue* with which he had been trying (unsuccessfully) to amuse himself. 'I must say that in general I am very pleased. Very pleased indeed. It's a little red and mushy and there are some purple veins which I can only assume are for decoration, but I can see that Bacardi has done a great job. A great job! It's very big for the price. As you know, I couldn't afford the largest – well, who can at three million dollars? – and in the end I decided against the Jean Genet. I mean I lurve all things French. Gimme an Yves over a Calvin any day! And of course they're fabulous in bed, although my only experience was that time on the Eiffel Tower with the tour guide, and you shouldn't generalise . . .

'Jesus Christ, that fat fruit from *Hard News* has just walked in and you should see the trousers! I suppose one doesn't notice them when they're under his news desk.

'Anyway, I decided against the Jean Genet: lovely head but it just wasn't me somehow. Bacardi tried to make me have the Mussolini but it was way too thin, and he's got Royals of course, but they weren't very tempting. Or stylish. In the end, I got it down to a shortlist of two and went with the Jean-Michel Basquiat. God, it's butch.

'I can tell you, honey, this is what they mean by sensible shopping! I'm on the brink of a new life. I just know it. The orderlies have already started cruising me and the cute anaesthetist tried to give me a blow-job, though it's way too early. Jesus, the pain; I can hardly touch it myself, and going to the john is like being stung in the groin by a swarm of killer bees.'

'Well,' said Pearl. 'I hope you'll be better in time for the Oscars. We've got to go. The suits are terrified that the Japanese are going to pull out. They need a show of confidence.'

'I know. I know. I'll be there.'

Pearl rang off and pressed the number for the Psychic Pals 24-Hour Help-Line ('Divine Experiences at Competitive Prices').

'Hi!' shrieked a voice. 'Please hold to speak to one of our clairvoyant operators. This call will cost four dollars ninety-nine a minute. Please hang up if you are under eighteen or you do not wish to be billed.'

This was followed by the plink of a New Age harp. Then a smooth Californian accent came on the line.

'My name is Narine,' it said. 'May I ask you your name?'

'Pearl,' said Pearl.

'Hi, honey. I'm your priestess for today. I am a genuine clairvoyant and the voices are already telling me that you are a very beautiful and a very special person.'

Pearl said nothing. She knew this already.

'Are you there, honey?'

'Yes,' said Pearl.

'Oh, well. I read the Tarot. The cards never lie but I feel it is my duty to warn you that only a few break through the web of delusion to face the shadow within themselves. Do you have any questions that you would like to ask me?'

'No,' said Pearl. 'Just tell me what you see.'

There was a snort, the sound of muffled laughter, and the click of cards slapping against a surface.

'I see you dancing for joy in the hidden garden of your soul. The Angel of Resurrection will blow his mighty bugle and you will fly. You yearn after strange gods, honey.'

'No I don't,' said Pearl.

There were Buddhists in Burbank and Swedenborgians in Glendale. She had seen Nazarenes and Mennonites and Pillars of Fire. She lived with metaphysical mayhem and strange gods were everywhere, but she did not yearn for them.

Here in Beverly Hills there were no strange gods. There was only Dirk's house: hard wood floors, blank white walls, glass, blue skies.

She unwrapped a Nature Valley Crunch Granola Bar and stared at her nails. They were long and yellow and had been built by a Korean girl.

'Ah,' said Narine. 'The Knave of Batons. Has there been some kind of scandal in your family, hun?'

'Yes,' said Pearl. 'My father is in prison.'

'May I ask what for?'

'Junk bonds,' said Pearl.

'Oh yes, here it is, the crack up of an estate and the Lovers reversed. You're going to have to be careful about moral lapses, hun. I see drinking and eating and over-indulgence.'

Good, thought Pearl.

There was a silence. In the background Pearl heard Narine order a sandwich. 'I want the baked eggplant with roasted red peppers, fresh pesto, tomatoes, melted jalapeno jack cheese, hummus, avocado, provolone, on a baguette, no – make that a pitta pocket, carrot hijiki on the side with low-sodium soy sauce and without the chilli flakes.'

Then, in the distance, there was the wail of a police siren and a radio DJ announced that *Jesus Christ Superstar* was a genuine spiritual experience.

Pearl looked at her watch. It was 1 p.m. Nearly time to watch *The World's Most Shocking Medical Videos* on Channel 14.

'Yes,' she said into the emptiness.

'I have wonderful news, hun. The cards say that you will meet the man of your dreams within the next thirty days and you will be united in the bliss of eternal love. Here he is: the King. He will treat you like a queen.'

Pearl cradled the telephone in her ear and opened a bag of Love Bites. Thirty days was not long to wait. Thirty days was nothing. Her father had got thirty years.

'What does he look like?' she asked.

'The cards cannot tell you that, honey. But I can tell you that it will be serious. He will want to marry you.'

'I don't want to get married,' said Pearl. 'I just want to have sex.'

'Oh,' said Narine. 'You must be from San Francisco.'

'No,' said Pearl. 'Sunningdale.'

Pearl was confused by this expensive prediction. She had no dreams and she found it difficult to imagine the kind of man to whom Narine alluded.

She did not want or need anything. She had it all. She did as she pleased, went where she liked, floated here and there, rooting down for a moment or two then pulling up again to travel where the breeze took her. She did as she pleased, slept with anybody and everybody, but these persons were not, as far as she could assess, the material of ultimate fantasy.

She was open. She had not formulated an image, any ideal as such. The scope was limitless; she could fall in with anything. She was fixed to neither location nor specific genetic make-up.

A procession of dandies and defects had long straggled through her life. She was not fussy. There had been fakirs and profiteers, deviants and drunks. Most sensed that she would sleep with anything, so anything came to call, drawn to a blonde girl who dared to be so unfashionably large.

There had been some wild moments out there in the Los Angeles land of liaison. She had licked fur and struggled with untouchables. She had been bound by Christians and penetrated by cineastes, but she had never gone with a goatee.

Now, according to Narine, he could appear at any time and he could be anyone. She would have to observe the opportunities, recognise him when he presented himself and make him welcome. But how would she know that he was the man of her dreams? What sign would there be? Would he be robed in some way? Would there be an unfamiliar physical sensation?

The doorbell rang.

Pearl lumbered to answer it, her flip-flops slapping against the polished wood.

There were three people standing on the porch: a girl, a blond youth, and an individual with a shaved head and several nose rings, who announced he had come to attend to the French armoire.

'The armoire has gone,' Pearl told him. 'Dirk sold it.'

'Well! He could have told me. I mean, we have a relationship. The appointment has been made for weeks! I could have gone to my yoga class which I will now miss. Gad! I work for Tomenicole and they have never let me down.'

He burst into tears.

Pearl gave him a party napkin with a gold fleur-de-lys motif.

'I'm sorry, honey,' he sobbed. 'It must be the ginseng and coffee and I have had my mother staying and boy, she has no boundaries. I mean, she was topless in my hall! What do you say to the woman who smells of your birth? Who brought you into this world? What do you say when you are faced with her *breasts*?'

He drove away in a black Mazda Miata.

The girl spoke. She had short, dark hair and wore a plaid shirt with jeans and Birkenstocks. Her eyes looked small behind the thick lenses of her black frames. There were several screwdrivers in her back pocket, she carried a bucket, and her hands were dirty.

'I'm J.T.,' she said. 'I've come to clean the windows.'

'OK,' said Pearl.

The third person – a tanned vision wearing white shorts and sneakers – had come to clean the pool. He was a surfer in the full meaning of the word and he gazed at Pearl with wide, blue eyes.

Pearl could not remember when she had last seen anything so beautiful.

'Fabulous house,' he said. 'Is it yours?'

'No,' said Pearl. 'It belongs to my uncle, Dirk Mannerheim. I'm looking after it for him. He's in Rio having his penis enlarged.'

'Oh,' said the vision. 'Good for him.'

They sat by the pool. Violent flowers breathed under the Californian sun: vinca, impatiens, bearded iris, all lush and vibrant. Verbena scents wafted over them.

Pearl slumped semi-naked on a recliner, breasts and buttocks spreading everywhere, round arms, huge legs, folds of smooth flesh, all fourteen stone of her.

'Man,' he said, staring at her vast proportions as some stare at carvings in a Venetian cathedral. 'Man,' he repeated, respectful and impressed. A tourist. 'You are all woman.'

'Thank you,' she said.

He was limbs and cheekbones and a smile that had enabled him to do as he wanted since junior school, not that he wished to do much.

He drank long beers, one after the other, and talked about the waves in Hawaii, and what it was like to be on the cusp of Pisces. He was 22 years old.

He said there were auditions but he didn't really go to them because he was exhausted from sitting in the sun all day. Sometimes he would stare at something and drawl, 'Man, look at that.'

When Pearl looked there did not seem to be anything except an armoured beetle or a butterfly or a bird with a blue head stabbing its beak into a corpulent nectarine.

'Are you German?' he asked.

'No,' she said. 'I'm English. Well, my mother is English. My father is American.'

'I'm English as well,' he said. 'And Irish and Australian. I have cousins in Sodbury. So you like L.A.?'

'Yes,' said Pearl. 'It's very nice. I like the food.'

'Would you like to have sex?' he asked.

'OK,' she said.

She took him in her mouth and noted his size with satisfaction; good and big and hard. No problem. About seven inches. She didn't like to waste her time with anything less; there was no point. There was more pleasure to be gained from eating a pizza without breathing. A small dick is a small dick is a small dick. As Gertrude Stein should have said.

Then he lay on top of her, sinking into the warm ripples of her flesh, resting his head between her huge, soft breasts so that all he could sensate was the beat of her heart and the smell of her skin. Thus submerged, he moved his pelvis and pushed himself into the opening that he knew would welcome him. It was tight and warm and wet; a good tight cunt in a big girl. The flesh closed around him and, as he pumped, so she easily came, and a chain of tiny, muscular caresses closed around him, pushing him further and further away from the present and into that head-land of dopey pleasure that he, the consummate lotus-eater, could always enjoy without guilt.

Arousal dizzied him. He loved novelty. All the other babes were the same shape. Boring.

He shuddered with enjoyment, melted momentarily with her, and withdrew.

'Nearly as good as the near-death experience I had on Venice Beach,' he said.

Then he left. Surf was up.

Pearl, adipose, reclined, felt the sun on her face, felt the last twitching of her cunt die away, and wondered if he was the man of her dreams.

The window cleaner, hot from her chamois work, asked Pearl if she could have a glass of wheatgrass juice.

'I don't have any,' she apologised.

'Oh,' said J.T. 'But you should take wheatgrass, you know. It has active cultures.'

'I could make you a delicious drink in Dirk's ten-speed powerjuice Crusha-Musha.'

'You have non-fat organic yoghurt?'

'Yes,' Pearl lied.

'And phytonutrient boosters?'

'Yes,' Pearl lied.

'Sounds real.'

Pearl threw half a pound of organic boysenberries, two bananas, a mango and a lemon sorbet into a jug with six shots of tequila. Then she switched the power to 'pulverise'.

The machine was equipped with rotating blades so sharp and so fast that they were, according to Dirk, strong enough to pulp a Prada handbag, or a baby, or 'anything else you want to get rid of'.

A green light flashed and the machine played the opening chords of 'Prelude to the Afternoon of a Faun' to announce that it had performed its function.

Pearl poured her guest a navy-blue froth. It tasted of fruit and spite and dancing on the tables but it did not prevent pathogenic disease.

'It's good,' said J.T.

She leaned with her back against the counter as if she was a man in a bar and threw the drink down her throat, also like those men who drink their shots as if they were medicine, quick and smooth, looking for all the effects.

And she found them. A pleasurable warmth rose up her throat, appeared as a flush on her cheeks and settled as a feeling of relaxed self-confidence. She felt ready to tell this strange English woman her life-story. Even the bit about the shark.

'I can feel those boosters making me feel better already,' J.T. said.

Pearl did not confess that the health rushing to her guest's head was more connected to alcoholic content than energising antidioxants.

J.T. rang up some of her friends on her mobile phone and soon Dirk's Jacuzzi was full of naked lesbians. A dyke soup, as it were, with piercings and giggling and Budweiser.

They all said they were English.

Uzanne said she was a gyander post-feminist and that she just graduated from college having majored in Booker T. and the MGs.

Octave had dyed purple hair and said she liked vampire sex and drinking blood. She described men as semen heads. Then her hair ran into the water and everyone's skin turned purple and the bodies heaved themselves out, saying, 'Fuck you, you fucking Goth.'

As Pearl was the hostess, a lot of people were polite and went down on her. This was well and good, but where was the man of her dreams?

J.T., in charge of the barbecue, made ostrich burgers. Then they all danced, and argued, and smoked, and danced and went home, driving their Ford Pick-Up vans down the hill.

Pearl and J.T. stood looking over the ocean of twinkling yellow and orange lights that was Los Angeles.

'So,' said Pearl.

'So,' said J.T.

They lay on Pearl's bed. J.T., still clothed, searched amongst the folds of Pearl's thighs for her clitoris and fingered it gently, then less so, manhandling almost, tough, as Pearl liked. J.T. knew what she was doing.

Her hand submerged with Pearl's unashamed flesh so that all was warmth and touch and smooth ripples. One finger went up, then two, then four, manipulating all those nerve-endings. J.T. knew where they all were and she played them with fantastic skill until Pearl seeped and writhed and was grateful as hell.

'I love your hair,' said J.T., pushing her fingers through Pearl's wild blonde disarray. 'And I love your tits,' she said, kissing Pearl's wide, brown nipples. 'They're so big, but firm, beautiful. You remind me of Jayne Mansfield.'

Pearl kissed J.T. She was a great kisser. J.T. lay on top of her, as a child lies on a floating lilo, enjoying the warmth and smell of musky arousal. In general people tended to go on top of Pearl. She was always the largest in any coupling and it was better that way.

'Take your clothes off, J.T.,' Pearl said. 'I want to play with you.'

The girl, surprisingly and unexpectedly, flushed.

'Go on. Show us that fanny of yours.'

J.T. stood at the end of the bed and slowly removed her plaid shirt, revealing pert, brown breasts and erect nipples. She was compact: thin, firm, narrow as an adolescent boy. Then she unzipped her jeans and brought them down over her legs, leaving tight Y-fronts, clean and white, sexy, though not the underwear that Pearl would have imagined for her.

J.T.'s dark-brown eyes stared hard into Pearl's blue as she deliberately smoothed herself out of the underpants and revealed a big, full on, perfect penis.

Not any ol' plastic dildo.

Not a lesbo-vibrator with three speeds.

No harness.

No fake.

The real thing.

J.T. had the real thing. It was smooth, it was beautiful and it was becoming well hard.

'Oh,' said Pearl. 'Lucky me.'

'You're OK with this?' said J.T. shyly.

'More than OK, my lovely. Excited and delighted.'

J.T. sat on top of her and placed her dick in Pearl's mouth, gyrating her boy-girl pelvis against her face. So Pearl took her in, her mouth playing over the manly hardness of the woman. And she moved loving, interested fingers over J.T.'s brown buttocks, inserting fingers here and there until she found what J.T. liked and knew where she wanted to go.

J.T. reacted like a gay boy. She liked to be anally penetrated – the bigger the better in her opinion – for all her sensation seemed to be there. She was just made for it somehow. And Pearl obliged, gently stroking the soft, brown rim while J.T. crouched on all fours, arse up at her, then Pearl probed deeper and deeper, taking J.T.'s muffled instructions and then bringing her to prostate bliss.

'Gad,' said J.T. 'I think I'm in love.'

She was very hard now, and wanting it. Suddenly, and with surprising strength, she heaved Pearl's legs above her neck and rammed her dick between them with a huge force, a force that Pearl had rarely felt in a man, let alone in any girl.

You never can tell.

All her wet nerve-endings closed over this great shaft, satisfying and vigorous and possessed of strange, unrelenting stamina that went on and on and on, bringing her to climax, letting her go, bringing her to another orgasm, letting her go again.

A man's organ with a woman's knowledge: who could want more? Her depth had been invaded, then touched, then loved. She wanted to cry.

And somewhere, in that transcendence that is a good fucking, when the person is wondering if they should just go on and on until they get fucked to death – which wouldn't be a bad way to go – where the mind is indulging itself in narcosis, and the dick has broken down some barrier or other that leaves only baby vulnerability, somewhere in this sensual mind-cloud, Pearl knew that she had found the man of her dreams.

Saving Julie Catharine McCabe

Reverend Billy Washburn sat at his desk, one hand gently rubbing the erection growing down his long, muscular thigh, the other hand thumbing through the concordance in the back of his Bible. I guess you could say the man didn't have his mind on his business, which was that night's sermon at the old-style revival being held at the civic auditorium. He was the selected speaker and, although he had the skeletal beginnings of his sermon in his head, he needed to flesh it out with examples from the Gospel. His hand under the desk kept pressing and rubbing the hardened flesh of his penis as his eyes stared blankly at the small black print on the page before him.

In fact, all Reverend Washburn could see at the moment were the enormous bouncy breasts of a teenaged girl he had 'touched' after last night's meeting. She was one of a number who had come to the front to be saved. However, at the exact moment he had laid his hands on her head, she had shoved a note in his shirt pocket. He was surprised by her actions but continued with his routine. After muttering a brief whisper of instruction into her ear, he pressed her backwards until she fell into the waiting arms of the attendant who stood behind the line ready to catch the newly redeemed. Her eyes followed his as he watched her luscious breasts bouncing within the tight confines of her pink pullover, her nipples alert and peaking into soft points that rolled deliciously in opposite directions. His glance caught hers as she stared at his crotch and, when she looked back at him, he took the note out of his pocket and read it before moving to the next supplicant.

'I want to be touched by your healing hands,' the damp, folded paper had read. Billy glanced up at Julie and raised one eyebrow. The note continued with, 'Please, meet me backstage after the revival. You won't be disappointed. With Sisterly Love, Julie.'

Julie was gently placed on the floor by the helper who moved behind the person next in line, and she watched Billy as he laid his hands on the shoulders of a balding, older man. Whispering instructions into the man's ear, he pushed the fellow backwards.

'Hallelujah! Confess your sins to the Lord and be saved! Can I hear an amen, brothers and sisters?' Billy joyfully shouted, his arms held high in the air in an attitude of victorious fulfilment. Out of the corner of his eye, he watched Julie raise her knees, causing her short, pale-grey pleated skirt to ride up her thighs. She decided to give undeniable credibility to her request. Julie slowly spread her legs, giving the Reverend a glimpse of the soft, blonde fuzzy down surrounding her naked, dusky-coloured sweetness. All the while the crowd roared in response to Billy's request, their voices mixed in a tangle of 'amens', 'praise the Lords', and 'hallelujahs'. Sweat began to pop out on Brother Washburn's face.

Saints be praised! he thought to himself, feeling the tension gathering in his balls as he moved on down the row. He nodded his head to the attendant and, within seconds, Julie was helped to her feet and ushered backstage to wait for Billy.

When he had finally got through the endless line of people waiting for his healing touch, Billy made his way to a deserted area backstage to find Julie sitting on the floor, leaning her back against the wall. She didn't see him standing there, watching her as her fingers plucked up and down the sides of her breasts where the sleeves of her sweater had rubbed the knit fabric into a frenzy of tiny balls. When he moved into her light, their eyes caught. He smiled to himself, acknowledging her gaze as it fell upon his huge erection. The Reverend watched Julie as she shivered and rubbed her thighs together, anticipating the feeling of that long bar of flesh between her love lips. Their eyes remained locked together as she placed her fingers between her thighs and slowly opened her legs to caress herself. Her redemption was at hand in the form of Brother Washburn.

'I believe the scales have been lifted from my eyes, Sister Julie,' Reverend Washburn whispered as he quickly crossed the distance to her waiting body. 'And I do believe this is the sweetest tithe I've ever received,' he muttered hotly as he kneeled by her side, his fingers making soft contact with her tight, wet slit. Julie sighed and pressed her hips against Billy's seeking grasp, gently rolling her head from side to side as he stroked the wetness that seeped between his fingertips and streamed across his knuckles. His cock throbbed as he felt her hotness, and in the back of his mind a voice hissed, 'Finally. It took her long enough.'

Billy knew Julie had come to his performance every single night of the revival. He was used to having a following of women, most of whom were housewives who had become bored with their husbands, and who sometimes had been able to convince him to drop his act long enough to indulge them in a quick lay in his office. Julie, however, was different. She was much younger than the others. At first he didn't realise that he was the cause of her frequent attendance. When she appeared on the third night, however, her eyes kept capturing him, pulling him back to her like steel filings to a magnet.

Billy knew, at that point, that the young girl had fallen madly in lust with him. He watched her reactions when he shook back his light-brown, soft, thick mop of hair as he strode across the stage, and he became acutely aware of how hotly she stared at the bulge of his cock as it pressed against the seams of his tight, black suit pants. When he took off his suit coat, loosened his tie, and rolled up the sleeves of his starched, white shirt, he saw her close her eyes momentarily at the sight of his thick forearms exposed to the audience's view. Oh, yes. The Reverend made sure she watched, her face rapt with attention as his expressions ranged from stern anger to gentle laughter, the smooth skin of his face radiating love to every person there, especially Julie. And when he grabbed the good book and shook it at them, he watched Julie cross her legs and pin her fingers between her upper thighs as she nearly wet herself with desire. He knew she was trembling at the strength of his long, thick fingers as they stayed firmly attached to the Bible. He wondered how long it would take before she came to him, like all of the others, and he wondered how he could have her without getting caught.

At Julie's school all the girls talked about that week was how they wished they had the nerve to ask Reverend Washburn to save them, wishing they could feel his hands on their bodies. They told tales in the bathroom about how hard they'd beg at his feet just to feel his healing touch. Julie lay awake the first night after the revival, and all of the following nights, her body hot with the flames Billy's presence had provoked. She had never felt like this, and that first awakening of her senses thrilled her body in those places she had been told by her mother were off limits to a boy's touch, as well as to her own. So it was in the darkness of her room, under the cooling breeze of her ceiling fan, that Julie made the first attempt to soothe her own desires.

It was too hot for the light, cotton nightgown her mother insisted she wear to bed, so Julie waited until she heard her mother's footsteps go back downstairs. She got out of bed, quietly shut the door to her bedroom and slipped the gown over her head. Standing in the light of the moon, Julie looked at herself in her mirror and watched with fascination as her slender fingers lightly ran over her soft skin, teasing her nipples into points of frantic heat that raced downward to gather in a pool of heavy want between her legs. Then, naked, her body literally trembling with unanswered need, she slid between the sheets. There, she closed her eyes as her hands crept between her legs and, with the lightest touch imaginable, she parted her love lips and began to stroke the centre of her sex.

Julie gasped with surprise at the first fabulous jolt she felt as her finger made contact with her swelling, tender knot. Again she circled it, this time more rapidly and, as the gathering heat became more intense, she became afraid to continue lest she die from the feeling. Letting the pleasure subside a little, Julie touched herself again, even daring to run her finger lower down to where her wetness seeped from her virginal cleft. Everything was quickly becoming a jangle of tingling nerves and wildly pleasurable sensations as her fingertips lightly rubbed and circled her soft sex. Her fingers strayed from the fuzziness of her spread lips to her inner thighs, lightly tracing the downward curve, then across the soft, inner flesh in small, hesitant circles, only to return again and tantalise the tip of her core.

Gritting her teeth against what she was certain

would be instant death – for that was what her mother told her would happen – Julie pressed the soles of her feet together, pulled her finger back up to her swollen kernel, and began to quickly circle it, determined to see to the end the wickedness she had begun. Within a matter of minutes her inner explosion was blossoming into a gargantuan wave of pleasure and, as she began to shake with the superhuman effort to contain her body's loud response, she silently cried out Billy Washburn's name, begging him to save her from dying from sin in her narrow bed. She was sure she was going to hell from wishing that he would pleasure her exactly like she was doing to herself that very minute. Her tears streamed on to her cheeks as she lay on her back and shuddered through her very first climax. And when it finally subsided, she realised that she hadn't died. Her mother had lied.

On the hardwood floor of the area behind the stage, Julie lay exposed to Reverend Washburn's softly tickling fingers. He heard her small intake of breath as he lightly pressed the tip of his index finger against her clitoris. Her hips jerked slightly as he lightly rubbed it back and forth.

'Will you save me, Reverend?' she murmured. 'I'm a sinner in need. My agony is great and only you can keep me from falling any further.' Julie's big blue eyes locked with Billy's hazel ones, her soft blonde hair falling in ringlets around her face. To Billy she looked like an angel. Her nose was small and perfect; her fabulously lush mouth was naturally pink and was softly parted as she ran her tiny tongue tip across her full bottom lip. In his imagination he could feel that tongue stroking across his glans. The shudder he felt at that vision ran clear through him; the intensity of watching him respond to her made Julie shiver. Billy's fingers crept under Julie's pink sweater and searched for the tight, hard peak of a nipple that had captured his gaze when he first saw her. When he softly pinched it, he rejoiced when Julie's breath again caught in her throat.

'Come with me, Sister Julie. I think we're the answer to each other's prayers,' Billy said, and he stood up. Extending his hand, he helped Julie to her feet, drawing her to him until her body was melting against his own. Then he turned her and pressed her forward into the warmth of the southern night. They walked the short distance to the river to the spot where the baptisms had taken place that afteroon.

'Have you been baptised, Sister?' Billy asked, his voice firm and commanding. Julie shook her head 'no' and lowered her eyes in shame. 'Then there's no time like the present to fully immerse you in the healing waters of the Spirit, Sister. Take off your shoes, and I will help remove your sweater and skirt,' he stated, the bulge in his pants beginning to ache for fulfilment.

'No clothes, Reverend?' Julie whispered.

'No, Sister. There shouldn't be anything to come between you and the water,' Billy Washburn explained, and he began to remove his own shirt and shoes. He watched Julie's face while he undressed, the moonlight making the hard muscles of his chest and arms look like they'd been chiseled out of marble. After he had taken off his shirt, Billy walked over to Julie and raised the hem of her sweater, slowly pulling it up her body and over her arms. Before he took it off of her completely, and while it still covered her head, he bent his mouth down to capture the softness of each of her breasts between his lips. The springy, slick, wet tenderness of her young nipples felt divine against his tongue, and to Julie, the sweet scorching desire that raced downwards from the contact of his mouth felt like the flames of hell ignited between her legs.

Billy heard her softly moan as he continued to nibble and pull each hardened crest between his teeth, leisurely working his way back and forth between them.

'Lordy!' he swore to himself as his nose and mouth nuzzled the soft skin of her abdomen. She wasn't like those other women whose breasts sagged from having too many babies and whose legs were as veiny as a road map from numerous pregnancies. Julie was young, unsullied, ripe and completely his.

'Are you moaning for the Lord, Sister Julie?' he whispered, as he finally removed the soft, pink sweater from her body.

'I'm on fire, Brother Billy. I'm in the worst kind of need, and if you don't help me through this, I know I will surely die an unfulfilled sinner,' she whispered back, her soft mouth seeking his.

Billy released the button of his pants and slowly slid the zipper down, pulling his shorts and trousers to the ground where he could step out of them. 'Come, seek the cool water, Sister Julie,' he muttered against her mouth, his lips travelling down the line of her jaw to the smooth skin of her neck.

He saw that Julie's gaze was latched on the thick, swaying heaviness of his engorged prick as he bent and stepped away to pull his clothes from his feet. She shivered with a mixture of pure lust and fear as he approached her again. This time they were both completely naked. Julie gasped with desire as she felt the smooth, nearly hairless, skin of his stomach and chest meet hers. Her nipples ached with need and, as if reading her mind, Billy lowered his head to again trap one pink beauty with his mouth. Then, lifting her off her feet, he carried her to the river where he entered the water in two, strong steps. She felt him stagger slightly as the strong current pushed against his calves. Billy continued to wade into the blackness and, when Julie felt the cold water caress her hips, she squirmed slightly in his embrace.

Brother Washburn laughed gently against Julie's soft hair. 'Ah, Sister, don't try to evade the inevitable. I've decided to baptise you against the river bank, where the water can hold us both accountable for your sins.' He laid her down and pressed his lips against Julie's parted mouth, drawing her sweet tongue into the turbulent suction of his kiss. She had never known that such fire could exist in the mere meeting of two mouths. His fingers once again sought the heat between her legs, taking all the time in the world to tease her core into a shimmery feeling she hadn't been able to produce with her own, inexperienced touch.

'It's wickedly sinful, isn't it, Brother Washburn?' she wondered aloud. 'What you're doing feels wickedly sinful, and when I did it to myself I didn't die like my mother told me I would. I lay there in bed, afraid to finish what I started, but I had to. Once I started, I couldn't stop doing it. Is it all a lie?' she asked, her voice full of heavy need and unanswered questions. The fact that she had told him about touching herself made Billy's cock leap against his belly, and his imagination was full of the sight of her fingering herself.

'Show me how you did it, little Sister. I can tell you if it was wicked or not by watching you,' he whispered, his mouth seeking the shell of her ear as he slowly rubbed his fingers around and around her swollen clitoris. He pulled away from Julie a little and she raised her hips to keep his fingers against her, her eyes bleak with need.

'No, Sister Julie. You must be brave and show me,' he softly insisted.

Despairing of making him angry, Julie did as he asked, and Billy watched as she placed her slender hand between her thighs. With her eyes locked on his gaze, she began to masturbate in the exact way she had been doing every night since that first one.

'Tell me what you think about when you're doing it,' Billy said, his hands straying to his own swollen cock, rubbing it gently and slowly in time with her movements. The coolness of the water gently lapped against his balls, making the tight feeling in his loins nearly double in strength.

'You, sir. I think about you,' she said, her voice nothing more than a bare sigh as it caressed Billy's mind. 'I think about your hands gripping the Bible and then you taking your fingers and rubbing me down here.' Julie glanced down her own body to where her sex lay open to his view. 'I think about your fingers on me, sliding inside me, and then I wonder about what you have lying between your legs,' she breathed, and then added, 'It's so big.'

Billy smiled to himself at her innocence as he continued to stroke his throbbing cock. She was the proverbial sacrificial lamb, but instead of being wary of the knife, she gladly leaped on to the altar and bared her body for it. He held his huge prick out of the water so she could see him rubbing it and then, kneeling next to her head, he asked her, 'Would you like to touch it, Sister?'

'I'm afraid I'll go to hell, or die, or . . .' She trailed off, her free hand already raised to stroke the tip as it glistened in the moonlight.

'It's OK, Julie. You won't die. You won't go to hell. Touching me will be like touching the Spirit. Touch me and you'll be saved,' Billy said, his voice growing more and more fervent as he became the preacher she was used to seeing. Julie's hand reached for Billy's hard penis, and he enclosed her fingers around the long shaft, containing her hand within his grasp as he taught her the motion of his pleasure.

'This will save me, Brother Billy?' she whispered.

'It will save you quicker if you kiss it,' he responded, his voice growing tight with need. Julie turned her head and dragged the tip of Billy's cock against her closed lips, rubbing the glistening drop of pre-come against her mouth before licking it off.

She was amazed at the slightly salty taste and, in her desire to find a more complete salvation, she opened her mouth and took him in. Billy's fingers again found Julie's heat and, once he had begun stroking her greedy cunt, she used both hands to rub him while he slowly pushed his hardness between her lips. The sudden spasms of her climax surprised him, and she cried out against his stiffness, her noise a mixture of pain and pleasure as he tried to thrust his fingers inside of her unopened body.

'You've come to me a virgin, Sister Julie? That's the greatest gift you can give a man. This act of submission will surely see you into heaven,' he said, pleased at what he'd found. He gently drew his cock out of her mouth and covered her body with his own, letting the water buoy them as he became more and more determined to make her feel every ounce of pleasure he could give her. Julie's body strained against his, her heat growing between her legs as he rubbed his hardness between her love lips, stroking her clitoris against him with the long, sweet movements produced by his clenching hips. He wanted her ready to climax, hovering on the brink, before he plunged into her, and after tonight he knew he would want her as often as she could come to him. He'd never had a girl this young and this willing, and the fact that she was barely seventeen didn't make any difference. Any thought of saying no to her had flown away long before now.

With a lift and a little shove Billy pushed Julie's body up on to the bank, leaving her hips barely floating in the water as he knelt between her thighs and pressed his mouth to the river-cooled mound of sex. She cried out in disbelief at the wonderful feel of his parted lips seeking her centre and, when his tongue made contact with her core, the gathering pleasure quickly grew. In the middle of Julie's increasingly delicious sighs which heralded her impending climax, Billy slowly licked the young girl's swollen clitoris, uncovering the little red knot hidden deep within, then lowered himself on to her and pressed home. Within seconds she was shaking as each consecutive wave of pleasure shattered within her and then engulfed her, and he came in huge, spasming jolts within her grasping sheath. His sperm jetted out, baptising her sex with each white hot spurt, and she wrapped her legs around his and pushed against him in order to feel him throbbing deep within her. Her small, tight cries of joy rang victorious in his ear as she sounded out her pleasure.

'Hallelujah, Billy! You've filled me with the spirit and saved me from the damnation of self-pollution!'

Billy thrust with all of his might into Julie's spasming body, at that moment truly believing he had saved another soul from the flames of hell.

'Can I hear an amen, Sister?' he whispered as his last shudder raced through his body.

'Amen, Brother,' she whispered back, her limp body already beginning to reawaken to the deep pool of lust he had just begun to tap.

He could feel her inner muscles clamping tightly around his already rising hardness. Lordy, she is a hot one, he thought, as once more he slowly began to move within her.

One of Billy Washburn's hands was still lying on the open book and his other was still fondling his hardness when the door to his office opened. Looking up, he saw Julie, her face a vision of desire as she quickly shut the door and leaned against it.

'Do you have a minute, Brother Washburn?' she softly asked, her voice full of hope.

'I was just thinking about you, Sister,' he responded and, getting up, he crossed the floor and pulled the young girl to him. 'Aren't you supposed to be in school?' he asked, his concern at being found with her almost overriding his desire to fuck her right there and then.

'Yes, but I cut sixth period. I told them I wasn't feeling well and I was going home. Brother Billy, I have a friend who wants to be saved. When I told her how you helped me last night she begged and begged to come with me today.'

Billy's stomach churned at the knowledge that she had told someone else about him but, faced with the prospect of claiming another soul in his mission to save people, he couldn't very well turn her down. He'd have to play it by ear and figure out exactly what Julie had told the girl.

'You know, Julie, I just hate to waste an opportunity to help someone, and I'll do it for you this time, but you have to promise me something first.'

Julie looked into Billy's eyes, her gaze so wide-eyed innocent that he didn't have the heart to fuss at her.

'Sweetie, don't go telling everyone about what we did. Salvation is a private thing. I admire your wish to bring people to the foot of the cross, but it should be up to them to figure out how to get there without you telling them everything. OK? Now, let me hear an amen from you, Sister!' And, grinning down at her, Billy hugged Julie's soft body to his as she answered him with a soft amen, all the time nudging her hip-bones in soft bumps back and forth against his erection.

He shivered to himself when he began to realise the depth of her lust. 'Now. Where's this friend of yours, honey?' he whispered, his mouth moving over hers in a soft kiss.

Julie turned and opened the door. There, wringing her hands, stood one of the most exquisite girls Billy had ever seen. She was smaller than Julie, her body more compact, but just as ripe, and her eyes were full of hope as she nervously rubbed the palms of her hands over her breasts and down her stomach. He remembered seeing her sitting with Julie the night before last, her dark head leaning against Julie's as they watched and whispered. He had wanted her to come forth. She had hung back while Julie pleaded with her to go to the steps with her. As it ended up, neither one had come forward. But now, ah, yes indeed! The Lord certainly moved in mysterious ways.

'Have you been saved, Sister? Ah, what's your first name, honey?' he asked the young woman as she crossed the threshold of his office.

'Clarissa, Brother Washburn. I'm Clarissa and I've been waiting for you to do it,' she answered, her low, husky voice racing through the man and jolting his cock into immediate stiffness. Billy took her by the hand and brought her around to his side of the desk, where he sat down on the corner and manoeuvred her between his legs.

Dear God! he thought. Her body smelled like lavender, and the nipples on her small breasts were already turning into little pebbles. He couldn't wait to taste her.

'Young girls are definitely habit-forming,' the voice in his head whispered.

'Sister Julie, please lock the door and come help me. Since you brought her to me, you will get to be part of this girl's salvation. I'm going to train you to do my work.'

'As you wish, Brother Washburn,' Julie replied, smiling slightly as she bowed her head in meek submission to his word.

Clarissa again began to nervously rub her damp palms up and down the front of her thin cotton blouse as she watched Brother Washburn. Her body trembled with a mixture of anxiety and blatant desire as he cleared off his desk. Billy tried to hide the fact that his hands were a little shaky as he thought of what he was about to do. The scattered papers were hastily gathered into messy stacks as he made space for her body. And he was achingly hard, his strong cock bucking against his trouser front as if it already knew that a hot, tight, virginal hole awaited it.

'Sister Julie, come help Sister Clarissa with her blouse buttons, will you?' he asked, hurriedly placing the final stack of books and papers on the floor. Julie stepped over to her friend and, softly and slowly, smoothed the light-pink cotton of Clarissa's blouse over her friend's small breasts before beginning to unfasten it from the top. He looked up at the two girls when Clarissa laughed a little nervously, and watched as Julie's trembling hands fumbled with Clarissa's buttons. Julie's glance captured his as she brushed her fingers over the tops of Clarissa's small, cotton-covered nipples. Clarissa shivered and pressed herself into her friend's warm palms.

'Does getting saved feel good, Brother Washburn?' Clarissa asked, her husky woman's voice sounding in direct contradiction to the innocence of her question.

Billy laughed a little as he crossed the office to check the lock on the door. Oh yes! Nothing felt better to him than this kind of salvation, especially with someone like those two young ladies, but he felt the need to sermonise a bit.

'Sister Clarissa,' Billy responded, 'sometimes you have to give up something little in order to gain something big. It's the giving up that hurts, but what you'll be receiving will give you more joy than you ever imagined.' Billy slowly walked back to the desk and watched as Julie finished unfastening Clarissa's blouse. His eyes glowed with enthusiasm for his calling and, as he watched, the steadily increasing fullness rose between his legs. The discreetly shaped V between Clarissa's own thighs began to gush and throb with an unworldly need to be touched.

'Turn around and I'll unhook your bra.' Wordlessly, Clarissa turned and presented her back to Julie who, after unfastening her friend's brassière, slowly slid the straps down over her shoulders and then let it drop to the hardwood floor next to Billy's desk. Billy noticed with satisfaction that Clarissa's arms were a mass of tiny goosebumps and that her nipples sprang to attention at the feel of Julie's fingers stroking her from behind. He enjoyed seeing her squirm in an effort to relieve the desperately tingly, wet swollen feeling between her legs.

Reverend Washburn watched as Julie's fingers lightly traced the shape of her friend's breasts, circling around the pouting nipples before spreading further out to stroke the firm white skin surrounding them. His mouth had begun to water and his hand strayed to readjust his swollen penis as it pressed against his thigh. He gave his hardened glans a reassuring rub before he stepped in to take over.

'Sit on my desk, Sister Clarissa,' Brother Washburn

stated and, grabbing his desk chair, sat down to wait for Clarissa to do as he had asked. Julie moved aside to watch. When Clarissa was seated, Billy rolled the chair forward until his body was nearly between her knees. Then he reached for her feet and gently untied and pulled off the girl's saddle oxfords and placed them on the floor. He rolled down her thick cotton socks and removed those as well, taking time to let his fingers trail over the bottoms and insides of the girl's feet as they rested in his lap, her toes pressing innocently against his hardness. He felt Clarissa trembling with anticipation and, in a movement that surprised him, she flexed and relaxed the ball of one foot until it moved against his rock-hard shaft. Billy looked into Clarissa's eyes, again stroked the underside of her foot, and was rewarded when she repeated the small, almost unseen movement. Releasing a ragged sigh, Billy leaned forward and parted her knees until they were on either side of his body and, gently taking her feet from his lap, placed them on the armrests on either side of him. He chuckled a little when he saw the bright-pink polish on her toenails.

'Why, Sister Clarissa, you're almost a grown woman,' he said to her, and then he looked up at Clarissa, who had braced her arms behind her and was leaning back on her elbows. Billy pushed his chair back slightly, causing her to extend her legs, and then slowly ran the palms of both hands up the insides of her ankles. She didn't look at Billy as he began to thread his fingers over and around the smooth muscles of her calves. Her head was thrown back and her eyes were closed. The white skin of her shoulders was smooth and soft and, as Billy gazed in wonder at the vision sitting on his desk, he watched the quick beat of Clarissa's pulse as it throbbed under the taut skin at the base of her neck. His own heart pounded loudly in his ears as he contemplated the girl spread before him, relishing the heady anticipation of committing another act of salvation.

Before he went any further, Brother Washburn stood up long enough to softly lick Sister Clarissa's dark-brown nipples as they pointed upwards and slightly to each side. Clarissa's body shuddered at the feel of Billy's hot, wet tongue stroking her hardened nubs. He heard her suck in her breath as the sensations raced from her nipples to her mound in hot, sweet surges, and he felt the tremors of arousal strain the girl's arms as she continued to hold herself up.

'Sister Julie, go stand behind Sister Clarissa and hold her, just like my assistant does whenever I'm working the revival,' Billy said as he sat back down in his chair. He hoped that Julie would again feel pulled to touch and tease her friend without having to be prompted, but if he needed to tell her what to do, that would be OK too.

Julie moved behind Clarissa and, much to Billy's admiration, began to do exactly what he had hoped for. Her fingers were already straying to the peaks of Clarissa's small, firm breasts as she relaxed against Julie's upper body and, as Billy watched for a few more seconds, Julie's eyes caught his own. In that one glance he was nearly consumed by the huge wave of her wildly gathering lust, her look nearly lashing his throbbing cock into spurting right then and there.

Billy ground his teeth against the rising sensations in his cock, bent his head in an attitude of prayer, and firmly intoned, in a voice tense with desire, 'Sister Clarissa, you are about to experience full salvation only brought on by an attitude of repentance and acceptance. In order for this to happen, you must agree to do exactly what I say. Can I hear an amen?'

And Clarissa answered him in a soft whisper without ever opening her eyes. Brother Washburn continued.

'By that affirmation am I to understand you are willing to undergo the rites and tribulations asked of you?'

Once more Clarissa answered, 'Amen, Brother Billy.'

Her husky voice brought Billy to his feet in a frenzy of desire. He pushed the chair back and Clarissa's bare feet fell off the armrests. Billy caught her legs under his arms and pulled her hips towards him. He wanted to take her right there and then; the urgency of the moment was excruciating. Grinding his teeth against the growing ache in his balls, he held his lust in check. Wrapping her legs loosely around his waist, Billy raised the girl's short skirt until it was rolled up to her smooth, soft belly. He let his fingers wander further between Clarissa's soft legs and, at his insistent pressure and a softly voiced command, she relaxed her thighs and let him have full access to the thin strip of pale-pink cotton stretched across her soft, swollen cunt lips.

Billy was nearly beside himself as he breathed in the girl's scent. It reminded him of warm, newly mown hay drying in the field. Sitting back down in his chair, he once more placed Clarissa's feet on the armrests and pulled himself closer to her. With one hand he released his supremely distended cock and stroked it slowly while he ran a single finger up and down the midline of her panties. 'Dear Lord, she's soaked herself,' he breathed, as his finger softly pressed against the protrusion between her wet, cotton-covered lips. He looked up to see Julie's eyes heavy with the heat of the moment. Her fingertips were still softly plucking her friend's small nipples.

'Sister Julie, please remove your shirt, skirt and undergarments,' Billy whispered hoarsely, and when Julie looked at him, she saw his hand already moving on his huge dusky rod. Without being asked a second time, Julie withdrew her hands from Clarissa's soft breasts, laid the girl down on Billy's desk, and slowly began to strip for Brother Washburn.

When she began to unbutton her blouse, Billy slipped his finger underneath the leg of Clarissa's panties and softly introduced it to her swollen sex lips. When he saw Julie unfasten her bra and take it off, he began to play with Clarissa's distended clitoris in small, soft strokes. Billy's finger sweetly tormented Clarissa's clit and she began to wiggle her hips against his touch, moving herself rapidly against his hand. He was sure she would climax before he was ready for her to feel his brand of salvation. Pulling his hand from between Clarissa's thighs, he quickly divested her of her underpants, and soon she was completely naked on his desk except for her skirt still bunched around her waist.

'Lean your breasts over Sister Clarissa, Julie, and let her see you like that. She must learn that viewing the flesh of her sisters and brothers is not sinful, like most would tell her, but instead is meant to be praised and worshipped as valuable and beautiful.'

In order to distract Clarissa from her impending orgasm, Billy ordered her to open her eyes. When she did, her gaze was immediately filled with the glory of Julie's breasts as they were proffered to her in both hands. Without prompting from Billy, Clarissa opened her mouth and softly and quickly inhaled the nearest pink nipple. Julie gasped with the thrill of being stimulated, and once more she locked eyes with Billy, who grinned in affirmation then bent his head to the tender task that lay in front of him.

'Sister Clarissa, are you ready to be moved?' he asked.

With her mouth completely full of Julie's hard nipple as well as part of her surrounding breast, Clarissa moaned her assent. Rising slightly from his chair, Billy Washburn lifted Sister Clarissa's hips until her bottom was nestled in the palms of his hands. Then he slowly brought his mouth to her sweet muff, his breath tickling the soft fuzz that covered the girl's swollen offering. Her wetness had begun to run down her crack and, with utmost gentleness, Billy's tongue ran interference, over and over, from tickling the entrance to her anus to concentrate on her throbbing clitoris.

Julie was desperate for attention. Her nipple was being licked to distraction, and every time Billy's mouth moved up Clarissa's cunt to softly lick at her core, Clarissa's suction became more rapid and more fierce. She shifted her body every few seconds, her restless sighs disturbing the near silence of Billy's office.

Guessing at the source of Julie's agitation, Billy lifted his head long enough to encourage his assistant. 'Finger yourself, Sister Julie.'

She heard Brother Washburn's thickly formed words as he continued to lick and caress her friend's swollen sex and, without a pause, Julie's hand raced between her legs.

Billy's face was once again buried between Clarissa's soft thighs, so he wasn't able to see how quickly Julie parted her love lips. He couldn't watch Julie's fingers slide over and around the distended lump of flesh. He couldn't see the joy spread over her face as she listened to the sounds Brother Washburn's mouth made as he licked and sucked her friend's slick cunt. And, because he was listening closely for the sounds of Clarissa's orgasm so that he could finally penetrate her, he missed hearing Julie's soft moans as her own climax crashed around her.

Brother Washburn's tongue found and uncovered the red heart of Clarissa's clitoris and, with several light, well-timed licks, he brought the young woman to the brink of her very first body-shattering climax. As Billy felt Clarissa's gathering shudders, he notched the head of his enormously swollen cock within her tight slit.

With a steady, unrelenting pressure, Brother Washburn drove himself into her until he was wedged clear up to his balls. The fingers of one hand kept up their light, rapid stroke against Clarissa's love knot, and he held her hips tightly against him with the other. Julie's lush mouth covered that of her friend's in a deep, hot kiss that literally sucked Clarissa's cries of pleasure into her own body.

Clarissa wound her hands around Julie's head, threading her fingers in the soft, blonde curls of her friend as the kiss continued and expanded while Brother Washburn slowly pumped himself into Clarissa's heaving body. Clarissa's hips were madly bucking and jerking against the desktop as she came in huge, shuddering undulations. He felt her inner muscles clamp around his cock with a strength that both astounded and wildly excited him, and he watched the girls intently as their mouths moved and changed with the depth of their stroking tongues. It was almost more than he could stand. His balls were straining to release their hot load.

'You're so tight, Clarissa, so good and tight. Ah, lordy!' he cried out as he watched his dark-red shaft stroking in and out of the girl's small, grasping slit. She was definitely as hot as Julie. As badly as he didn't want it to end, he knew he had to finish.

Gripping Clarissa's bottom with both hands, Brother Washburn began to furiously pump his hips in and out between the soft white skin of Clarissa's parted thighs, bucking and humping her until his raging cock took over the beat and finally exploded deep within the orgasmic spasms of her tight hole.

'A baptism of fire and water, Sister Clarissa,' he muttered against her breasts as he fell against her, his cock still continuing to jolt deep within the girl's slick, hot depths. 'Let me hear an amen!' He chuckled as his

fingers softly tweaked a nipple and his mouth bur-
rowed between Julie's breasts as they hovered in front
of his face. Both girls answered, their voices softly
shaking with the emotion they felt.

Billy slowly withdrew his still-swollen penis from
Clarissa's body, the tip streaked with his own spending
and small streaks of her virginity. Grabbing the handkerchief from his shirt pocket, he quickly wiped up the
traces of her undoing before she would have a chance
to see them and become scared. As he softly mopped
her tender mound, he again began to tease the girl's
clitoris. She lay on his desk, her legs wide spread, her
stomach quickly rising and falling with the shuddering
rhythm of her breath. She moaned softly as he found
and uncovered the small hooded centre of her sex, and
Billy was nearly undone at the quickness of her response
to his touch.

Bending his head, he began to lick the swollen tip,
sometimes trailing his tongue to catch his own seed as
it trickled from her body. She began to climax again,
and Julie quickly covered her friend's mouth with her
own as the second orgasm in the young woman's life
took over her now rigid and shaking body.

The sweetness of taking the two friends together
wasn't lost on Billy. He couldn't afford to lose either
one of them, as addicted to them as he had become,
and with a word of caution from Billy to not tell anyone
about what had happened, they dressed in silence as he
thought up a way to continue seeing them both.

As the girls were leaving, Billy kissed Clarissa lightly
on her upturned mouth. With a soft pat on her bottom,
he whispered his admonition to her. 'Don't tell your
mama, Sister Clarissa. Salvation is a private thing, and
you should keep this matter to yourself. Don't tell your
friends, either. I'll deny ever having seen you, if you do.
Anyway, most people would only laugh at you and say

you were lying.' He kissed her again, and this time running his tongue quickly around the inside of her lower lip. Clarissa shuddered at the erotic feeling. Feeling empowered, Billy continued. 'If you want, you both can come backstage after tonight's revival, and I'll see about baptising you in the river, privately.'

Clarissa answered, 'I think Julie would like to come, too. But I forgot. You already baptised her last night. Can she be baptised more than once?'

'It's unusual,' he answered slowly, his voice full of mock gravity as he thought over the delightful variations in taking two girls at the same time, 'but not unheard of. I'm sure it will work out just fine. You two wait for me where we were last night, Julie, and I'll get there as soon as I can. Now, you all run along and let me get my sermon written, or this revival will never get off the ground.'

With that, Reverend Washburn opened the door to let the girls out into the soft evening light of near summer. Before Julie passed him, he grabbed her by the arm and drew her into his embrace. His kiss was deeply promising, and his hands went under her skirt to range over the tight globes of her bare bottom before coming around to lightly stroke her soft, fuzzy mound.

'Thank you for your trust, Sister Julie,' he whispered in her ear as, shivering with need, she leaned her head against his shoulder. 'You won't regret this, I swear.' And, inserting his fingertip between her wetness, he slowly thrilled her swollen clitoris until she was nearly faint with desire.

'I still need saving more than Clarissa, don't you think?' she begged, her body already so hot for him that she lightly rocked her hips against his stroking fingers.

'Yes,' Brother Washburn answered as his lips nibbled on her tender earlobe. 'You definitely need saving on a daily basis, Sister Julie.' His fingers tickled her wet, open sex. He wanted to pull her back into his office and finish what he'd started. 'Oh, lordy, sweetie, you sure do. Now, go on and let me get things done, or I'll never get to be with you tonight.' After kissing her again, he softly closed the door behind him and went to sit down behind his desk.

Once more his erection was straining against his trousers as he picked up the book and began to try to concentrate on verses for his message. He stared at the small, black letters on the page but he couldn't see them. All he could see was the naked body of the girl who had occupied his desk and, once again, his hand strayed between his legs as he unzipped his fly and began to rub his hardened shaft. The words gave him little comfort and, the longer he sat there, the more he longed for his own salvation.

Public Washrooms, Private Pleasures

Verena Yexley

Kate stood casually at the end of the hall leading to the public washrooms. This was the first of three they had located in the small mall, and they would get to the others in due time. She scanned the area for possible intruders while giving the appearance of waiting for some lingering companion. There was never any debate about the need for a lookout of sorts – she wouldn't actually attempt to stop someone else from going down to use the facilities, she'd just watch the action if it happened to be a woman. It was always so much more exciting when a patron did come along after she or Mike had begun their quest for stimulation. If he were caught in the women's washroom she would watch the fallout, or if it became too threatening she would help him make a hasty retreat. They would scramble away, becoming the Bonnie and Clyde of public toilets!

As she waited, a woman came out of the ladies' facility and walked calmly down the hallway, straightening her skirt and rearranging her bundles. She gave no indication of being disturbed or upset as she walked past Kate, a sign that she had not discovered the man using the ladies' stall to take a leak. Kate knew there were only two stalls inside, meaning Mike had been standing beside this woman while he did his thing. She knew this also meant he'd be just that much more aroused when he came out, setting her own pulse speeding at the thought. If he had found it especially enticing, he might have risked keeping himself exposed while he washed his hands, on the off-chance that he still might be seen. Pushing the envelope like that would mean she had some pretty nasty work ahead of her when it was her turn to relieve herself. Their friendly competition could become quite tricky as they took turns seeing how far they could go, trying to top each other with the level of risk.

Mike sauntered out a few minutes later, looking for all the world like a cat who'd just tasted the pet canary. The smile on his face could only be described as beatific. As Kate walked towards him down the hall, she saw how his eyes shone and the light film of sweat beading his dark upper lip. He was a pretty ordinary-looking man most of the time, only 5′ 11″, well-tailored sandy brown hair, plain brown eyes and a fairly nondescript body, especially when he was in the business suits he favoured when they played their games. But now, only minutes after satisfying his first stirring of need, he looked to Kate like a male model for some advertisement guaranteeing sexual satisfaction with their product. His brown eyes were already being eclipsed by his expanding pupils, giving him an air of danger when coupled with the dusting of dark stubble he never seemed to be completely rid of, even when he shaved twice a day. His body movements were always so much more fluid when he was getting turned on, but at the same time she could see how his chest and neck were expanding, constricting him within his shirt and tie. He'd be positively explosive by the time they had made a complete circuit of the mall, so much so that he might want to get her naked before they even got home. How she loved this man!

When they were close enough to touch, Mike took

her hand and led her farther down the hallway, towards the emergency exit a few yards away from the washroom doors. He positioned Kate against the wall and put one hand flat against it beside her head. Anyone looking at them would assume they were a couple having a serious conversation and would not be able to see Kate's face hidden behind his extended arm. They were having a serious discussion all right, it just wasn't what anyone in their wildest dreams could imagine two such middle-class professional people would be talking about.

Kate knew exactly what Mike needed her to say and she wanted to tighten the bolt holding his desires in check. He leaned his head towards hers and they shared a brief chaste kiss. When he moved his head away, Kate began to describe the woman who had come out of the washroom while Mike had been in there. A middle-aged lady, neatly dressed, with pantyhose and casual pump shoes wearing a longish wool skirt. She'd had on some indistinguishable blouse and a black jacket and was carrying a purse and a few parcels. She knew Mike didn't really want these details, although having to create an image of the woman was important sometimes. He was waiting to hear where this was leading.

'She probably had a really hairy pussy, Mike, don't you think so? An older lady like that, overweight and all, hustling around a mall on Saturday morning, trying to buy satisfaction when what she really needs is something nice and juicy in that hairy pussy of hers.' Kate all but whispered this description into her husband's ear, occasionally letting a little more breath than was absolutely necessary escape her mouth and caress his face.

'If she'd known you were there, honey, she would have wanted to suck on you even while the pee was still streaming out of your beautiful dick. You know how women really want that slick hard cock of yours. You know I want it, I want it all the time, especially when I can watch you use it to pee.' Kate was getting just as turned on as Mike from her addition to his adventure. This was her own speciality – being able to make up erotic story details on the spot.

Mike was positively glowing with lust as he looked down at his lovely wife while she told him the story of this anonymous woman who'd squatted beside his stall while he stood with his cock in hand and watched his stream hit the porcelain bowl. That he had been so blessed to find this creature, this soul mate, was a gift for which his gratitude would never be enough. Kate wasn't anybody else's idea of a stunning beauty, but for Mike she all but walked on water. He looked into her blue eyes and didn't see the dull shade someone else would see, he saw the rich deep blue of the ocean, and right now the pulsing black of her broadening pupils gave her an exotic look he loved. Her hair might be fine textured and mousy brown to the average glance of a stranger, but he knew how rich the colours were close up and how silky it felt as it slid over his naked body or tumbled through his fingers. A casual glance would indicate a woman of medium height, slightly overweight but well dressed in a business suit, the skirt tight to her largish hips, the jacket open, revealing an equally large bust straining under the button-up blouse. She looked most like a typically thir-tyish Canadian professional woman, overweight and uptight. Mike was pleased by her deceptive looks; it made what they did together so publicly seem even more secretive because the woman he saw doing what she did was not who others saw.

Unless, of course, they caught her in the act. Then men were blessed with the vision of her Mike had every day. If the man were willing to watch and not touch he could be given a sight of pure rapture. Kate would change right before his eyes and become the vixen of sex the man most desired. She was so blatant with herself when caught and being watched, she was every man's dream of the perfect wife: looking straight-laced to any casual observer, but hiding a smouldering slut available only to him.

With these visions of her floating past his mind's eye, Mike ran his free hand across Kate's blouse and motioned for her to take her turn. They had both noticed the man who had just entered the facilities and he wanted Kate to get in before he had a chance to finish a quick evacuation. Before he let her leave, Mike bent his head to hers again and licked her lips with his tongue, leaving a trail of wet across her mouth. The contact streaked through both their bodies, making a straight line for their mutually aroused genitalia.

With a last smile at her adoring partner, Kate plunged onward and pushed open the door to the men's washroom while Mike stood casually against the closest wall outside. He would easily be able to hear if anything untoward was happening and could instantly be at Kate's side if she needed him. In actual fact, however, over all the years they had been developing their unconventional games, no man had ever threatened to censure Kate or call for assistance. When she was caught they always seemed rather eager to accept her story of either a flooded women's facility or a greater need to relieve herself than she could hold while waiting for room in the women's toilet. The eyeful of pussy she gave them was as much to blame for this as the purely erotic image they suspected most men enjoyed while watching an unknown woman pee, most especially if they were handling their own cocks. No, Mike wasn't at all worried. Kate could handle herself just fine and he could always quite legitimately enter and pretend to be an innocent bystander himself, something they did if the facility was very large.

When Kate first pushed open the door, the man they had seen minutes earlier was standing with his back to her, directing his stream into one of two urinals. She watched his flow for a moment, delighting in the heat the sight elicited between her already damp legs. She walked with ease over to the single empty stall to the side of him and was rewarded with an unintelligible noise as he noticed a woman gazing at his arc of urine. With a smile that would put the Mona Lisa to shame, she looked the stranger straight in the eye and innocently explained that the women's was full and she really had to go. The man seemed to want to tuck himself away, but it was clear he was well into midstream and not able to stop the natural course of events his body had begun. With a last blatant glance towards his hands, where she could just make out some pinkness against the blue jeans he was wearing, Kate entered the small open stall.

This was the kind of cubicle she most liked – so small you'd have to be a contortionist to get down to business with any finesse. It would allow her to relieve herself in her most preferred manner, albeit at slightly greater risk, perhaps, but that was the way she liked it. Without bothering to close the door, Kate stood facing the toilet and began hiking her skirt up her thighs. Its length and snug fit meant she had to raise it right up over her bum, displaying her gartered legs and the tiny underpants she wore. Knowing the man had finished his business and was watching her reflection in the mirror in front of the stall, Kate leaned slightly forward to display more of her crevice as she wiggled her panties down her thighs. When they were low enough for her to take her pee, she turned around to the front of the stall. Sure enough, the stranger was barely keeping up the pretence of hand washing and was now just staring at her exposed flesh. She saw his eyes widen as she turned her uncovered pussy towards him and he visibly gulped when he noticed one of her hands was holding the uppermost part of her slit open. He was riveted as she sat down on the cold toilet seat and spread her legs open as far as they would go, limited by her panties pushed only to her thighs.

Kate smiled at the stranger while she put both hands at the top of her mons. She used them now to open her pussy so that she would be able to watch herself pee and hopefully delight the man watching her. It took only a moment of concentration for her flow to be coaxed free and she shivered visibly at the first touch of urine coming from between her thighs. Pulling herself as wide as she could within the restricted position she held, Kate looked up at the lucky man who was being given this wonderful gift. Part of her mind was focused on the sensation of fluid running from her while another part was marvelling at the rush of pleasure being watched by this stranger was causing. He too was finding it quite stimulating: Kate could see the evidence of that clearly bulging under his jeans.

When she had pushed the last little drop from her bladder, Kate reached for the toilet paper and carefully tore off five sheets. It was always only five sheets, unless it was the kind of dispenser where you had to rip off tissue on a jagged edge, then she estimated the least amount she would need. Why this mattered she had long since forgotten; it was just another necessary aspect of the ritual they played out in public washrooms. She watched her hand as it moved between her thighs and reached back to her asshole and wiped slowly forward, rubbing over her clit as it finished the half-circle motion. Using one hand to hold her skirt out of the way, she then stood up and looked over her shoulder at the yellowed water in the bowl. With a small knowing smile touching her lips, Kate looked again at the man who'd just witnessed a story none of his friends were ever likely to believe. With her wares still exposed, she turned around and bent over much more than necessary to reach the handle for the flusher. As her urine swirled away down the mysterious hole, she held one leg of her panties and began tugging them up her large round hips. When her ass was covered by the skimpy material, Kate turned back to the quiet stranger now leaning heavily against the basin. This could sometimes prove to be the most difficult part of her game – convincing the man that the show was over and nothing more was going to come of it. This time, however, there was no problem as Kate brushed out the creases in her skirt and said simply, 'Boy, that feels better.'

The fellow showed a sense of humour as he walked to the door saying over his shoulder to her, 'You're not kidding.' Then he left.

Mike was waiting outside the door when Kate emerged from the men's washroom. He hardly needed to be told she had pushed the envelope way out there – he had seen the look on the man's face when he'd come out moments before. The guy had actually looked to Mike as if he'd wanted to share his secret but instead had shaken his head and with a clearly bemused smile on his face walked down the hall and re-entered the bustling mall. Mike knew his lovely wife had kept the door open. He could always tell: the average guy didn't get that particular look just because an unknown woman was peeing in the men's bathroom with him, unless, of course, the guy shared any one of the fetishes Mike and Kate embraced.

Knowing how raw her nerves would be after such a successful venture, Mike didn't immediately touch her.

Instead, he nodded his head towards the opening to the mall and walked silently beside her until they came to the end of the hall. Even then he only took her by the elbow and began to steer her towards the food court, occasionally squeezing her elbow with his hand as he felt the shivers of pleasure her adventure had stirred through her body. She had been pretty hot going in after his first use of the facilities; now, knowing she had been blatant in her exposure and watched by a stranger, Mike figured she'd be ready for an orgasm if he stimulated her even just a little bit. He would, once they were sitting down drinking, but he wouldn't touch her for ages yet. He would get her primed with conversation and the two other sets of washrooms they had to visit.

After they got their drinks, the couple found a relatively secluded set of seats where they couldn't be overheard. When Mike looked closely at his wife he could easily note the evidence of her aroused body. Her face was shining, not with perspiration, but with that glow so often ascribed to pregnant women; she got it when she was horny. Her mouth was swollen, the lips full and almost pouty, her pupils all but obscured the blue of her eyes and the top two buttons holding her blouse closed across her breasts were tipping into the button holes, ready with little effort to pop open and let her swollen breasts have the freedom they seemed to be straining towards. Just looking at her when she was so voluptuous and aroused made Mike's cock give a little jerk in his pants, and knowing what had turned her on so much would have made his knees buckle if he'd been standing. God, he loved this woman!

Kate watched her husband watching her and knew, just as he had with her, what was going on in his mind. He was taking in all the signs of her arousal and feeding his own lusts from it, as was she. They were so perfect together, symbiotically able to find nourishment from each other's peculiar ideas of sexual arousal. There was no limit to the naughty things she would willingly do to turn Mike on. He could demand anything he wanted and she would do it even if it scared her. The public exposure and the inherent risks of getting caught had not been the original intent of their bathroom escapades, but had proven to be extremely juicy additions. They both actually had a fetish for the process involved in the act of peeing and had discovered it was a wicked turn-on just to watch each other in the beginning. Eventually that had grown to include peeing on each other, which was where all this morning's games would lead them once they got home. The possible participation of strangers in the washrooms was only something they could hope for, but never actually counted on, especially with the women. Too few ladies seemed willing to stand and watch Mike pee, and fewer still were ever willing to hold him or lick him while he did it. But, with Kate's ability to create stories for him at will, she could become all those strangers who really wanted to watch and touch but were just too shy to do so.

Getting as lucky as she had earlier with the man watching her in the toilet had pushed a lot of Kate's arousal buttons, but she suspected she was getting ready to get into some more intense experiments. After today's adventures it might be time for her and Mike to visit one of the large shops selling sex toys and look for ways to experiment with pain. She had begun to imagine having nipple chains, possibly linked to a piercing in her pussy, as the unknown men watched her pee. Just thinking about it now was enough to move her to suggest they finish their drinks and go to the next set of washrooms.

Mike wanted to fill himself with more fluids before

he took his turn, so it was easy enough to decide that Kate would go first at their second stop. This was a busier toilet than the other had been, as it was closer to the food court and took the bulk of the patrons. With all the men coming and going at such a steady pace, they decided Mike would go in and confirm the vacancy of the stall. It wasn't too difficult for the men at the urinals to believe that the women's facility was too busy for this ordinary-looking woman as she stepped in to do her thing.

Unfortunately, just as Kate was wondering whether or not she should close the door to the stall, a uniformed security officer from the mall came in. He nodded to the other men standing around and looked a question at Kate. With a brusque 'can't wait', she whisked herself into the small area and manoeuvred the door shut.

The bit of anxiety she'd felt at the guard's initial entrance was quickly transformed into added excitement as she imagined him watching the open area at the bottom of the stall door. With experienced hands, she rolled her skirt above her relaxed and somewhat protruding belly, creating a spot for it to stay without necessitating she hold it up. With both hands free, she undid the garters holding up her stockings. She carefully pushed first one then the other now unhooked stocking leg down to bunch at her ankles, knowing the guard would be keeping an eye on the stall. Next she pushed her panties all the way down her legs until they too were bunched at her feet. Once she sat, she spread her feet as far apart as they would go and relaxed her bladder. The pleasure she got from letting her urine slowly drip from her insides and cover her cunt was strictly her own satisfaction. Whether the men in the john with her were excited didn't matter this time; she was more than willing just to enjoy the feel of her warm liquid as she slowly let it escape in small spurts.

The image she had created with her underclothes lying dishevelled on her shoes might or might not intrigue the guard. It really didn't matter to her.

She let her pee seep from her body slowly while keeping a keen ear for the sounds of the men at the urinals, easily hearing the contact of their liquids hitting the drains in the floor. The combination of her own fluid touching her, and the vision of all the unknown men holding their cocks and letting their pee arc out of them infused Kate with intense animal arousal. She wanted to throw open the stall door and have all the men there look at her beautiful pussy as her light yellow water cascaded out of and over her delicious lips. She imagined the mall guard using his club to push her cunt lips farther apart so all the men could have a good close-up look at her juicy, bright pink pussy. They would come close enough to smell her particular urine smell and smile at the delight of her.

As that last image faded, Kate realised she had been in the stall longer than was perhaps prudent, given the proximity of someone who just might want to take issue with a woman using the men's facilities. At the same time she saw a very familiar pair of expensive men's loafers passing by the bottom of the cubicle. That would be Mike letting her know he was there and perhaps telling her wordlessly it was time to get out. It was always possible that someone who had been the willing or unwilling recipient of their perversions earlier had told authorities and a warning might have been circulated to area malls. Kate didn't really care: no one was going to charge her with anything, and she could always stick to her argument of there being no room in the girls'. Women were another matter, and the partner of a man who did get to see Kate might always lay a complaint without knowing what Mike did in the ladies' room. No matter, she had gotten a lovely buzz from this scenario and was more than ready to let Mike have his turn.

Once outside the room, Mike filled Kate in on events after she had closed the stall door. He had come in moments behind the guard, also concerned that Kate's last conquest just might have complained or told someone from the mall. As it was, the guard appeared only curious at a woman's willingness to enter such a male domain until he saw what Kate was doing with her underwear. Mike watched his wife's breathing increase as he recounted the obvious arousal of the mall guard when he saw Kate lower her stockings to the floor. When her panties had followed, Mike had seen the guy's dick grow under his uniform pants. Not only that, but the fellow had nodded his head at the two other young men in the room and before long Mike had joined them in watching Kate's feet and ankles below the stall door as she squatted to take a pee. Mike suggested that there may have been more going on than even he suspected but without giving their game away he had thought he should not risk finding out just then.

Kate wanted more than anything to go back into the men's toilet and let her husband pee on her. She didn't think she could wait for him to visit two more women's facilities before she got a piece of him. The idea that he had shared her voiding with three other men was enough to make her legs weak. Her panties were thick with her juices and her nipples were desperate to be squeezed, hard. It frustrated her to know she could have had an avid audience if she hadn't been so scared of what the guard might have done if she'd left the cubicle door open. She could almost come on the spot at the thought of Mike sharing her display with these unknown men. As it was she settled for a quick press of her hand against his hard cock as they strolled over to the food area to replenish her empty bladder.

She knew Mike had unloaded himself while watching out for her and realised she didn't want to hold off her own needs for his turn at the game. She told him how much she really wanted to do it again with him in the room, something they didn't often do but were finding a lovely incitement today. Mike didn't mind, knowing he could always crowd himself into the stall with her and release his needs that way. In fact, after the last adventure he was just as happy to watch his wife being watched by other men while he peed in the same public room with her.

During the next twenty minutes Kate consumed two extra large cups of cola then walked around the mall for a time while all that liquid settled lower in her bladder. Arm in arm with Mike she strolled among the mass of harried shoppers, enjoying the secret only she and her husband knew about. She could feel her swollen vagina pulsing under her panties and whenever the crowds were thick enough she would snatch a feel of Mike's engorged penis. She would have loved to be able to walk through the mall with his member sticking out from his pants so she could touch it skin to skin at her leisure. Dismissing the notion as not an option, she contented herself with the occasional caress she could indulge in publicly. As they meandered, Mike was able to point out the two men who had been in the washroom with him and the guard. Both men had watched the couple walk past, and husband and wife realised they would now know Mike had been aware of what his wife had been doing in the cubicle. That too turned them both on to the point where Kate felt she just had to go into the last unvisited site.

This facility was probably the most isolated of the

three the mall boasted, farthest away from the shops and food court. No one appeared to be heading towards it or coming from it when they first checked out the men's room. It didn't really matter to either of them not to have an audience. There were lots of things they could do together in this public place that would satisfy their aberrant desires. If someone came along and caught them in the act, they trusted their professional appearance would qualify them as newlyweds who just couldn't wait to get home. They'd found the average person might 'tut tut' but would generally forgive the indiscretion, with occasionally cautioning words about public lewdness laws.

Kate pushed Mike up against the sink and started to rub her body against his. She wanted to feel the friction of his jacket against her nipples and unwrap the hardness beneath his suit pants. She unbuttoned her blouse and pushed his head down to her erect nipple hidden beneath her bra. When he started to suckle her like a baby she felt a gush of wet soak her already damp panties. When he bit into her stimulated nipple her knees buckled and Mike's hand around her ample waist was all that kept her from sinking to the floor. As he bit into her breast, Kate reached a hand down to the front of his pants and squished his firm cock against his own thigh, causing his mouth to open involuntarily as he loosed his hold on her breast and gasped his excitement at her touch.

Kate had reached the point where she knew if she wasn't going to have an unfamiliar audience involved while she urinated in this men's washroom, she would be quite content to do it with Mike there, and then head for home. The things they could do in the car on the way would only make them crazy to get at it in the privacy of their apartment. Pulling gently away from her aroused husband, Kate left her blouse open and headed for the empty enclosure. While she stood within its confines, they both heard the heavy tread of feet coming from the corridor outside. Their eyes lit up as they imagined men approaching and Mike readied himself by one of the urinals to start his game of pretend as the man or men entered.

When she saw the three men who came into the washroom, Kate smiled somewhat smugly to herself. It was really not much of a surprise to see the mall security guard and the two others who had shared her visit earlier at the other set of facilities. Once they had seen her and Mike together afterwards walking through the mall, it probably hadn't taken much imagination for them to realise there was something rather naughty going on with this couple. The guard might have had access to remote cameras and already noticed how Kate and her husband kept appearing at all the toilets. Heck, he might even have seen them both entering the 'wrong' facilities throughout the mall. In any case, the three unknown men were all in this toilet now and it looked as if they were quite ready for whatever game Mike and Kate might have in mind.

Kate nodded her head towards the door and the security officer walked over and turned the latch to lock position. While he was busy at that the other two men propped themselves on the sink counter, apparently content to wait for the event to unfold. When the lock had plainly latched, Kate began to take her skirt off. She pulled it down over her feet and stood in front of Mike and their three unknown companions. She folded it neatly and carefully hung it over the wall of the cubicle. Standing partially naked in this men's public washroom was causing Kate's eyes to close, making her appear to swoon as she reached for balance against the stall partition. With her free hand she began to unbutton the rest of her open blouse, keeping her eyes closed as wave after wave of lust and appetite crawled across her wanton body. Knowing she would still get to empty her full bladder in front of all these men later, Kate wallowed in the beguiling removal of her clothes.

Certain of their continued undivided attention, Kate easily dismissed from her mind any thoughts of the men's pleasure. Aspects of her own pleasure would surely come from knowing they watched, these three unknown men and her adoring husband, but what she did, how she touched herself, how she moved, would be done the way she would if alone and solely pleasing herself. She removed her suit jacket and laid it on top of her skirt. Standing now in only panties, garters, stockings and her half-opened blouse, Kate began to unbutton the blouse the rest of the way. When it was completely undone she took it off and put it with the other pieces of clothing hanging over the cubicle wall.

She felt decadent as she stood before the motley group of men, thinking of how naughty she was being taking off her clothes in a men's public washroom. The thought alone was a powerful aphrodisiac, but to be actually doing it, to peek from her closed eyes and see the urinals and the obvious mess of the facilities with her unfamiliar audience was making her desperate for more stimulation. She rubbed her palms across the material of her bra, her nipples sending bolts of desire to her cunt. With the picture of where she was and what she was doing in front of these strangers in her mind's eye, Kate was sure she could make herself come before she even got to the best part. It took more willpower than she thought she possessed to control herself and continue to the end she most desired.

She reached behind her back with one hand and unsnapped her bra, bending her torso slightly forward to take it off and allowing her abundant breasts to spill free. She imagined she could feel the heat of the men as they absorbed the sight of her large and lovely breasts and waited for the uncovering of her delicious pussy. But, before she had a chance to begin removing the few remaining bits of clothing, Kate felt a presence in front of her and could hear the rapid breathing of an unknown man. When cold hands filled themselves with her heavy tits she gasped with the contact and the thought that she didn't know whose hands they were, squeezing and rubbing her erect nipples. She opened her eyes just enough to see the uniform of the mall guard and his head as he bent to suckle the nipples he was pinching with both hands. Over his shoulder she had a brief glimpse of her loving husband and saw his lewd smile as he watched the stranger suckling her breasts. Seeing just how much Mike was getting turned on, it was easy for Kate to encourage more of this fondling from the man in front of her.

Even with the door to the stall left open, it was a tight squeeze for Kate and the guard, but when a second man stepped in to take one of her breasts in his mouth Kate was forced to have the two of them pressed up against her and found she could feel two hard bulges rubbing against her legs. As two unfamiliar men suckled and fondled her tits, Kate reached down between their bodies to grip the cocks hidden beneath their pants. When both her hands were full, shards of white light danced behind her eyelids as she pressed the engorged dicks against the men's own legs. The vision of them using these lovely rods to create the soft yellow arc only men could make caused Kate to gasp for breath and push both men away from her chest.

She opened her eyes to see the shining glow of lust coming from the two men she'd just disengaged from her nipples and the other two standing against the sink looking like little boys waiting for their turn. Motioning for the guard and the other man to move farther away, she ran her hand over her stomach and across the fabric of her panties. She slipped a finger into the side of one elasticised leg and pulled the panties to the side to expose her pubic area. She ran her finger through the manicured pattern of her pussy hair and shivered as she thought ahead to the moment when she could stand completely naked in the toilet stall.

With no particular intent to be seductive now, Kate unstrapped her stockings and quickly pulled them down and off her body. In moments she was standing in nothing but her panties and garter. The air touching her body felt like a million fingertips with tiny flames scorching her flesh with desire. This was exactly what she wanted; this was a dream come true. With her eyes still closed and one hand against the cubicle wall for balance, she turned her back on her rapt audience. When her shins bucked up against the toilet Kate used both her hands to pull off the last obstacle between her and complete public nudity. Standing naked with so many eyes raking across her voluptuous body was driving her to desires even more nasty than the ones she'd known she had. She bent forward over the bowl and ran her hands over her bare buttocks, spreading the cleft open between them. She felt so dirty, for a moment she imagined the men had paid to come sniff her very private parts and almost fell forward at the thought. Opening her eyes while she held her asshole and pussy open to the men, Kate looked into the toilet bowl beneath her and realised she could barely wait to pee in front of them all.

Straightening up fully, she turned to face the observing men. What she saw then thrilled her beyond description. Her adoring husband and his newfound friends were staring at her with their solid cocks in their hands. Four beautiful cocks, different in so many ways, but sharing the same desire to be more active participants in what she was doing. Kate moaned at the sight, relishing the images she created in her mind as she flitted ahead in her imagination to what might come next. She drank in the sight of these ensorcelled observers, finding Mike looking somewhat dazed but still managing to convey his pleasure with her behaviour.

When their eyes met he nodded his head at her, silently telling her she should sit down on the toilet. As her bare bottom touched the seat she told herself again what a very dirty girl she was being, finding her thoughts alone enough to almost send her to orgasm. It seemed, however, that Mike had other plans to get her there. He stood in front of her to the side of the stall, not blocking the view of the other men. In a voice thick with lust held barely in check he told her to open her legs, wide. He entered the stall then and kneeled in front of her, reaching towards her very available pussy. Using his thumb he entered the very top of her crack and ran it through her cunt until he found her large opening. Looking up into her face he told her how wet she was as he pushed his thumb into her farther. Speaking still for her ears only, he told her only a slut would be so wet and as her husband he would have to do something very serious about that.

When Mike was standing again he motioned the other men forward around the entrance to the cubicle. Kate was going mad as she watched four grown men surround her with their oh so delicious cocks straining in their hands. With the audience of unknown men looking on, Mike stood directly in front of his wife and began to pee. With obviously experienced hand movements he directed his spray towards Kate's clitoris. She reached down to open herself to him and began a concentrated effort to force her own liquids to flow. The sound of the two streams of urine filled her to bursting, the touch of his fluid on her cunt making her gasp for each breath. She tried to spread her legs and pussy lips wider but they were already too far apart to be comfortable. Not that Kate thought about comfort: she would sit like this for ever to maintain the mind-shattering eroticism of the moment.

The wet assault on her swollen cunt stopped and Kate ground herself on to the wooden seat in a vain effort to stimulate herself. Frustrated by the absence of her husband's urine on her, she looked to him, intent on having him come back and finger-fuck her while she finished emptying her bladder. Instead, she saw him motion the guard to his recently vacated position in front of Kate and indicate the man should emulate him. Looking every bit a man saturated by carnal thoughts, the guard wasted no time in letting loose his stream of urine. Less accurate than Mike, but in some ways more arousing, his wet arc was hitting her on her belly. Kate arced her hips forward to try to direct the cascading stream down through her pussy.

When another splash hit her, this time on a breast, Kate reached up to hold both breasts out for washing. In her mind she was telling herself she had been a bad girl for letting her cunt get so wet with desire, just like Mike told her. He was having his friends punish her by washing her in their pee. When she felt her knee jostled she realised her eyes had closed again and opened them to fill herself with the image of her public punishment. What she saw was one of the men squeezing into the very small space to the side of her seat and his cock coming to rest on her shoulder. She rubbed her cheek against the intruder and softly told him to pee on her.

The man shuddered as he first spurted then streamed out his yellow fluid over her shoulder and down her breast.

Breathing in the smell of the liquid the men were covering her in, Kate knew she couldn't wait any longer. She started panting for them to pee on her, telling them what a bad girl she was and that she must be coated in their wet urine. Stringing together the filthiest thoughts she could come up with, Kate kept up a continuous flow of words, holding herself ready for the final act. Within moments of telling the men to please cover her with their come, Kate felt the shift from light warm liquid to hot thick sperm. She rubbed herself wherever she felt the contact of heavy come on her naked body. With her eyes wide open she watched as the three strangers covered her with their spunk.

She was aware that her mind was completely shattered at the glorious vision she was creating as she felt the ecstasy grip her stomach. She felt the relief building, burning through her womb to her vagina while she watched Mike move the now depleted audience out of his way. Standing as close to her face as space allowed, Mike jerked his hand and loosed his load of semen on to her face and into her mouth as she parted her lips to receive it. The noises coming from her throat escalated as her body was gripped by the satisfying wave of orgasm she had been waiting for. With her legs still wide and her body literally covered head to foot in four men's pee and semen, Kate exploded again and again until she had to calm herself or risk losing consciousness.

When she could unglue her heavy eyelids and open her eyes, Kate was thrilled by what she was seeing. The four men, with cocks still dangling from their pants, had torn the cloth from the hand-drying dispenser. Each of the men held a length of material and were wetting it in the sink. A smile began to play at Kate's lips as she sought to make eye contact with her husband. She made purring sounds deep in her throat as Mike looked at her with adoration in his eyes and told her, 'It's time we washed you, honey.'

The Bad Gal LaToya Thomas

They've been trying to get me to say that I hadn't known what I was doing; that I hadn't been of sound mind; that there's a man somewhere who forces me to dress like this and keeps me on drugs so I can earn the cash to buy more. That sometimes this man makes me go out and pick up young men and bring them back to my apartment so he can watch. Is he my pimp? A ponce? Some kind of sicko that has got me involved in all this against my will? 'No,' I insist, but still they refuse to believe I'm telling the truth. They've read so many stories in the local paper they think I'm a victim. They can't believe I gave my consent.

I've had plenty of opportunity to give in and humour them; to say that this pimp mostly makes me go with older married men, 'cos they've got more cash and they want a bit of exotic black ass. I could get away with saying that teenage boys aren't really my thing 'cos sixteen- and seventeen-year-olds don't have the cash for it and they wouldn't dare touch what they can't afford.

But I've said nothing of the sort. So now I've been sat banged up for hours saying nothing while the social workers try to get an inner-city sob story out of me. The thing is, I hardly look like a victim. The cops have already tried to slam a drugs charge on me but I'm squeaky clean. No evidence of anything on my perfect skin. I even wiggled my butt at them earlier in case they wanted to check if I was packing rocks up there. The scrubbed-faced blonde one who brought me in declined my offer. Just as well, man. I didn't fancy her rubbing round my minus-plus. She's one of those types who have that lame goody-goody appearance. Bad, 'barely there so why bother' jewellery, you know, like small pearl earstuds and stuff, and an overneat, short layered hairstyle. It's the look of no imagination – and it makes me glad to my soul that I have what I have. I love my weave-on four-tone hair and body jewellery. I got two belly-button piercings, both nipples, a small gold eyebrow bar, as well as my diamond nose stud. My body is cared-for and toned. My caramel skin shines with health, and I glow with loving myself and being worshipped. I can make a boy come in his pants just by licking my lips. My friend Carol is always telling me I could give the bus driver a hard-on just by asking for my fare.

I bet that cop has never given anyone pleasure. I bet she doesn't even know what pleasure is. Her pussy is frozen, man. A guy could get himself a frostbitten cock in there, boy. I laugh for a couple of seconds. The bastards can't take my humour away from me but they have taken my mobile. God knows what messages they're picking up. The cops are probably wanking off to it. I could tell in their eyes when they brought me in that they wanted to fuck me. I know that for a fact. All men do. And wearing what I'm wearing makes it more so. I stand tall enough to be at eye-level with most of them. I never give them the sweet stuff – the coquette look – and that kinda threatens hard men. They see me as a challenge. They don't want to love and protect me; to make love or have the kind of sex with me that you see on those Lovers' Guides. They want to chase me and hunt me down; get me by the neck and have it rough. They can't stand that my spirit might be stronger than theirs. But they can't ignore me 'cos they can smell my sexy stuff. It gets their cocks hard and makes them want to fuck me and hurt me. They want to slap me and dominate me. You know, I've never known a hard white man that wasn't a brute inside. And that bitch who got me busted, I swear she's gonna regret it. Still, it was quite a laugh seeing the look on her face as her precious little boy was losing it in my sweet pussy.

My brief's got to show up soon. Fucking Sunday afternoon, man. Trust me to get pulled in on a Sunday. If I hadn't made so much noise, it would probably have been all right. How was I to know that one of them lived on the same level as me? That his mother was that fucking freak-out who always gives me filthy looks in the walkway along our estate. If only I hadn't gone to the shop in my fineries, and *they* hadn't been standing around outside, looking so bored. If only I hadn't started sparring with them. Yeah, well, we all know how easy it is to look back and regret things. Well, fuck that, man, 'cos I enjoyed what I did, and it ain't so serious really. I'm such a pushover for a new experience. I'd not tried it fives-up before. And all of them were so hard and young and nice-looking. I swear boys nowadays are better at keeping themselves clean and nice, you know. When I was a young girl, boys my own age were rough, man. They always had stinkfoot trainers and bad underwear and stuff. Now, them all got Calvins and body lotions for men and that. And, I tell you, I'd been feeling horny all morning. I wanted stiff cocks in me; to suck on 'em and watch 'em being rubbed up. Mmmm. So there I was coming out the shop, and this big, cold gust of wind caught my full-length fun-fur coat and blew it right up and showed all the boys what I had underneath – like, not much.

You can imagine. Nuff noise. The feistiest one comes up to me and he says: 'You is fit, man. I wanna ... you know,' and grabs his crotch and his mates start squealing with laughter and dancing around. He stands there jiggling his young slim hips around while his pals slide their butts off the wall and start dancing around him. The cheek, man. I was vex. I was about to shout for them to watch their manners, but something wicked got a hold of me and I couldn't be mad with them. So I calmly put down the shopping bags and walked up closer to the feisty one and opened my coat and showed him everything. And I said to him: 'So you want a little bit of China Blue, then?' I always use that name. It was the name of a ho' in a sleazy movie I'd seen years ago. It sounded so good I kept it. I like those hooker names like Roxette and Chelsey and stuff. I didn't want no corny thing like Coffee and all those other cheesy black-gal names. Yeah, China Blue was my favourite. These days I always keep the front bit of my hair bright blue and oiled down. I look bad gal 'cos I is bad gal. And if you have a problem with that, I feel no way about it.

So the others now get bold enough to start asking me questions like, 'So, who are you, China Blue?' and 'China Blue ... is you a ho?' Then peals of laughter as I stand there looking as if I'm waiting for them to impress me. Then one grabs my tits and he can see through the slinky material that they're high and firm and the nipples are hard – partly from the cold and partly from me being really ready for sex. Then the feisty one grabs at my ass. I'm wearing a skirt that's shiny and a two-tone apricot/pink colour. I don't know what the material is, but it feels like some sort of plastic. It's dancehall wear, really. And my shoes are black patent with high heels with the backs cut out of the foot and ankle. They look like hooker shoes, I suppose.

So there I am at eleven in the morning looking like I'm fresh from a dance. Full make-up, no knickers and smelling sweet and musky. And those boys were capti-vated. Their pupils were dilating and they were all getting stiff. I could see it. Two or three of them had their hands in their pants, adjusting stuff. And it was making me wet, and I was so excited, man. It was their enthusiasm that did it for me; and their total inability to control themselves.

'So what are you doing?' I ask. 'Is this all you have to do? Hang around outside the Spar?'

'Yeah, man, it's dry round here. There's nothing, guy, nothing.'

And just at that moment I felt really sorry for them. I wanted to brighten up their day. Give them something to talk about for months. So I invited them back to mine. I know I shouldn't have, and that I'd probably regret it and have them following me around and calling at my door for the rest of the time I'd be living there but, well, it was a snap decision. I wanted to play a part. And get my pussy rammed by all that young cock.

Straight to my flat, then, and at first things felt like they could get a bit tense. I hadn't expected them to be quite as nervous as they were, but I guess it had been quite a while since I'd had anything to do with sixteen-year-olds. Even the feisty one kept going to the bathroom, and they were all rushing about the flat getting drinks and looking at my pictures and CDs and stuff and avoiding the issue, basically – the reason why they were there in the first place. When one of them started asking me about music and what clubs I went to, it was time to regain control. It was all getting too much like a youth club and, believe me, I had no intention of being their social worker. I didn't want to be friends with them; I wanted to fuck them. So I had them all sit down on the sofas while I told them how it was gonna be.

I stood up and told them, 'We'll go into the bedroom 'cos there's more room there. You might think you're all going to get a turn with me separately but I want you all at the same time.'

Well, my God, that made them look fear. Then two start giggling. One of them said in a serious voice, 'Tony, man, no looking at my cock, right?' The one called Tony looked back at his mate in horror.

'What you thinking, Darren, man. That I is batty boy or something?' Then much sucking of teeth and 'Get off, man', 'No, you get off, man.' Foolie boys. Then it dawned on them that one had to be last, and a muddled wailing started of, 'I'm gonna be first.' They were look-ing at things in a typically male way – start to finish, one after the other.

'If you're gonna argue, no one's getting any,' I shouted. I felt like a teacher in a primary school, dishing out birthday cake or something. 'If you want my pussy, you wear Jimmy hats, right. I got them, don't worry. If you wanna ride bareback I can suck you.' None of them were looking me in the eye, even though I was rubbing my thighs slowly and walking up and down past them. They wanted the action, but they knew they were being told righteously that they had to do things the way I wanted. I was so in control. And they were all so scared of fucking up, even if one or two were still looking cocky. Then things were quiet for a bit while they sucked on bottles of drink and reached out to touch me. I kneeled in front of them and let them all have a turn of feeling my tits and ass.

When the time was right I got up and slowly walked towards the door. I was almost out of the room before I realised not one of them was following me. 'So, are any of you up for it, then? Or shall I put the TV on instead?' I asked sarcastically. Then, finally, movement. The boys were looking at each other and in a state of excitement so great that they couldn't even speak.

My room was immaculately tidy and the huge bed was made. There was room enough on that bed for six people – just. So I lay on the bed and rucked my tight plastic skirt up so that when they started trooping into the room they could all see there was nothing underneath that skirt except my sweet wet pussy. Then I rolled over on to my knees and bared my backside at them and rubbed it. And I did all the porno moves. The tongue came out and the fingers went in. And I told them I was so horny, and I was wanting them to fuck me. I was loving it. They were all rubbing their crotches. Then one by one they were unbuttoning and unzipping themselves and pulling out their wood.

'Ah, man, I'm so ready,' said Tony. 'I'm gonna shoot my fucking load in this sweet pussy, man. I want to do it really bad. Really gonna come hard. I'm gonna rump her, and fucking soon, I can't hold it.' Darren may have been worried about Tony looking at his cock, but Tony's concentration was most definitely fixed on what was between my legs. Sweet things.

Then he grabbed me and forced me down on the bed and pushed his young hard white cock in my face, and rubbed it across my maroon-coloured lip-glossed mouth. It smelled of musk and man, and it was so, so hard.

Well, by this time I could barely stand it myself. I snaked my hand down between my legs and started curling my fingers over my wet clit. I have to be careful with this business 'cos my nails are, like, three centimetres long or something.

'God, man, I've never seen a woman play with herself before!' one of them shouted in total shock.

'Well, you can get real close up to it if you like,' I

invited. 'What's your name anyway?' I asked. I weren't gonna have no boy watch me rub myself up without me knowing his name. That would feel well strange.

'I'm Linton, China Blue. You see me, I check for you. I got wood in a brief and I is hot for you.' And we all start laughing at his little rap. And I'm laughing really loud until Tony forces that cock of his in my face and I has to shut up. Then Linton climbs on the bed and he's unzipped himself. Out the corner of my eye I can see he's rubbering up, so I'm relaxed that they're having respect for me in that way. As he bounces on the bed my head shakes a bit and it makes me swallow about two centimetres more cock than I'd anticipated. And that's it. Tony is hissing words I can't make out through his gritted teeth. I open my eyes again and I see he's losing it, and then suddenly a warm gush at the speed of a bullet shoots from his cock and down my throat.

At the other end Linton is nudging himself into me and boy it's big!

'Get the fuck out the way, Tony, man,' he orders, and Tony gets off me and the bed, looking satisfied.

'I'm gonna put a tune on, man,' he says, all calm.

Then, just for a few seconds it's me and Linton: the experienced woman and the feisty boy. The three others are standing there hard and expectant, rubbing themselves slowly with excitement in their eyes. The bass starts coming from next door as Linton's ramming himself up into me. I swear I've never heard it that loud before. The fool's gonna blow my speakers if he ain't careful. But the thud goes on and I'm carefully circling the flat of my finger around my clit, just drawing out the pleasure as long as I can, 'cos I would go off like a rocket if I didn't exercise a little self-control. But he's good, that Linton; he's really good, and then suddenly another boy is coming towards my face with his stiff load in his briefs. And he tugs it out and just starts jerking furiously. I look him in the eye and say it's OK, that he should wait his turn, but he can't, and before I can get the message through to his young eager brain, he's shooting it all over my smiling face, pulling on his balls as he milks the last couple of drops of sweet boycum.

I'm sorry, but that was too much for me. I start coming and, I tell you, I was loud. I was louder than I had ever been. I look up at Linton and he's going, 'Oh, oh, yeah,' and the both of us are making so much noise, man.

I don't know how many minutes pass before I bring myself to my senses. Then I start to notice the bedroom door opening slowly. Expecting to see Tony back for seconds I look up and straight into the eyes of a woman – a furious-looking woman – and, before I know it, she's got her hands around sweet lover-boy's neck and is pulling him off me and out of me. My pussy is still throbbing and I'm in the most compromising position.

'You fucking twisted bitch,' she screams at me. 'What do you think you're doing? That is my only son and you've ruined him! I've never seen such slackness in all my days!'

'He don't look ruined to me,' I says. 'And if you can't figure out what is going on, I'll spell it out for you. I was having a fives-up with my little gang and –'

And I get cut off in my speech. She starts flying at me. I'm screaming and fighting back and hitting at her. It's a real cat-fight, and Tony's back in the room trying to calm things down. The two that didn't get their fill look so sore and hard done by, man. With much kissing of teeth they slouch off, their virginity intact. Then, before I know what's happening, two Old Bill are in the room. I hear their radios before I see them. And I reach for something to wrap around myself while I ask them if they're getting a good enough look. Cheek. And as I'm led out the house a few minutes later (at least the bastards let me get dressed) I find out that the front door had been left open the whole time. That was the big mistake. Linton's mother had thought there was murders going on up here and had phoned the police at the same time as the neighbours had complained about rough ragga blasting out on a Sunday morning.

So I was well and truly caught bang to rights, man. And now I is sitting here bored and thirsty and brimming with ideas of revenge. But, I tell you, I've learned my lesson. And this is my advice: if ever any of you bad gal gonna do it five-ways with the yout', remember to close the bloody door behind you!

Wheels on Fire
Mathilde Madden

I first noticed her in the library. I noticed the way
sunlight from a high dusty window bounced off
her hair. I noticed the dress she wore: a tight, fitted
white cotton dress with a print of red cherries on it.
She was a little prim looking, like a school teacher;
just a nice-looking woman standing next to me, as I
reached for a book on a high shelf, stretching in my
wheelchair.

The book I wanted was almost out of reach, but I got
a fumbling grip on the spine and pulled, and at that
same moment she leaned over quickly and whisked it
from my tentative grip, no doubt in an attempt to help
me out.

That annoyed me. 'I can manage,' I growled through
my teeth.

She ignored my complaint and turned the book over
in her hands. 'Jackie Collins,' she noted in a stage
whisper.

I realised I was staring at her lips; they were the
same colour as the cherries on her dress.

'It's for my mum, OK.' I kept my voice low.

'Well of course it is. A beautiful man like you
wouldn't need to read about it.' Her tongue flicked over
her lips, turning the matt to gloss. She bent down
slowly, so her eyes were level with mine and I could
see straight down the top of her dress. Her voice
dropped even lower. 'You'd be surprised, though, just

how dirty these books can be. I think it's quite amazing that you can find the filthiest things right here in the public library.'

I felt my face redden as she suddenly dropped the book into my lap and walked away without another word.

I sat there for several moments, my heart beating fast and my mouth dry, but I didn't move. Six months ago I wouldn't have even questioned such a blatant come-on. I would have followed her and given as good as I had got, shown her just where such deliberate prick-teasing could lead. But not now. After all, I was in a wheelchair these days. Pretty girls like her didn't come on to pathetic cripples like me.

So it couldn't have been a come-on; I must have been mistaken. No doubt she just felt sorry for me and thought she'd talk to me for a few moments. Brighten up the day of the poor boy whose legs didn't work any more.

Pushing the girl out of my mind, I leisurely found the other books I wanted and checked them out. Then, balancing them in my lap, I wheeled my way carefully down to street level by way of the substandard ramp outside, a new addition to this ancient building.

As I zigzagged I saw her again. On the low wall at the bottom of the steps sat the girl in the cherry-print dress. She was eating an ice cream, a 99, and didn't seem to have noticed me. I was planning to wheel straight past her, but as I did so she said, 'Hey.' So, not wanting to be rude, I stopped my chair right in front of her.

'Oh, hi.'

'Come to the park with me.' She winked and jerked her head towards the iron gates over the road.

'I can't,' I muttered, turning my head to look at her. 'I'm in a hurry.'

She stretched her leg out and stuck the chunky high heel of her brown shoe into the spokes of my wheel. 'Go on,' she said, pulling the ice-cream-smeared chocolate bar slowly out of her 99. 'I'll let you have my flake.'

I didn't reply, but just looked down at the chunky heel jammed in my spokes, trapping me. What could I do? I looked at her cherry-print dress and her cherry-red lips. I met her eyes and something in her expression seemed to captivate me. Silently I nodded my head.

As she leaned forwards and slid the chocolate bar into my mouth I felt as if I were falling under her spell. I had no choice but to obey when she whispered hoarsely, 'Don't bite it now.'

I watched her expression as she inched almost the entire thing into my mouth, a fraction at a time, and then slowly began to pull it out again. Then in it went again, then out, gradually picking up speed. My breathing quickened. I hadn't had so much as a chaste kiss from a girl in months and now, suddenly, I was fellating a chocolate bar for this one, outside the public library.

And I couldn't remember the last time I was this turned on.

All the time we stared at each other. I was trying to will her on with my gaze, begging for more, wanting nothing in the world except to let her fuck my mouth, to her satisfaction, with this makeshift phallus.

But then she sighed and must have shifted position, because I heard her heel click against my spokes and the sound broke the spell. I remembered in a rush why things like this didn't happen to me any more. I remembered that I was sitting outside a library in a wheelchair. I remembered what was wrong with this picture. I bit down through the flake and pulled my head away.

I chewed the chocolate, licking more of it from my lips and wiping the spills away with the back of my hand.

'Thank you,' I said coldly, when my mouth was almost empty.

She seemed unconcerned by my sudden change of heart, and just smiled seductively at me. 'Well, that's my part of the bargain over with; now it's your turn.'

'What?'

'The deal was, I'd give you my flake if you came to the park with me, so, off we go.'

She hopped down from the wall and, making no attempt to push me, I noted, started across the road.

I followed her through the Victorian wrought-iron gates, my wheels crunching on the gravel as I trailed her around the rose garden.

She didn't say much as we followed path after path, just pausing to point out the certain blooms or, once, a squirrel. Most of the time she just let her eyes slide over me, looking down as if she couldn't bear to tear herself away. I felt self-conscious under her gaze, finding myself bowing my head and hunching my shoulders. But deep down inside me, I liked that feeling. There was something between us, something in the air, and it scared me, but I knew I couldn't resist it. Maybe that was what scared me the most of all.

At one point she leaned over and plucked the petal from a very dark red rose.

'Look at this one,' she said, her eyes glowing. 'It's exactly the colour of blood, but it feels so soft.'

She rubbed the petal briefly on her cheek, before leaning forwards and trailing it slowly across mine. Her face was inches away from mine, and I felt sure she was about to kiss me, but she didn't; she just said, 'Let's go to the pavilion and get some tea.'

And we did, settling ourselves at a sticky table and making perfunctory conversation about nothing. She picked up my library books from the table and looked through them.

'So,' she said, 'are all these books for your mother?'

'No, just the Jackie Collins, like I told you.'

'You need to drop it off today?'

'No, I'll do it tomorrow, on my way back from physio.'

'Right.' She drained her teacup and placed it carefully in the saucer. 'Let's go to your place.'

'Why?' I used the last part of my resolve to try and resist her, reminding myself that whatever she said it was just pity. Just an offer of a pity fuck for a poor cripple. And I didn't need her pity.

She looked hard at me, her face completely matter-of-fact. 'Because every time I look at you, I want to get on my knees and run my tongue along your footplate, until you're desperate for me, rock hard and writhing in that chair like an animal in heat.'

I stared, thoughts of refusing her 'pity fuck' suddenly drained away. I couldn't speak.

She smiled. 'And I'd rather not do that right here.'

I don't remember how we got there, but it hardly took any time at all.

I hurriedly showed her around my flat, which she surveyed with a polite lack of interest until we reached the bedroom.

We both stared at my unmade bed. For minutes.

'You can get into bed without any help, right?' she whispered eventually, as if not wanting to disturb the charged atmosphere our mutual heavy breathing had cast in the small room.

'Sure.'

'Well, go on then.'

And within moments, we were in the bed, both naked, and her mouth was clamped on mine. She was rough, driving her way inside and sucking brutally on my lower lip.

Her skin against mine felt so good. It was all I could do not to come just from the sound of her rapid heartbeat and the feel of her heat.

She moved from my mouth, nipping her way across my cheek until she reached my ear. 'I want to fuck you with my mouth,' she hissed.

I laughed. 'Don't you mean you want me to fuck your mouth?'

'No.'

She rolled me onto my stomach, with an impassioned sigh. Once I was positioned the way she wanted she straddled my legs and bent down to flicker her tongue across my exposed buttocks.

I flinched, uneasy, not sure if this was something I wanted, but somehow I couldn't find the words to tell her to stop. So I quivered there beneath her, as she let her tongue dart everywhere. Absolutely everywhere.

I gasped when she nudged at my hidden little hole, at the same time splaying me, with one hand, so that I was open and wanton for her. And then I found myself moaning as she teasingly let her tongue lap over that hot little mouth, again and again, until it was so hungry, so wanting, that I was thrusting my hips up to meet her every caress. Aching. Aching for something. Anything. More.

Responding to my desperate thrusting, she pushed the very tip of her tongue gently inside me. I was so needy and desperate for her by that point that I bucked like an animal, half begging and half sobbing, my face buried in the pillows while my desperate erection ground against the mattress.

Thankfully my frustration didn't last long. One of her hands snaked underneath me, forming a lubricated fist around my aching cock. I thrust into the warm soft well gratefully. Seconds later her tongue, which was starting to feel hopelessly small inside me, was replaced by a finger, then two, and the most amazing sensation, as she stroked her way inside me with her other hand, fucking me decisively. I'd never felt anything like it.

And in moments, with her hands manipulating me from every direction, I was spasming for her, soaking the sheets beneath me, half screaming, half blacking out.

She held me for a long while after that, brushing my hair away from my face, waiting until I had recovered. Eventually I found I could speak again. 'If that was a pity fuck,' I breathed, 'then I think I do need your pity.'

She propped herself up on her elbow and looked down at me. 'It's only a pity if we don't do that again,' she said, emphasising her point with a brief kiss before clambering from the bed and walking naked into the kitchen of my tiny, specially adapted flat. I heard the ancient pipes squeal and then she returned with a glass of water, and slipped back into the bed so we could share sips in silence.

'I need to go to the loo,' I said, when the glass was drained.

'Do you need any help?'

'No, I can manage.'

I manoeuvred myself from the bed to the chair and wheeled myself into my bathroom. When I returned she was sitting up in bed, grinning. 'Stay in the chair,' she said distantly, as I parked up next to the bed.

'Why?'

'You look so beautiful, naked in your chair – please, I want to see you come in your wheelchair.' She flipped back the bedclothes and crawled across the bed in a couple of quick movements, stopping to kneel up right next to me.

'Are you going to make me come again?' I asked in disbelief.

'More than that.' She licked her lips. 'I will suck your cock every time I see you naked in that chair and that's a fucking promise.' My sudden erection twitched.

And then with one final hungry look she buried her head in my lap, sucking greedily, almost before I had time to engage the brake.

Her tongue swirled around the head of my cock, coaxing and teasing me to my second orgasm.

I barely had time to question whether I would be able to climax again so soon before I exploded in her mouth. I felt my fingers tightening against the rubber tread of the tyres, nails digging in so hard I was surprised I didn't end up with a puncture.

She lifted her head, wiping the spills from her chin and smearing them down my chest. As I went to wipe them away she snapped, 'Don't move.' I froze obediently, again feeling I had no choice but to obey.

She flopped down on her back, watching me through lust-lidded eyes. Hitching up her knees, she let them fall apart, exposing herself blatantly to me. I felt my breath catch as I saw how pink and wet and ripe she was. She held my gaze as she let one of her hands trail between her legs.

She smelt so delicious I could almost taste her, but I understood her game by now. I knew she wanted to direct the action.

'I bet you'd like to fuck me,' she murmured as she let her hand glide over her dark, shiny pubic hair.

'Yes,' I moaned, helplessly. 'Oh God, yes.'

'Mmm,' she cooed, 'but I'm afraid I can't let you right now. I'm torn but, if you come and fuck me, I won't be able to look at you. And you look so beautiful, naked in your chair, sated, with your come smeared over you. Tell me you don't mind waiting.'

There was that hypnotic tone to her voice again. I could hardly bear it. But I swallowed hard, trying not to shake with frustration. 'I don't ... I don't mind.'

I could scarcely believe it was possible after coming twice in quick succession, but my cock stirred as I watched her movements become more vigorous.

'Have you ever come in your chair before?'

'No, never.'

'Really?' She was panting so hard now she could barely get the words out.

'Really, I've never. I haven't done anything like this since – since I've been like this.'

'You never ... you never even made yourself come, though? You never played with yourself while you were sitting in the chair?'

I shook my head. 'No. I only do that in bed.'

'You should.' She was bucking against her hand now, squirming hard on the bed. 'I'd like to see that. I'd like to see you touch yourself. Do it now, just so I can see what you do.'

'I can't.' I hated to deny her, but there was no way I was going to get anything further out of my cock at this moment.

She smiled. 'Just touch it. Play-act for me.'

I reached down and took my very tender cock in my

hand, stroking it lightly, doing what I hoped would put on a good show for her.

I'd never thought of myself as an exhibitionist before, but soon I was throwing my head back, moaning and biting my lip, acting the slut, just because I wanted to make her come harder.

And she did, as I writhed and moaned for her; she did the same for real, arching up into her own hand, and screaming something about me being the most beautiful thing she had ever seen.

Much later, in the middle of the night, I woke to find her rubbing herself against my leg, sliding, wet and needy, against my unfeeling thigh. When she realised I was awake she began kissing me roughly and, every time her mouth was free, asking me to tell her, again and again, that I couldn't move, that I couldn't feel her wetness coating my useless, broken legs, that I couldn't walk.

'Again.'

'I can't walk.'

'Again.'

'I can't walk.'

'Again.'

'I. Can't. Walk.'

And she came, screaming, twisting both my nipples hard, so I screamed too.

I don't know what kind of effect she had had on me, but the very next day at my physio session the therapist asked me if something had happened to change the way I felt about myself. I couldn't help it. I ended up telling him all about her.

Well, not all about her. In fact not even half of it. I simply told him I had met the most wonderful girl and was happier than I had ever been. He suggested I ask her if she wanted to come to some of my sessions, see how I was getting on.

But she never did. We had other things to do.

Like find new ways for her to play with me in my chair. One evening she wheeled me into the kitchen and stripped me, then painted my body with warm, shiny chocolate. She wrote the word 'slut' and 'cripple' across my chest while I moaned for her, and I writhed when hot splatters dripped from her fingers and landed on my stomach.

Painfully aroused, I pleaded and begged, but there was nothing I could do to relieve my frustration. She had ordered me to keep my hands on my tyres and I did so. I was always powerless to disobey her orders. So I kept my hands in position, even when she leaned forwards to lick me clean and drew one nipple, hard, into her mouth, nibbling and teasing until I was a frantic squirming mess.

And then she was licking me clean of come as well as chocolate.

She did indeed, one night, get on her knees and lick my footplate. And it was one of the most erotic things I had ever seen. She moaned softly as she ran her tongue along the bright metal and caressed the tread of my tyres with her hands.

I was frantic for that mouth to be on my cock, long before she had done all she wanted.

She asked me things no one else had ever asked. Breathless, late-night conversations that scared me and made me want her even more: 'If you weren't in your chair, how would you move?'

'What do you mean?' I rolled over so I could rub against her, pressing close in the dark.

'I mean, well, would you crawl around? What could you do?'

'I couldn't really crawl; I could pull myself along. My arms are pretty strong.' I felt her shiver against me.

She swallowed slowly, then said, 'So, sort of on your belly?'

'Yes, just like that.'

'I'd like to see you doing that.'

'Why?' I asked with a teasing smile.

'I just would. Show me.'

So I did. Suddenly the lights were on and I was in my chair, wheeling myself into the living room where there was most floor space. I let her gently tip me onto the carpet and watch me drag myself across the floor on my stomach, as best I could, naked and utterly vulnerable.

'Tell me why you're doing that,' she said, her voice so ragged it was barely recognisable.

'For you.'

'No, no, tell me why you have to move like that.'

I changed my path and started to drag myself towards her, meeting her eyes from way down on the floor. 'Because I can't get up.'

I could tell how much this was turning her on and it aroused me to see her almost frozen to the spot with desire. My cock was painfully hard against the carpet as I continued towards her.

She stared at me in silence after that, until I reached her and ran a passionate, wanting hand up her bare leg, trying desperately to reach her cunt. As my hand grazed her upper thigh she took half a step backwards, pulling deliciously just out of my reach. And I whimpered. Begging. Helpless. Everything she loved.

Then she growled and flipped me over roughly, and we fucked until I felt sure she had worn away the carpet beneath me.

So I never actually asked her to come to my physio

sessions, and she never showed any interest anyway. When the taxi came to pick me up she would just snuggle down deeper in the sex-stained sheets and I would drag myself away, reluctant to miss even a second of her beautiful half-hidden curves.

It was two weeks after we had first met that we had our first and only conversation about my physiotherapy. That night she straddled my already bucking, needy body and tied my wrists to the bed frame. I struggled a little, gazing up at her handiwork. 'Is that really necessary?' I asked, laughing. 'I'm not going to run away, you know.'

'I know.' She grazed the pad of her thumb down the sensitive side of her forearm. 'But the less you can move, the more I like it.'

'Would you like it if I couldn't move my arms at all? If they were like my legs?'

'Yes,' she said huskily, rocking her hips against my erection.

Encouraged and relishing the pressure I went on. 'What about if I couldn't move any part of my body? If all I could do was blink?'

She leaned forwards and licked my temple. 'If all you could do was blink, I'd blindfold you and then fuck you through the mattress with an enormous strap-on.'

I moaned greedily as she kissed me on the lips. 'But I wouldn't be able to feel it,' I muttered into her mouth, as she pulled away.

'Well, I'd have to describe it to you, wouldn't I?' She scooted back down my bound body as she spoke, dropping kisses onto my chest between words. 'Blow by blow.' And her lips closed languorously around my cock.

'So when I can walk again, is this what you'll do to me? Tie me down every night?'

She slid her lips from my cock with a pop and sat back on her heels, frowning. 'What do you mean?'

'I mean, to keep me helpless. The way you like it.'

She frowned at me. 'No, no,' she said slowly, shaking her head. 'What do you mean: when you can walk again?'

I stared at her and she stared right back, her mouth open.

There was a moment's pause before I spoke. All I could say was, 'Oh my God.'

'I thought you knew,' she said quietly.

But I hadn't known. I hadn't known until that moment. I spoke slowly. 'I thought you liked to make me helpless. I thought you liked having power over me. I thought that was your thing. But that's not it, is it? It's all about the chair. It's all about the fact I can't walk. That's it, isn't it?'

'Did your physio say you'd get better?'

'He said I might. Actually I've been improving since . . .' My voice trailed off, strangely soft. 'I even thought you'd be pleased.'

But now I realised that that wouldn't please her at all.

I realised, with a sickening, creeping dread, that the thing I wanted most in the world was the one single thing she didn't want. And she didn't care about me; hadn't chosen me for her power games because of who I was. Just what I was.

It was as if a strange sexual spell had suddenly broken; as if suddenly, after almost two weeks of continuous fucking, I felt ashamed to be naked in front of her.

I didn't need to say it out loud. Without speaking she slipped off the bed and picked her dress up from the floor.

'I'm sorry,' she said, fastening the buttons so fast she fumbled over most of them and ended up taking twice as long. 'I should go.'

'Yes,' I said, glancing up at my still-bound wrists. 'Would you mind untying me first?'

In reply she picked her way across the room and set me free with a few deft moves. I pulled myself upright.

'I'd better go,' she said again.

'Yes,' I said. 'I think you'd better.'

And she left. It was the first time I'd slept alone in two weeks. My erection wouldn't go down all night. But I couldn't bear to touch it in case I thought of her.

The next morning I found a note had been slipped under my door, asking me to meet her back at the park, in the tearoom.

When I arrived she was sitting there, sipping her tea. She was wearing a blue dress. It was the first time I'd seen her in a different outfit. That cherry-print dress seemed to have been crumpled on my bedroom floor for the whole two weeks we were together. A black coffee, the drink I had ordered in this same tearoom with her two weeks ago, sat across from her on the table.

I wheeled myself over.

'I'm sorry,' she said. 'I shouldn't have reacted like that. It was just such a shock. I'd assumed it was permanent.'

'Really. Well, they don't really know.' I took the dripping filter contraption off the top of the cup, placing it messily on the table, and took a sip of the too-hot liquid underneath.

'Yes, of course. I mean they don't know for sure if you're going to get better or not, do they? And even if you do, well, I'm sure it could be OK.'

'Could it?'

'Yes. Maybe.'

I fixed her with a stare. 'Well, forgive me if I don't see how, because it's not me, is it, with you. It's just the chair.'

'No. It's not that simple.' She ran her tongue over her lips. Suddenly my mouth felt very dry, but I knew the coffee would still be too hot. 'The chair is part of you. I want every part of you.'

'Yes, especially the parts that don't work.' I saw her swallow hard, but ignored it and went on. 'Admit it – that was what attracted you, wasn't it? If I could walk you wouldn't be interested.'

'Well, so what? You can't. So what does it matter?'

'So what! So what if you're not interested in me for me, just because of some sick fetish?'

'Why is it sick? We have a good time, don't we? I have a fetish for wheelchairs, you're in a wheelchair. What's the problem?'

'I want you to want me for me. That's the fucking problem.'

'I do. And that includes all the things about you that make you different from other people, including the fact you can't walk. So can't you want me for all the things that are different about me, including the fact that you not being able to walk turns me on?'

I looked at my lap for a long time. 'No,' I said eventually, not looking up. 'No, I can't.'

I kept my head bowed and heard her chair scrape against the tiled floor. I listened to her chunky-heeled footsteps walk away, before I looked up. So I don't know if she cried. And I don't think she knows I did.

Sometimes, when I go to the library I see her there. Standing in shafts of dirty sunlight, running her finger along a high shelf, clunky brown shoes clip-clopping on the old parquet flooring. We never speak. I wouldn't know what to say.

But if I do see her, I always end up touching myself when I get home. There's no point in resisting her if I want to sleep at all. It's the only way to get her out of my head.

And I do it naked, in the chair.

The Last Deduction Alison Tyler

An audit. A tax fucking audit. Nadine couldn't believe it. She'd filed her forms on time, didn't make a shitload of money, kept careful – well, adequate – records of her expenditures. Why was the IRS harassing her?

'They always go after the little guys,' her friend Daphne explained. 'Waitresses, like me, or freelancers, like you. They know you're too poor to afford an expensive accountant and that you'll probably be too scared to challenge anything they say.' Daphne shot Nadine a sympathetic look. 'You'll be fine, hon. You're so honest. I'm sure they won't find anything out of place.'

'But I don't have all my receipts,' Nadine confessed, impatiently brushing her dark hair out of her eyes. 'I mean, I have a whole shoeboxful of scraps of paper –'

'Give *that* to the auditor,' Daphne said righteously. 'Make him work for it.'

'And some of my deductions might be a little...' Nadine's voice trailed off.

'A little what?'

To answer the question, Nadine pulled open the doors to the closet where she kept her writing materials. Like a hostess on some X-rated game show, she pointed to a battery-powered vibrator with harness, a bone-handled crop and a pair of high-heeled fuck-me pumps with tiny studded ankle straps that glistened in the light.

'You put *those* on your itemised return?'

Nadine nodded.

'Under what heading?' Daphne snorted. 'Office supplies?'

'Miscellaneous research items,' Nadine said, adding emphatically, 'I used everything here for my latest book. Every single piece.'

'And I'll bet Steven loved each minute of it,' Daphne said as she stood to take a closer peek, her green eyes wide in disbelief.

'Forget Steven,' Nadine said. 'Help me figure out how I'm going to explain what I do to a tax auditor.'

'You're a writer. Tell him that you need a wide variety of experiences in order to get in touch with your characters.' Now Daphne was slipping into a pair of bright-red feather-tipped mules and admiring the way they looked on her delicate feet. 'Did you write these off too?'

'Of course. They were for a story called *The Death of the Marabou Slippers*.'

'I wish I could be there,' Daphne said, looking longingly at the pink and black-rubber coated paddle, the thick silver handcuffs, the ball gag. 'I can just imagine the guy's face when you show him what's behind door number one.' She started to laugh. But Nadine didn't think it was funny.

Was it really necessary to have bought all the different toys? Nadine debated the question because it was one the auditor would undoubtedly ask her. If she were a mystery novelist writing about a murder, would she go and buy a gun? No, but she most definitely would hit the shooting range and pump round after round of ammo into some defenceless piece of paper. To her way of thinking, that sort of quest for knowledge was the equivalent to slipping a plastic butt-plug up her heart-shaped ass before trying to write about what that experience felt like.

Besides, her ex-boyfriend had loved it. At least, at first. As she prepared for the audit, she thought about the different kinky times they'd shared together. With Steven starring in the role of her personal sex slave, she'd experimented with a whole assortment of erotic toys. Acting the part of a dominant woman wasn't unique for her. She had done that from time to time anyway, taking charge, being on top. But pushing the limits of that fantasy, getting down and dirty without fear of reprisals – well, that's where the real research came into play.

Closing her eyes, she remembered the time she'd fucked Steven with a massive black strap-on. Made to look anatomically correct, the tool was ribbed with veins and sported a rounded mushroom head. Just sliding the accompanying leather harness around her slender waist had turned her on. Having Steven on his hands and knees getting the head of the plastic prick all dripping with his mouth had made her knees weak. That was something she'd never have known if they hadn't played the scene out together. She'd been forced to pull herself together, to act the tough, female dom. Telling him to get as much spit on her tool as he could, because she was going to ream his ass when he was finished. It had been difficult for her not to stop mid-scene and write down dialogue for her book, but she'd managed to wait until he'd come.

Extreme.

That's what the experience had been. And it was why the two had ultimately broken up. She couldn't shake the pleasure at being on top. No reason to go back to anything else. She wanted the power – and, oh, did she have it when she put on her slick, expensive boots, when she wielded the toys that Daphne had so tentatively pointed to.

Yet how was she going to explain all of that to a tax auditor?

'Ms Daniels?' the man in the suit asked, arriving right on time on the dedicated day. The meeting was taking place at her beach-front condominium, because Nadine worked at home. 'I'm Connor Monroe,' the man continued. 'Your auditor.'

My auditor, Nadine thought, irritated by the man's clean-cut good looks, the Boy Scout quality of his carefully pressed suit and polished leather shoes. She was especially irritated because she found him appealing. Connor Monroe seemed more like a male model than someone who served the government in its most hated capacity. If *she* were to create a character who worked for the IRS, she'd have made him heavy, balding, old. Not Connor. He had short dark hair, stone-coloured eyes and a sleek, athletic build that was apparent even with his suit on. In other circumstances, Nadine would definitely have flirted with him, batting her long eyelashes over her deep-blue eyes, stroking one hand sensuously along the curve of her hip to give him ideas. She knew all of the ways to behave in order to make a man want her, but this wasn't the time.

Holding open the front door to her apartment, Nadine tried to put a pleasant expression on her face. 'This way,' she said. 'I have my papers in the bedroom.'

Inwardly, she smirked at his obvious hesitation, letting him suffer for a moment in silence before continuing. 'That's where my office is. I'm not rich enough to afford a two-bedroom condo yet.' Why not let him know that she was angry? He couldn't penalise her for a bad attitude, could he?

As the man followed her down the hallway, he spoke, sounding as if he were repeating a memorised line from a script. 'I know an audit is a frightening proposition for some people. But it's just a regular practice at the bureau. Not any sort of punishment. Think of this as a routine, like an annual visit to the doctor.'

Nadine let herself smile since he couldn't see her face. In her research closet, she had lots of toys for 'doctor' visits. A box of regulation rubber gloves. A naughty nurse's uniform. A real stethoscope. Playing doctor was something she knew a lot about. She thought about one of her last nights with Steven. How she'd examined him, spread his handsome rear cheeks open as if to take his temperature and then tongue-fucked his ass until he'd shot his load on her mattress, creating a little lake of come beneath his flat belly. No need to share that bit of information with Mr Uptight IRS Man.

'Here we are,' she said, opening the door to her room and gesturing inside. In preparation for the meeting, Nadine had made her bed neatly, the black satin comforter hiding the evidence of her silk leopard-print sheets – another write-off. The room looked as utilitarian as it possibly could, with her paperwork spread out on her writing desk. What receipts she did have were well ordered, and the shoe box was there as well, lid on firmly to hide the mess contained inside. Wasn't that an echo of every part of Nadine's life? The surface looked one way – but take off the lid and see the inner turmoil within.

Regardless of her attempts to make the place look more official, it was obviously the bedroom of someone who liked sex. A dusky, romantic room, with flocked wallpaper and feminine touches in the prints on the walls and the rose-coloured rug on the hardwood floor. The auditor, *her* auditor, looked around, taking in the intricate brass frame on her bed, the two candelabras that stood on small round tables nearby, perfect for wax play when she was in that sort of a mood. How she liked to tilt the candlestick, to let the hot liquid wax drip in pretty patterns along a naked chest...

She shook her head, trying to clear the image of doing such a dirty thing with the taxman. He was here to discuss her payments ... not her panties. Still, she wondered whether he was feeling a pull between them as well. Or did she just have sex on the brain because she'd been looking in her research closet prior to the audit?

'I'm not out to ruin your day, Ms Daniels. We really had only a few questions,' the auditor said, sitting at Nadine's antique desk and waiting while she perched on the edge of her bed. He opened his leather briefcase and pulled out a copy of her tax return, pointing to several lines that were highlighted in bright yellow ink. 'And, honestly, the problem wasn't that we didn't agree with the deductions, it was that we didn't understand them.'

He smiled again and Nadine thought she saw something shimmer in his eyes. A look that didn't match the Boy Scout image at all. His expression made her feel flushed and she looked away.

'Vagueness is something the IRS can't handle,' he continued self-deprecatingly. 'We expect things to fit into neat categories. Phone. Entertainment. Rent. Travel. So, this $6,500 deducted for miscellaneous research supplies. That raised a red flag.'

Nadine sighed, her worst fears realised so quickly in the afternoon. She was going to have to open her toy chest and reveal the different items she'd used as the foundation for her latest novel. Might as well get it over with quickly. Without a word, she stood, walked to the closet and pulled open both of the mirrored doors.

'I'm an author,' she explained, lifting the different implements and placing them on her comforter, one after another, as casually as if they were pens and paper, any other equipment of a serious writer. 'I throw myself into my work, learning every aspect of my characters' lives. My most recent novel took place in an SM environment.' Carefully, she set out the high-end vinyl dress, the handcuffs she'd bought for the equivalent of a month's rent, the shoes with heels so high they couldn't possibly be walked in. But that was OK, since they weren't created for walking. She noticed that the auditor's eyes had opened wider, but he didn't speak.

'If I were writing about pet care, I'd buy grooming materials. If I needed to learn about the art world, I'd have purchased books about Monet and Picasso. I hope you're not going to judge me based on the content of my work.'

The auditor had stood and was now observing the growing pile of items on Nadine's bed at closer range. She noticed that he had the same look on his face that Daphne had had when she'd picked through the toys. Intrigue rather than disgust. She also thought she saw a bulge in his trousers that hadn't been there before.

'Do you understand now, Mr Monroe?' Nadine asked, her husky voice low. 'I had to file everything under miscellaneous, because the IRS doesn't provide neat categories for whips and chains. For bondage gear. For handcuffs –' As she said the word, he hefted the pair, interrupting her.

'Connor,' he said softly.

'Excuse me?'

'My name's Connor. You don't have to call me Mr Monroe.'

Connor. She liked that. And she also liked the way he was playing with her toys, rifling through them as if with a private purpose, stroking the shiny material of the vinyl dress – perfect for water sports – holding up her corset and then looking at her, as if picturing her in it. 'This is all for a book?'

She nodded. '*Paradise Lounge*. It will be out next month.'

'And your character is –'

'A dominatrix,' she said, and again she noticed that flicker in his eyes. Was he getting turned on? She found that *she* was, and she shifted in her faded jeans, feeling suddenly too constrained. As she watched, Connor slid one of the cuffs around his wrist and closed it. Then he looked at her.

'I think I understand now,' he said, 'but maybe you could explain what you do a little more in depth for me. So I get the full picture. I'm a bit anal that way. I like to possess all of the facts before I write up my reports.'

Nadine could barely contain her laughter at his use of *that* word. And didn't need any more encouragement. She felt the heat between them and she recognised fully the looks he was giving her. 'Strip,' she said sternly, without hesitation. 'You don't want me to mess with your nice, expensive suit.'

Connor did as he was told, like a good boy, and the metal of the handcuff chain made music as he took off his jacket, shirt and tie, then kicked off his slacks, socks and shoes.

'Boxers too,' she said, admiring him for a moment. My, but he had a fine body, even better than she'd expected. Tightly muscled legs, flat stomach and, most importantly for Nadine's particular fixation, a round firm ass. 'You can't really appreciate the image I'm going to create for you unless you give yourself over to it totally. That's how it is for me anyway. I lose myself in my characters. Plunge hard and deep until the rest of the world disappears.'

With his eyes locked on hers, Connor slid off his

boxers and then stood, waiting. Oh, he was erect. So hard that Nadine felt a moment of weakness. What she would have liked to do was go on her knees in front of it. Meeting a new cock for the first time was always an exciting prospect. Nadine adored that initial taste, learning how the man's bulbous head would fit into her mouth, stroking the underside with the tip of her tongue, gripping into his ass to pull him forward, harder, at her pace. But not yet, she reminded herself. Take your time. Play it out.

Steeling her inner yearnings, she took hold of the other handcuff, pulled the man forcefully on to her bed, threaded the chain through the headboard and captured his free wrist. He allowed himself to be manipulated without a word, letting Nadine know that he understood she was in charge.

'Now,' she said, 'you want a demonstration of my research equipment.'

'No.' He shook his head, then motioned to the rock-hard monument between his legs. 'A demonstration of your mouth.'

That made Nadine smile, her cherry-red lips curving upwards at the corners. The man had attitude, which she appreciated. But she wasn't about to reward him from the start. Where was the fun in that? No, she wanted to make him pay for the fear she'd had from the moment the IRS had contacted her. That starkly written letter sending panic through her. Nadine hated to feel panic.

'We don't play that way,' she said. 'Not by your rules, but by mine.'

'And they are?'

'That's the fun part.' Nadine grinned, stripping out of her own clothes and sliding into the short vinyl dress and her favourite pair of leather boots, feeling the power start to build within her. She sensed that Connor was memorising the look of her body nearly naked, but she didn't give him a long time to observe her. 'You get to figure out the rules as we go along.'

Connor tilted his head at her, as if he didn't know what she meant.

'You ought to comprehend that concept,' she said snidely. 'Isn't it how the IRS works? Secret rules that you auditors get while the rest of us poor people are forced to guess what on earth will make you happy.'

But what would make Nadine happy?

She considered the question as she glanced over her implements of pleasure and pain. Her auditor continued to watch as she hefted the different devices. The strap-on cock. Yes, she'd had fun with that in the past. Steven liked to be taken, bent over the bed and thrust into, his ass cheeks spread wide, the only lube a bit of spit that Nadine worked up and down the rubber dildo with the palm of her hand, jerking the cock the way a man would.

'Was that one of the items on your tax return?' Connor asked meekly.

Nadine nodded. 'Used it for research for Chapter Twelve.'

Next, there was the wooden paddle, perfect for heating the ass of a naughty boy. This particular paddle had a satisfying weight in her hand and she considered it with an almost loving expression, remembering the scene she had written with the paddle virtually the star of the chapter. She thought of the night she'd tested it on Steven, actually bringing him to tears before letting him come.

'And that was in the miscellaneous items as well?' Connor asked. Nadine heard the note of fear in his voice, but gave him extra points for staying in control of himself. He didn't ask whether she would use the paddle on him, didn't beg her not to. She nodded in answer before moving on to an oily-looking black leather belt, slipping it between her fingers and then leaning forward to use the very lip of it to tickle Connor's balls. He arched his back at the move and a bit of pre-come made the tip of his cock seem to shine.

It wouldn't take much to push him over the edge, Nadine knew. She could do just about anything and he would cream for her. Yet she wanted to have some fun, to make the experience worthwhile. Finally, she decided on one of her five-star toys: a vibrating wand shaped like a cock. Combined with a little of the lube she always kept in her bedside table, she would enjoy introducing this pin-striped man into the world of submission.

'Roll over,' she said.

He tilted his head at her and rattled the chains, indicating that he couldn't.

'Don't mess with me, Connor. There's enough slack,' she said knowingly. 'It might hurt a little bit, the chain rubbing into your wrists, but you can do it.'

Obediently, Connor followed the order, twisting his body on to his stomach, shifting as if to make room on the mattress for his erection. Then shifting again because it was obvious he liked the friction.

'None of that,' Nadine said fiercely, her open hand connecting with his ass in a stinging slap. 'You get off when I tell you. *If* I tell you. Not before. Understand?'

Connor sighed but said nothing.

'Do you understand?' Nadine repeated slowly. 'That's rule number one. I'll give that one to you for free. You answer when spoken to.'

'Yes, Ms Daniels,' Connor said, voice slightly muffled. Mmm. He was learning already. Not calling her by her first name. Choosing Ms instead of Miss. Nadine lifted the leather harness that went with this particular sex toy and fitted the large synthetic penis into its resting place. Then she fastened the harness around her slim hips. She did the work behind Connor, so he couldn't see her, could only hear the metal of the buckle connecting. Having a cock on always made Nadine feel different inside. Gave her a little bit of a swagger. But there was still plenty of woman in her, and she wouldn't start with poor Connor without giving him the foreplay he might need before she fucked him.

On hands and knees behind her auditor, she held open his firm bum cheeks and licked once up and down between them, then made a tight, hungry circle right around the velvety rim. Connor sighed and ground his hips again into the mattress, but this time Nadine didn't tell him to stop. Instead, making her tongue hard and long, she pointed it and drove it home.

'Oh, Christ,' Connor groaned, thrusting hard against the bed.

She didn't have to ask whether he liked it. The way he moved made it obvious that he wanted her to fuck his ass and he wanted her to do it now. Sure, sometimes she had played longer with Steven, making him deep throat her massive hard-on before screwing him. But this afternoon Nadine couldn't wait. She wanted the feeling of gripping into his shoulders and sliding the length of her cock deep inside him. First, she reached over Connor's body, opening the drawer on her bedside table and snagging the bottle of lube. Kindly, she spread it along the length of her pinkish cock, her fingers working it and getting extra grease on the tips. To prepare him, she slid two fingers into his ass, opening him up. Teasing him a bit with the intrusion.

'Please –' he said, and she knew somehow that he meant to say 'please stop'. This was all far too new for young Mr Monroe. The fact that he didn't continue with the request let her know that he didn't want her to stop. Not really. And he didn't have the balls yet to say,

'Please fuck me.' So he left it just at that one word. Nadine didn't mind. With both hands, she spread him even wider apart, then placed the huge, knobby head of her joystick at the entrance of his ass.

An evil grin on her lovely face, she found herself repeating the same speech, altered only slightly, that he had given her upon his arrival. 'I know an ass-fucking is a frightening proposition for some people. But it's just a regular practice in my boudoir. Not any sort of punishment. Think of this as a routine, like a visit to the doctor.' Then she reached for the remote control device that went with the toy, holding it tightly in one hand. Now, she was ready.

As she slid the cock in, the power flooded through her. Jesus, but she loved taking a man. In the oval-shaped mirror over her bed, she saw the way she looked as she fucked him. Her glossy dark hair framed her pale face, and her eyes turned a smouldering blue of the ocean in turbulent weather. With one hand on his waist to keep herself steady, she made the ride last. Giving him a taste, then pulling back. Slamming in deeper and holding it. Connor let her know the rhythm that he liked based on the sounds of his moans and the way he echoed her thrusts with his body against her comforter. He was going to come all over it, make a sticky white pool on the black satin, but she didn't care. Because once he got off, she had other plans. Methods to make this afternoon last.

It had been way too long since her last fuck.

Taking Connor hard, she used her free hand to reach around her until she found the mess of toys still spread out on the bed. Her fingers brushed against the handle of the wooden paddle and she hefted it, such a nice weight, and then let the weapon connect with Connor's right cheek, leaving a purplish blush there. Pretty colour. She gave the left cheek a matching blow to even out the hue and, as Connor started to moan, she kept up the spanking. That sound was such a turn-on. The clapping noise, like applause, of a sturdy paddle meeting a naked bottom. She continued to both fuck and punish him until he said, 'I'm going to come, Nadine –' a perfect time to switch to her first name, it made it seem that much more personal '– now.'

With those words, Nadine hit the button on the remote and the instrument inside Connor's asshole began to move, startling him as those sexy vibrations worked through his body. 'Oh, fucking hell,' he groaned. He arched and then shuddered, his whole body releasing, and Nadine threw herself against him, still inside deep, so that he felt the length of her body pressed into his skin. In this position, the base of the vibrator buzzed against her clit, sending her wet pussy into spasms that lasted as long as she kept her cunt pushed forward. Oh, yes, that was perfect, the pleasure that had kept her on edge as she was fucking him now spread throughout her body, making her skin tingle in waves that radiated outwards from the hot zone between her legs.

Sealed deep into Connor's ass, her hair spread out over his shoulders, her vinyl-clad breasts pressed into his back, she held him. This was the way she liked to be held when she came during anal sex. It was comforting, soothing, to be wrapped in another's arms. But after a moment, she pulled out, tore off the harness and stripped.

Out of breath, Connor rolled over on the bed, chains clinking, and watched her. Even lost in the post-climax bliss, it was obvious that he was admiring the curves of her body, her flushed, perfect skin. Nadine felt his eyes on her, but didn't pose for him. She was busy planning round number two. Naked, she stood in front of her closet, and then she found what she was looking for.

'What's that?' Connor asked, pointing as Nadine

lifted the bone-handled crop with the braided leather tip.

'This?' Nadine repeated softly as she approached him. 'This is my last deduction.'

Outmanoeuvred
Juliet Lloyd Williams

Shannon eased her body slowly over her right leg and felt the muscle at the back of her thigh stretch. She did the same over her other leg, then routinely went through the other stretches, warming her body, preparing for the exercise to come. Beside her, Laura was doing the same and grinning widely. Shaking her head, Shannon couldn't help smiling back. 'Ready?'

Laura straightened and stretched her arms high over her head, pulling her T-shirt taut across her chest. 'Too right I am.'

There was a tap on the window behind them. 'Good luck,' Louise mouthed and gave them the thumbs up.

'Let's do it,' Shannon said.

They kept the pace of their jogging slow to allow their muscles to warm properly. The roads were empty; the early morning and slight drizzle keeping everyone in their beds. At her side Shannon could hear Laura breathe, hear the slap of their feet on the pavement as the pace picked up. A warm glow settled over her body in spite of the weather. She lifted her face to the moist air and felt the dampness cool her. She smiled, thinking she would love to take off the rest of her clothes and feel the coolness settle on her hot body, to feel the dampness prickle her skin, bud her nipples, arouse the heat between her thighs. Not now, though; now they had to run.

The road rose slightly and became a gravelled path

as they reached the start of the incline. For a while they ran silently along the mountain path, feet crunching on the gravel, sometimes squelching in the occasional patch of mud that hadn't dried out in the past couple of sunny days. Ahead the path forked: one led to the small lake, the other into the woods. Shannon jogged to the right, following the path into the darker covering of trees. Behind her Laura followed.

Only the whisper of the breeze shifting the trees and the birds' early-morning songs disturbed the silence. Calm and still. Just the two of them.

Ahead a bird screeched loudly and flapped into the sky, disturbing the other birds so that they all soared into the air, squawking unhappily. Had they disturbed them, Shannon wondered briefly, or were they still too far away to bother the birds? Was it something else? What?

It took a couple of minutes to reach the place the birds had been and, looking around her, at first she could see nothing out of the ordinary. Then, out of the corner of her eye, she saw something move. For several seconds she couldn't make the shape out, then she realised. A man, partially hidden by the trees and barely noticeable until he stepped from his hiding place on to the path into full view of the two women. Behind her Shannon heard Laura inhale sharply. A man in fatigues. Army. A snapping twig, a rustle of leaves to the side of them and more male bodies lined the way. All soldiers.

Shannon felt a surge of excitement shoot through her. How many were there? Her first impression was five, maybe six, but she didn't stop to count them; she carried on running, straight towards the first man, who remained motionless. With trees lining the path it would be difficult to pass him. As she drew closer she was able to see him clearly: tall, muscular, a harsh lived-in face and a grin almost as wide as his shoulders.

Lust raised its head, making her heated body hotter. Would he move? Or would he stay there?

He folded his arms across his broad chest and widened his feet. He wasn't moving. Laura moved closer; Shannon could feel her touch her shoulder briefly. Then she understood why – the other men had fallen into step behind them and she could hear their feet pounding closer and closer. Her heart stepped up a beat and she moved faster, aware of the adrenalin rushing through her system. A few yards away the soldier stood, unmoving except for his eyes as he watched the men gain on the women, and the wide grin as he ogled the two female forms.

As she drew closer, Shannon saw the challenge in his expression. A challenge she couldn't resist. To her left she noticed a gap in the trees and decided to take it. The ground sloped sharply away beneath her feet; it made her legs ache as she struggled to stay upright on the slippery grass. Behind her she heard Laura gasp. Turning briefly, Shannon saw Laura held by a couple of men and, judging by the grin on her face, she wasn't finding it at all unpleasant.

'The other one's mine,' the man blocking her path yelled. He swore as he followed Shannon through the trees. Above her harsh breathing and the pounding of her heart, she heard him gain on her. Smiling, she slid further down the grass, using the tree trunks and branches to keep her balance. He'd have to work to catch her.

Branches caught at her as she passed, snagging her clothes and her hair. Her feet thumped against the ground and her arms flailed in front of her, trying to clear the way. He was closer now. She could hear him breathing, feel him behind her. And it was delicious. The thrill of sexual excitement, of being chased, was exquisite beyond belief. Jogging alone made her horny.

How many times had she masturbated in the shower on her return? The hot glow, the rapid thump of her heart, the pressure between her legs were so sexy. Anyone who didn't find exercise sexy must be mad.

A hand caught her arm. Wriggling, she tried to free herself without stopping. The fingers loosened and she was free. For a second there was nothing, then a huge arm clamped around her waist and she was wrestled to the ground with a sweaty male body landing heavily on top of her.

Before she could struggle or even find her voice, a large hand slid between her thighs and captured her groin. She moaned in pleasure and he squeezed hard. Pure bliss. The pain receded and pleasure took over as her body shook with orgasm, leaving her writhing beneath his hard body. Even as the tremors died away, he kept his hand on her mound, squeezing gently, squeezing every last drop of pleasure from her.

'Horny bitch,' he murmured, his mouth mere inches from hers. 'Aren't you?'

She couldn't speak, could barely catch her breath. Her hand found his cock through his trousers and gently closed around the swelling. 'Horny bastard,' she gasped.

He laughed, loud and confidently, and hauled her roughly to her feet. 'We're a pair well met then.'

With one hand firmly wrapped around her arm, he dragged her back up the banking. Long silvery sighs of pleasure and masculine grunts met them. The noises made the hairs on the back of her neck tingle and arousal, barely assuaged by her earlier orgasm, started to flicker once more. As they came up over the banking she could see a naked Laura on her hands and knees, breasts and body swaying as one soldier thrust into her from behind, his hands clasped tightly around her narrow waist. Another squaddie kneeled in front of her, holding her hair in one hand, forcing her head up. In his other hand he held his prick and was teasing her open mouth with it. And from her moans she was enjoying every second of it. Another two men looked on.

'Caught the other one, sarge,' one of the men jeered, who was watching the action with his flies open, rubbing himself frantically. The youngest of the group merely looked on in amazement as the sergeant turned Shannon to face him and dragged her T-shirt over her head, then dropped it on the ground.

'Feisty one, this,' he told them as he dragged her breasts over the top of her bra. 'And she's mine first. Isn't that right?' he murmured in her ear. He didn't move as he waited for her response. Shannon could only nod in acceptance. In the back of her mind she appreciated his offer of a way out but she wanted this as much, maybe more, than he did.

The way he was talking made her squirm. It was almost as if she wasn't there. That she didn't matter to him. All he cared about was the pleasure he would take from her body. It was a new and brilliant sensation to be thought of purely as a sex object; it was something she had never experienced before. She knew then there was nothing she wouldn't do. And it thrilled her so much she nearly came.

'See,' the sergeant was saying, 'she's so horny she'll come if you touch her tits. Try it, Private.'

His language, crude and so male, made her squirm even more. Then she was roughly turned around, with her arms held tightly behind her back. The youngest soldier took a hesitant step towards her.

'Go on, lad,' the other soldier encouraged. 'Think of it as part of your education.'

His face paled as he moved towards Shannon. Her body began to shake as she imagined his hesitant fingers on her body. Was he a virgin? How old was he?

Probably not twenty, but a virgin? A movement to the side caught her eye. The soldiers had finished with Laura and she'd flopped on to her back with her legs together. The sergeant had noticed it too for he said, 'Keep her legs open.'

Laura complained most vocally as her legs were prised apart.

'They're to be available at all times for whatever we want,' he continued. His harsh voice made Shannon weak with longing. The tension was unbearable. Why didn't the young one touch her? He was so close she could feel his breath on her but still he did nothing.

Slowly his hand reached out to tentatively touch her erect nipple.

'That's it,' one of them encouraged.

One finger trailed over her nipple, teasingly unaware of how it made her squirm and made her even wetter between her legs. Encouraged by her gasp, he cupped her breast and weighed it in his hand. When the sergeant nodded, he tightened his fingers and squeezed. Her mouth fell open and she began to pant and mewl with pleasure.

'She's going to come. Squeeze both of them, lad, and watch her come.'

Both hands dragged her breasts further out of the bra and closed over them. He tightened his fingers and she wriggled, trying to get closer.

'Keep still,' the sergeant hissed in her ear, 'or I'll have you punished.' He bit her earlobe, making her squeal. The lad stopped and watched them carefully.

'Please,' she moaned.

'Right!' the sergeant snapped. 'Punish her.'

The men whooped excitedly.

'Get her blindfolded.'

Her arms were still clasped tightly around her back and something dark covered her eyes. Then it fell silent.

There was a rustle as someone stepped closer. Laura's gasp sent fear hurtling through Shannon – fear of the unknown heavily tinged the pleasure. What were they going to do?

'Gag that one,' the boss ordered. 'Phil, stick your cock in her mouth to shut her up.'

Shannon heard Laura moan happily as Phil obviously did as he was ordered. Her mind filled with images of Laura on her knees, sucking Phil's cock, of the punishment she herself was due. Could she take any more stimulation?

Her arms were released for a few seconds then dragged over her head and tied to a branch. The branch was too high and she was forced to stand on her toes. Her arms ached, her legs ached, but still nothing happened. It was too much.

'Just bloody well do it!' she yelled. No sooner had the words left her mouth than a hand struck her arse. He'd slapped her. The swine had slapped her. Anger more than pain made her scream.

'Go on, scream. No one will hear you,' the sergeant taunted before nipping her ear once more.

Rough hands dragged her shorts to her ankles. There was a loud swish and something hard and rough connected with the soft flesh of her buttocks. Stripes of pain burned through her, mingled with pleasure. After four lashes her tight shorts were dragged roughly up over her warm buttocks, enclosing them in the tight material, and the man who had been whipping her moved in front.

'Might as well warm the tits up as well,' the voice murmured. He waited indeterminately long seconds before carrying out his threat. The flesh on her breasts was softer than her buttocks and stung more. Her nipples burned like fury, but it made the pleasure sharper, more urgent.

'Now touch her, lad. See how she likes pain with her pleasure.'

Someone, the youngest, moved before her, and the hands cupped her stinging flesh once more. The slightest touch there made her want to moan with pleasure; she was so sensitive. He tightened his grip and squeezed, gently at first, till her body strained at its ties, then becoming tighter and harder. Her stomach coiled, readying itself for the release to come. She squeezed her thighs together, much to the men's amusement and ribald comments. One breast was released and she moaned in dismay, only to gasp happily as a wet mouth replaced it, cooling the heated flesh. Being suckled and rubbed between her legs, she came with a huge cry of pleasure.

Her body still shaking, she was quickly untied. She collapsed in a heap but barely had time to catch her breath before she was shoved on to her back and her legs splayed. There was a rumble of laughter from the men; she stiffened, unable to see what was happening. Something cold touched her nipple and was quickly removed. Her mind filtered through all the possibilities but she couldn't think of what it could be.

Fingers grabbed the material between her legs. It was wet from her juices and he knew it. She felt a head touch her thighs, heard one of the men inhale deeply, felt him rub his nose to the wetness, savouring her excitement.

'Enjoying yourself?' She wanted to deny it but how could she? He'd touched and smelled the evidence of her enjoyment.

'Now let's see exactly how turned on you are.'

She lifted her hips for him to drag her shorts and panties down but he didn't; he merely laughed. He tugged on the material, pulling it away from her groin. She tensed, aware of every sound, every movement.

There was a ripping sound – her shorts. He was tearing the seam at her groin. But instead of ripping it as she thought, he was cutting it. When he'd finished, he sighed and pushed her thighs further apart. Tearing along the seam wasn't good enough: he'd cut a chunk out of her shorts and panties. She could feel the air cool and damp at the junction of her thighs. From mound to anus there was a two-inch rectangle of material missing. Enough for them to see all of her. But seeing wasn't enough.

A cock thrust into her, hot and hard and deep, through the gap in the material. Even before he spoke she knew it was the sergeant who was thrusting so wickedly into her, twisting his hips, making her ripple around him. Every inch of her ignited once more at his lunging; she hadn't thought it possible. It was so strange to be wearing shorts and be fucked at the same time.

'You love it, don't you?' he murmured in her ear. 'Love every dirty second of it.'

His words were driving her wild. She wrapped her arms and legs around his hard body, pulling him closer. His breath mingled with hers, his face merely inches from her. She wanted him to kiss her, to drive his tongue into her mouth as his cock was driving into her pussy.

He teased her, nipping her ear, biting her jawline, making her moan, making her squeal. Slowly his mouth edged closer to hers, his tongue circling her lips then plunging inside to toy with hers. He tasted of coffee, strong black coffee, and strong male. Then he was gone. She groaned in dismay.

'Want to come now?' he muttered.

He wasn't having it all his own way, Shannon decided. She tightened her internal muscles around him, smiling when he groaned loud and urgently. In the background she was aware of the cheers, the mutter of the others. So what if they were watching – it added another dimension to her pleasure. Being watched and fucked. She'd give them something to cheer about. She trailed a hand over the clothed muscles of his back, down past his shirt. Rucking it up, she dug her nails into his muscled flesh, revelling in his moans and the marks she'd leave there. Both her hands clasped his buttocks, pulling him tighter towards her. Her one hand moved closer to his anus, and he knew it. He snarled as she let her finger tickle the sensitive skin and scratched the puckered hole.

'Damn you,' he gasped, then bucked into her hard and came, his snarl of pleasure drowning out the other raucous noises. His body was heavy on her as he lay there for several seconds, too dazed to move. Slowly he shifted from her.

'Don't move,' he ordered. 'Legs open. Private, get between those legs and taste her.'

Shannon couldn't see the private's face but could imagine only too well what a picture it must have been, for the others laughed.

'Go on, lad. Taste her. Lick the sarge's come from her.'

'Get your face between her thighs.'

'Lick her out.'

'Make her come again.'

The teasing seemed endless but gradually Shannon heard him shuffle towards her. She held her breath as she felt him slide between her legs, his clothing rubbing previously unknown sensitive areas. His hands on her clothed thighs made her jump. His hands shook as they stroked the smooth skin underneath, transmitting his nerves to her as he slowly moved closer to his goal. The nervousness heightened every touch. Tentative fingers smoothed the ruffled curls at her groin, feeling the rasp against his skin. Her whole body began to throb anew.

Her two earlier orgasms were forgotten – all she could feel was the tentative touch of his hands at her groin; all she could remember was the sergeant's mind-blowing thrusts deep inside her. Now she needed more. She needed the private's hands on her, his tongue tasting her, worshipping her. And because it was new to him then it made it better for her.

His fingers parted her sticky sex lips. She heard his swift intake of breath. Her mind reeled as she saw herself through his eyes – saw the red, glistening folds of flesh swelling under this man's gaze, saw the wetness trickling from her mixed with the sergeant's come.

'Get to it, lad.'

The others were losing patience with the timidness now, wanting action. She wanted to yell at them to give him time, let him take control. Indeed, he wasn't going to be rushed. When the next man jeered, Shannon felt him turn to the watchers.

'Fuck off!' he yelled.

Good for you, Shannon wanted to say. You stick up for yourself. It worked, for the men fell silent.

His fingers slid over her wet flesh, tentatively discovering each fold, each nook, each movement drawing Shannon into a swirl of pleasure. More confident men had drawn less of a response from her. This man was enjoying every sensation, taking in every inch of her and revelling in it.

'Do you like this?' he asked as his fingers slid over her clit. She moaned and he laughed softly to himself. 'You do? And what if I do this?' His tongue replaced his finger and she stiffened. 'You like that a lot, don't you?'

Shannon could only nod as words failed her. Her mouth was dry, her limbs heavy with sensation, her mind numb with pleasure. His tongue traced every inch his fingers had, then circled the entrance to her vagina.

Slowly his tongue lapped at the juices, both hers and the sergeant's, and she heard him moan in enjoyment.

'I knew you'd like it, lad,' a voice murmured close by. 'How does she taste?'

'Un-be-liev-able,' the lad replied.

'Slide your fingers into her. See how tight she is,' the sergeant encouraged.

He did as he was told and Shannon tightened her muscles around them. He sighed happily.

'Like to feel your cock in there?'

'Yeah!'

'Then shove it up her and make her moan. You'd like that, wouldn't you?'

Shannon nodded her head vehemently.

There was a rustle of clothing. Then the touch of a heavy penis against her thigh. Automatically she reached for him; he was hot, velvety smooth and rock hard. She couldn't wait to feel him inside her.

'Lift her legs. Don't let her control anything,' the sergeant urged.

Her legs were raised, hooked over his arms.

'It'll be better, deeper like this.'

She was so wet, so open to him, he slid in easily. Ecstasy. His hesitant movements sent chills down her spine. His thrusts were erratic but touched the very fibre of her. His breathing increased, becoming interspersed with low moans. Everything increased her pleasure. He was nearly there. Now to make it really special for him. She slid her hand between their bodies and found her clitoris. As he plunged into her, she rubbed herself and fell headlong into pleasure. His gasp as he felt her contract around him pushed her further into ecstasy, then he stiffened and came with a long moan.

'God, that was fantastic,' he murmured when he could breathe again. 'I could feel her come around me.'

'This one's an expert, aren't you? We're not finished yet. Phil's desperate to get his cock into you. He's fucked your friend in the mouth and up her arse. And she loved every dirty second of it. Now it's your turn.'

The blindfold was ripped off. Shannon blinked in the bright light. All around her there were bodies in various states of undress. Laura was curled on top of one soldier, dozing. Shannon smiled: no stamina, that girl. She was pulled to her feet, and she wobbled as her legs almost failed to hold her. Phil (she assumed) stepped towards her, his cock spilling out of his enclosed fist.

He backed her against a tree, and stepped between her open legs. Dragging one leg past his thigh, he rubbed his cock along her slit. Then, without a word, he pushed into her. The tree was rough against her back and she savoured the scratchiness against her skin but she wasn't there long as Phil made her wrap her legs around him and then turned and walked away. Each step brought her down hard on his cock, driving him deeper into her.

Then he stopped. Why? His hands slid down her back to her buttocks, holding them open. She felt her breath snag in her throat. Something cold and metallic slid into her. The tip of a tube of cream: someone was lubricating her arse. The cream was cold then her sensitive flesh started to tingle. She wriggled in Phil's grasp to try and assuage the tingle but it didn't work.

Someone gently touched the curve of her spine, tracing a finger over her vertebrae. It made her shiver. Phil's cock twitched inside her. The cream tingled and a tongue traced the path the finger had made. Wet and hot. She twitched. The cock jumped. The cream burned.

'I'm going to have you up that nice tight arse of yours in a minute,' a voice taunted. The sergeant's. 'But first let's see how you like this. Something to cool you down.'

She stiffened, wondering what 'this' was. It was cold and hard as it touched the rim of her arse. She felt the resistance of her anus give to allow the intruder entrance. It was cold, very cold. It sent a shiver through her. It wasn't very long or thick but when Phil bucked his hips she felt it move inside her, wiggling from side to side, touching the sides of her rectum, making her bowels quiver. She couldn't help moaning at the sensation of being filled in both orifices.

'Like it? Like having a handle up your arse?'

Arrogant swine! She couldn't deny it – she was enjoying it. It was gently removed from her, only to be replaced by the tip of the sergeant's cock, which was much thicker and longer than the other object had been. Slowly he pushed into her, just an inch. The coldness was replaced by heat. She moaned low and urgent. Beads of sweat puddled on her brow. Phil thrust and she was pushed backward, slowly and inexorably, on to the sergeant's thick cock until he was in to the hilt. She was squashed between two men, two cocks filling her in the basest of ways. Phil thrust first, his face crunching in pleasure, then the sergeant drew back and thrust into her. One after the other, not stopping, not breaking the rhythm that was tearing her apart. One after the other they pushed into her, pushed her pleasure beyond its limit. Hard male bodies rubbed against hers, making her yield to them. The sensation was mind-blowing. She was full of hard men; their sweat teased her nostrils, their moans filled her ears, their bodies thrust hard into hers. Orgasm crescendoed over her, driving everything else away, and replacing it with a pleasure that made her scream.

She came around to find herself wrapped in one of the men's jackets. She snuggled closer to the warmth, the scent hitting her nose – it was the sergeant's jacket. Beside her Laura stretched and slowly stood up. She passed Shannon her once white T-shirt that was now covered in leaves and dirt. Shannon struggled into it then realised they were alone.

'How long have they been gone?'

'Not sure,' Laura said. 'About ten minutes. You all right? I've never seen you like that before.'

Shannon closed her eyes, remembering the sensations the morning had brought. She shivered. 'Exquisite. Absolute bliss. What a morning. Come on, we'd better get back.' She looked down at the gap in her shorts. 'Good job this T-shirt is long.' Laura grinned.

They walked back slowly, their energy spent, savouring the memories, the feel of sated flesh. For Shannon, the sensation of being clothed but having a naked pussy was strange, her sex lips rubbing together as she walked.

Louise was waiting for them. 'Were they there?' she demanded as they stepped into the living room. She smiled at Shannon's nod. 'I told you they would be. Well? Tell all.'

Shannon sank on to the sofa and slowly parted her legs to reveal her naked flesh. Louise's snatched breath made her smile. 'It was brilliant.' She rubbed her hand against her sore flesh. 'Superb.'

'What's Sergeant Croydon like?' Louise asked, barely able to tear her eyes from Shannon's ripped shorts.

'Divine! He fucks like the devil.' Shannon caught Laura's satisfied smile. 'Doesn't he?'

'It certainly looked that way to me.'

Shannon rose. 'I'd better get a move on. But first things first.' She picked up the phone and dialled. When it was answered, she said, 'Captain James here. Get Sergeant Croydon in my office as soon as he gets back from manoeuvres. There's something I have to give him.' Her hand touched the jacket he'd left wrapped around her. There was something else besides the jacket he deserved. The picture formed in her mind – Sergeant Croydon draped over her desk, naked arse up awaiting the slap of her ruler. And maybe she'd take her vibrator along, to see how he liked having something up *his* arse.

After this morning she could have him up on a charge of insubordination. She knew what she preferred – and knew how to get it out of him, too.

The Jewel Carrera Devonshire

'Darling!' Anthea sweeps towards me across the elegant marbled hallway of her Belgravia town house. She plants two kisses in the air beside my cheeks. 'That dress is divine,' she purrs.

She should know. She designed it.

My boss has no difficulty recognising her creations. She could pick one out in a coal-mine without a torch. But pretending a dress is not hers is one of Anthea's favourite games. It allows her to sing a sly chorus of her own praises, giving her a veneer of modesty that fools no one.

'And you look lovely in it,' continues Anthea with a beneficent smile. She turns me towards a towering gilt-framed mirror and we both survey my reflection. I have to agree. The dress is fabulous, and it does suit me very well. It's cut from fine crêpe de Chine in the darkest possible blue and falls to just above my ankles. Boned and lined to perfection, the fabric flows over the curves of my hips, slithering deliciously over my thighs and bottom. It scoops too low to wear a bra, but is so well tailored that it easily supports my breasts. They rise up – plump and luscious – above the plunging neckline.

'But it needs something else,' says Anthea, frowning as her gifted mind grapples to identify the missing ingredient. 'Some decent jewellery perhaps.'

Jewellery is Anthea's passion. Fortunately, after thirty years at the top of the international fashion business, Anthea has made a substantial fortune and is well able to indulge her taste for expensive trinkets.

She reaches behind her head and unclips her necklace – a single tear-shaped diamond suspended on an aged gold chain. Standing behind me, she fastens the necklace around my neck. I feel an almost erotic thrill as the flawless stone slides down my throat and nestles at the top of my cleavage.

'Oh, Anthea.' I reach up to touch the magnificent gem. 'May I borrow it? Just for tonight?'

Anthea laughs. 'Of course, darling. But do take great care of it. And now, let's take your wonderful dress and your wonderful necklace out for an equally wonderful night on the town.'

The evening is everything Anthea promises. A treat for her staff at the end of an exhausting but highly successful London Fashion Week, Anthea entertains me, and the rest of her team, in grand style. Dinner in one of London's most illustrious restaurants is followed by a whirlwind tour of the city's fashionable clubs.

When I return to my flat in the early hours of the morning, I fling myself on to my bed. But I'm too excited to sleep. I lie quite still, the memories of the evening spinning in my head. I remember the diamond against my skin. The powerful charge I got from wearing it. I remember how its sparkling beauty had drawn attention to my breasts. And how I had enjoyed the admiring glances.

Slipping my hands inside the top of my dress, I ease my tits from the bodice. Bound by the fabric, they cleave and bulge attractively. As I look down I can feel my breath against the creamy white curves. I watch my nipples harden as arousal grows.

I draw up my knees and the dress tumbles up my legs, sliding slowly up my stocking-clad thighs. I run my hands over the sheer nylon, enjoying the contrasting tones of the steel-smooth fabric and the firm flesh beneath. Above the stockings I am naked and my bare skin tempts me. My fingers float up my legs to drift over the down of my pubes.

For a while I'm content with this gentle tease, but as my desire builds I need more. My sex grows heavy with want and I ache for relief. I can't resist any longer. I press one finger down between the plump lips to meet the throbbing bud that is my clit. My finger swirls, tormenting the tiny erection into a hard point. I dip my thumb deeper into the oily wetness, sighing at the moment of penetration.

I turn on to my stomach, and I feel the slightest roughness in the sheets against my nipples as my breasts fall forwards on to the bed. Parting my thighs, I moan out loud. At first I move slowly, my body undulating to a languid tempo. But soon I become more savage. As I near my end, I can't help thrusting my hips, and I hump my own hand, my need to climax becoming urgent. The position is undignified and my masturbation is not pretty. But I don't care. Nothing but my orgasm can stop me now.

I plunge my dress between my thighs, and the fabric saws at my sex, splitting the swollen flesh. This is the trigger to my orgasm and I reach my peak, my sex spasming gloriously against my knotted fingers.

As the last ripples of my climax fade, I reach up to touch the chain around my neck. It is only then I realise the jewel has gone.

There is nothing else to do. I must buy another diamond. Anthea ranks carelessness as a cardinal sin and I can't face explaining the loss of the jewel. I spend Saturday morning scouring the West End for a replacement. At last I see it – a stunning tear-shaped gem – resplendent in the window of one of Bond Street's smartest jewellers. A liveried doorman stands aside as I step into the shop.

There is just one other customer, a man, looking at a display of gold-encrusted glassware. He catches my eye and smiles. The smile is fleeting but full of promise and something about it sends a ripple of pleasure through me.

I ask to see the stone. An assistant brings it to me, placing it on the satin-topped counter with a flourish. I reach out to caress its cool, smooth surface.

'How much?' I ask. The jeweller regards me with barely disguised contempt.

'Ten thousand pounds, madam,' comes the snooty reply. My heart sinks. There's no way I can afford that amount of money.

'Oh,' I stammer. 'That's more than I'd hoped. I'll have to leave it.' Hot tears prick my eyes as the shop assistant moves to put the jewel back in the window.

'No, wait.' I hear a voice and turn to see the customer standing next to me. 'I want to buy it.' The impulsive shopper tosses a platinum credit card on to the counter.

He is tall and broad. His expensively casual clothes hang stylishly on his well-proportioned body. As he leans forward to sign the credit card slip, his dark hair flops forward over his handsome face. I stare after him as he tucks the jewel into his jacket pocket and leaves the shop.

But outside on the pavement he's waiting for me. He's leaning against the shop window in an attitude of studied indifference.

'I really wanted that diamond,' I say. A flicker of amusement crosses his lips.

'I know. And you shall have it. In return for spending tonight with me.' His bizarre proposition takes me by surprise and I stare blankly at him, unable to think of a reply.

'What's the matter?' He lifts a graceful hand and runs the tip of his finger over my mouth. Involuntarily my lips part and I taste his skin against my tongue. 'I have something you want,' he says. 'You have something I want. It would be a fair exchange.' He fixes me with dazzlingly blue eyes. 'What's wrong with that?'

'Nothing,' I reply. 'I'm just a little shocked.'

'And if you can shock me tonight, you can have your diamond.' His name, he tells me, is Sebastian.

Shocking he wants and shocking he shall get. I've prepared for my date with great care and, as I check my reflection, I am more than satisfied with my appearance. My make-up is perfect. My eyes are rimmed with black, my lashes mascara'd to an impossible length. My lips are painted deep crimson. I fluff up my blonde hair to create a look that's part Barbie doll, part porn star.

My outfit, purchased hastily this afternoon in one of Soho's less respectable shops, is a million miles from my usual understated style. My feet are squeezed into ridiculously high-heeled black patent boots. Rising to halfway up my thighs, they force me into a slightly unsteady gait, giving me an air of rakish abandon. I'm wearing black fishnet stockings, which rustle seductively as my thighs brush together. When I move, I catch an occasional glimpse of white flesh between their deep lace tops and the hem of my black latex skirt.

I have never worn rubber before but now, as I see what it's done for my figure, I understand its charms. Polished to a glasslike shine, the latex emphasises every curve of my body. As I ease my hips forward, the swell of my mound is clearly visible beneath the glossy fabric. My cropped top is also made of latex, lashed tightly together at the front by a leather lace to create a wonderfully deep cleavage. My breasts are barely contained by the tiny scrap of rubber and they almost spill out of the indecently restrictive garment. The outfit is finished by a black leather collar around my throat. I look like a tart. And I love it.

Waiting for Sebastian, my stomach flutters with excitement at the challenge that faces me. I want the diamond. I want to win. But most of all I want to play the game.

When Sebastian arrives, he makes no comment about my appearance. We speed off through the London streets in his long, low sports car.

Sebastian takes me to a smart restaurant in Mayfair and my outfit causes a stir as I stride across the crowded room in my spiky boots. There's a lull in the conversation as I pass tables of corpulent, suited diners. Men gawp, forks laden with food poised in front of their open mouths. I imagine them dashing away from the restaurant to masturbate frantically. Or fantasising about my latex-encased body as they fuck their fat wives.

We dine well. Good food is washed down with quantities of champagne.

'Where to?' Sebastian asks after the meal.

'Perhaps a film?'

'Anything you fancy?'

'Oh, yes,' I say.

The private cinema club in a seedy back street is almost deserted – its only customers a few drab-looking men dotted around the darkened auditorium. As we enter, no one looks away from the movie. I too am transfixed by the action as we find our seats.

On the screen is a close-up of a large cock pumping mechanically into the anus of a woman. As the shot widens, we see her squatting above her lover, her head thrown back, her mouth open in pain or pleasure. Her fingers are thrusting into her sex, her thumb rakes feverishly against her clit. She may be faking it, but her masturbation looks very convincing. I long to be touching myself in the same way. Her partner pushes her away as he nears his orgasm and we see him come, his spunk arching up to splash against the lips of her wide open cunt. Two rows in front of us, a balding businessman groans as he too climaxes into his coat.

I slip to cramped space on the floor between Sebastian's legs, my back pressing against the row of seats in front. In the darkness he can't see my face, but he understands my invitation. With one hand he reaches down and unzips his flies. He slips his hand inside his boxer shorts and takes out his cock. Turned on by the porn film, he is already semi-erect. As he fingers himself, I watch in fascination as he fills and thickens further still. I lean forward and feel the head of his prick bounce lightly against my lips as he masturbates. I breathe in the manly, warm scent of him.

The film and the touch of his own hand fuel his need and he shifts his hips, eager for more. I bend over him and lower my lips over his now solid shaft. He lets out a little moan of pleasure as I take him into my mouth, my lips sliding down to the shadowy base of him and then back up the glistening surface to the very tip. I devour him, feasting greedily on his succulent flesh while he watches the film. Curling my fingers around him, I use one hand to double the sensation. I reach down into the darkness and stroke myself, my free hand picking up the rhythm as I wank us both.

Quite suddenly, he reaches down and grabs my hair, holding me still against his cock. I wait, knowing what the stillness means. Then a tremor runs through him and I feel his cock jerk as his come foams across my tongue. His orgasm is long and strong and he pumps spurt after spurt of delicious liquid into me. I gulp it down, enjoying the flavour of him. As I swallow the last drop, I too begin to climax into my hand.

When finally we are finished, I stand up and kiss him, pushing my tongue past his lips while the taste of him still fills my mouth.

'Shocked?' I ask. But Sebastian only smiles.

Walking back to his car, we talk about the film. I hear his breath quicken and his voice deepens with renewed desire as we discuss what had turned us on.

'What was your favourite bit?' I ask. He laughs, almost shyly, and does not reply.

'Go on,' I coax, 'I'm not easily shocked.'

'I liked the bit where she peed herself.' He speaks quietly, his voice hardly above a whisper. 'The expression on her face as he watched her do it was really lovely. She looked so vulnerable. So exposed. It's such a private act; I'd love to see a woman soak her knickers like that.' I stop walking and he turns to meet my steady gaze.

'Really?' He holds his breath as I back into an unlit doorway and slowly lift my skirt. 'Like this?'

I plant my legs apart and lower my body into a squat, my thighs spread wide. He recognises the position.

'Jesus,' he mutters. 'You're going to piss.' I let myself go. He watches as I urinate, golden liquid flooding through the black lace of my panties. The release is almost orgasmic and I groan again as relief seeps through my veins. The final drips splash from me in little spurts.

I have barely finished before he grabs me by the waist and shoves me deeper into the shadows. Then, ripping my wet underwear to one side, he pulls me on to his rampant cock. His climax begins even before he is fully inside me.

Later, at his riverside loft, we lounge on sumptuous sofas and sip cognac. I sit opposite him, deliberately placing myself where I can offer him the best view. I spread my legs wide. Now I am wearing nothing under my skirt but he doesn't react as he eyes my naked mound. His phone rings and, with a polite 'Excuse me', he takes the call.

I yawn ostentatiously, letting him know that if he won't amuse me, I will do something to amuse myself. As he talks, I reach up to unfasten the lacing on the front of my top. It's so tight that, when I untie the knot, the latex slides open almost on its own. He carries on watching as my bosom comes into view. I shrug off the top and my breasts sway as I shake my shoulders. Still talking into his phone, he surveys my bare tits, and I can tell by the slight smile on his face that he approves. I reach down and caress the ample curves, lifting one breast and then the other, letting him see them shift and ripple beneath my touch.

'I've received the paperwork,' says Sebastian, 'I'll sign it in the morning.' My hands move further down the plane of my stomach and over the diminutive skirt. Bracing my legs apart, I slide my fingers through the curls of my pubes towards my clit, which is again yearning for attention. I let my finger flutter in the lightest possible caress. The pleasure is intense. As I sweep my finger over the tiny bud and the hot opening of my sex I can't contain a sigh.

'Yes,' I hear Sebastian say, 'the deal should be concluded by the end of the week.'

My lids flutter and then close as sensation leaps through my body. But I can feel his eyes on me as I lie back and roll my hips. I hear a slight unsteadiness in his voice as I raise one hand to my mouth and lick my fingers. I run my tongue the length of each, savouring the taste of my own wetness. Then I slide my damp palm back down my body and use one finger to fuck myself. Sebastian's call ends, but I am too turned on to stop touching myself. I arch my back and grind against my hand, giving him the show I know he wants to see and which I am now compelled to perform.

Sebastian speaks first.

'What are you doing?' There is a hint of outrage in his voice.

'I'm sorry,' I say, feigning contrition. 'Is it rude to masturbate in front of a man on a first date?'

'Yes,' he mutters. 'Oh, God, yes.'

I open my eyes to see Sebastian standing over me. His cock is in his hand. Once again, it is hard and huge. He rubs it furiously, holding it close to my face – so close that I can hear the moist slapping of skin against skin. He is staring fixedly at my hand as my fingers move lazily in and out of my sex. His face begins to distort and, hunched over his swollen cock, he masturbates hard. I wonder what it will look like to see him come at such close range.

Neither of us hears the door open. But, aware that we are being watched, I look up into a pair of eyes that are the same blue as Sebastian's. They belong to a girl, who stands as if frozen. By embarrassment or fascination I cannot tell.

'Sorry, Sebs,' she says, 'I didn't realise you were ... entertaining.'

Hurriedly, Sebastian shoves his cock back inside his trousers. I make only a token effort to cover my own bared breasts and pussy.

'This is Diana,' he stammers. 'My sister. She's staying

with me for a few days.' Sebastian's introduction is almost dismissive, as if he has never noticed Diana's obvious good looks.

Diana has clearly been out partying. She's wearing a short pink dress, which flashes at least a yard of tanned leg. Her feet are bare and a pair of high, strappy shoes dangles from one finger. Her sleek magenta hair is trimmed into a neat bob – the kind of cut that falls back into place, no matter how wild the night.

She sits, perching on the edge of a chair, and we chat. But underlying our polite conversation is the knowledge that I am naked beneath my slut's outfit. Diana, I can tell, is curious. When she gets up to go, I know she does not want to leave.

'I'll just get myself a drink then I'm off to bed,' she says, throwing a knowing smile at Sebastian as she crosses the room. She moves with easy grace, long limbs rippling like a fit thoroughbred. After sloshing an inch of Sebastian's cognac into a glass, she turns to go.

'No, wait.' I lean forward and place my hand on Diana's knee. She jumps slightly at my touch, and for a moment I hesitate. But, as I inch my fingers to the inside of her thigh, she makes no attempt to move away.

'Stay,' I whisper. 'Just for a little while.' I slide my hand further up her leg. Her flesh is warm and slightly damp. I meet her gaze and see alarm in her eyes. But behind it there is something else. The first spark of desire. As I move higher I'm not sure if I feel her step slightly further apart. Emboldened, my hand rises again. Diana holds her breath. So do I. Finally I reach her mound and, almost casually, as if by some wicked accident, I run my finger gently over the satin-covered swelling. The sensation of female underwear against my fingertips sends a new and thrilling buzz through me. I linger, stroking, coaxing, until Diana's eyes close and she begins to sway against me, her hips taking up a beat as old as time.

I reach up to take the glass from Diana and place it on the floor. Taking hold of her wrists, I ease Diana's body over mine. Poised above me, she looks into my face, awaiting my next move. I reach up to the fine straps of her dress and inch them over her shoulders. As the fabric slides down her arms, her breasts are slowly revealed. One deep pink nipple then the other is bared. The sight is breathtakingly lovely and for a moment I can only stare. I reach down and dip my finger into the brandy. Then, with a wet fingertip, I trace a tiny circle around each dark nipple. I marvel as the liquid-chilled tips pucker and point.

Sebastian groans as I pull Diana towards my face and begin to lick, lapping at the pert, brandy-flavoured breasts with long, slow strokes. I draw one erect nipple into my mouth and flick my tongue against her in a teasing caress that I know I would so enjoy myself.

Diana arches against me, and I feel the subtle but insistent pressure of her mound against my stomach as she seeks the contact she so clearly now needs. I move my hands down her body, and lift her dress to reach her minute, and now very damp, panties.

As I ease the fabric away from her sex, I am gratified to hear a soft whimper from Diana. The whimper becomes a low sigh of pleasure as I slip one finger into the wetness. Instinctively, I know what to do. I touch her as I would touch myself, the pace and pressure increasing as Diana's pleasure builds.

It is almost too strong. She leans heavily against me, sliding down my body and on to the floor in a daze of ecstasy. Sprawled face down over the edge of the sofa, Diana looks magnificent. With her dress flipped up over her bottom and her panties in a little bunch around the tops of her thighs, she is ruthlessly exposed. I am transfixed by the full lips of her pussy. She is as tempting as sun-warmed fruit and I long to sink my teeth into her delicious flesh. I wonder if Sebastian feels the same. I glance up to see his erection pushing up hard against the front of his trousers, distorting the fabric into a strong bulge. Oh yes. His feelings are clear. He stares at Diana's inert body, his eyes glazed and fixed on the dark shadow of her sex.

I run one hand casually over the curve of Diana's buttocks, letting my fingers stray towards the pink crease between the tops of her thighs. Her flesh parts like a ripe peach as my fingers move lower. The inner folds glisten with her juices. I move my hand underneath Diana's trembling body and she writhes against my fingers as I find her clit and begin to fondle it once more.

'Look,' I say, easing her thighs further apart so Sebastian can see clearly how splendid she is. 'Don't you want her?' Sebastian is staring at her, eyes dark with lust.

'But she's my sister.' I raise an eyebrow. Surely he's not shocked?

Diana has no such qualms. She moans with increasing passion as I continue to stroke her swollen clit. She's so high, I know it won't take much to sweep her away. Soon she is trembling with need. She is desperate to be fucked – even by her own brother.

'Please, Sebs,' she whimpers. 'Please put it in me. Please fuck me.'

Still sitting on the sofa in front of us, Sebastian observes her mounting arousal with an interest he can't disguise. I watch him struggle with his conscience. But desire is spurring him on and he's not in control. Unsure, he shoots me a nervous glance. I nod, giving him all the encouragement he needs.

He looks back at Diana's proffered body. He can't

resist her. He kneels behind Diana and, scrabbling to untangle himself from his clothing, guides the tip of his prick to her waiting cunt. I watch as he slides into her. Diana sighs with bliss as he slowly fucks her, burying his cock deep, his hard stomach pressing against her upturned arse. Their faultless bodies flow together, rising and falling as one. The silence is broken only by the occasional low moan and the faint, almost imperceptible slurp of cock dipping through willing wet cunt.

But soon I too am overcome by the need to be filled. The divine cock slipping in and out of Diana becomes necessary to me. As necessary as my next breath. I climb astride Diana, my booted legs straddling her bare thighs. On my hands and knees over her, I ease my skirt up over my bottom and part my legs to offer Sebastian my sex above Diana's. Faced with two cunts from which to choose, Sebastian can't conceal his delight.

'Oh, girls,' he sighs. 'You are so beautiful.'

He takes his prick out of Diana and stands up behind me. I feel him ease into my surrendered sex, a craving emptiness slowly and perfectly filled. As he begins to thrust against me, my body is rocked, pressing my clit against Diana's lovely bottom. My breasts slide over the smooth skin of her back. I reach down and slide my hands under her, wanking her with my new-found expertise. She moans and her trembling pleasure thrills me. My power over her is a strong aphrodisiac – it is as much as I can do to hold back the orgasm that threatens to engulf me.

Greedy as a schoolboy in a sweet shop, Sebastian is finding it hard to make up his mind. Bending his knees, he lunges into Diana again. Then it's me. He plunges into one and then the other, enjoying us both to the full.

It is Diana who climaxes first. At first it is the merest

shiver, then her orgasm builds and powerful spasms ripple up my fingers. As I feel her coming against my hand, I can restrain myself no longer. Grinding myself against the pert globes of her arse, I reach my own orgasm, moaning with pleasure as each delicious wave washes over me.

And now Sebastian is free to give way. It is Diana he chooses as he reaches his end. I feel him shake as he pours himself into her forbidden body.

The next morning I awake in Sebastian's bed after a dreamless sleep. Yawning, I stretch my legs against crisp linen sheets. Sebastian and Diana are gone, but on the pillow beside my head is a small leather box. I open it and see the diamond, cushioned in blue velvet. Next to the box is a card. I pick it up and read: 'You shocked me!'

Nearly a week passes before I see the diamond again. Anthea wears it to work. It sparkles enticingly against her black cashmere sweater, as beautiful as ever. I can't tear my eyes away and I find myself staring at it as Anthea moves about the office.

Catching me looking at her, she walks towards my desk. For a ghastly moment I wonder if I've been rumbled. But Anthea is smiling at me. She covers the gem with a manicured hand.

'You like it very much, don't you?'

'Yes,' I stammer. 'Very much.' I know I won't be able to relax until I'm certain she hasn't noticed the switch and I risk a question.

'Is it part of the collection you bought at that Cartier auction last year?' Anthea tosses her head and laughs.

'Good Lord, no!' she says. 'I got it from a stall at Camden Lock market. Only paid five pounds for it. But it's so pretty you'd almost believe it was real, wouldn't you?'

'Yes,' I say, the word catching in my suddenly parched throat.

'But if you love it so much, you must have it.' Anthea lifts the chain from her neck and presses the diamond into my hand. My fingers close around the cold stone. 'Please. Keep it,' she whispers.

And I will.

After all, I earned it.

Strawberry Sunday Maria Eppie

Glastonbury, the year it didn't rain. Me and the two Michelles – Meesh and Shell. Me, skinny and tall, tanned and red haired. Shell, short and dark and a bit clever. And Meesh, one hundred per cent blonde babe. Three girls in a tent. Not on the pull or anything. Quite the opposite. We had an agreement: no skanking, just three girls out for a laugh. Supposedly.

We were so crap we couldn't get the tent up (some complicated geodesic affair). The boys on the neighbouring pitch (dark-haired moptops affecting Manchester accents of the mad-fer-it, livin'-it-laaarge, Gallagher brothers variety) asked us if we needed a hand. Shell, who fancied herself as Riot Grrrl, went right into one, so they told us to fook off and look up equality in't dictionary then. That didn't solve the tent problem and I was contemplating sleeping in the car when finally Meesh batted her baby blues. The Gallaghers relented and started slotting poles together manfully. Turned out that they were nice boys (northern posh) called Damien and Jeremy.

Once we'd got them organised, we stretched out on the shady side of the tent, happily enjoying a smoke. The idea was to shelter from the sun but as soon as the Gallaghers finished banging in pegs, Meesh instructed Jeremy to begin rubbing sun oil into her creamy-white skin. (Not being a bronzed Nordic blonde, her hair came out of a bottle.) He kept shooting smug little looks at Damien, who was trying on statements like, 'I'm a feminist, actually,' in his real voice now (minor public school) to ingratiate himself with the still glowering Shell. I contributed to the fun by unhitching my bikini top so I was down to cut-offs, and tantalising them as I sprawled on my tummy and toasted myself. Then I tuned out and took in the view. It was burning hot; all the grass had turned to dust. A shanty town of tents sprawled away, as far as the eye could see. And everywhere boys.

I don't know if they'd been specially bussed in, but they were all over the place – gorgeous and scantily clad. Most of them wandering round in shorts and headscarves in a choice of styles – pirate or PLO were favoured. Shades were de rigeur. Sunbathing gets me horny anyway but, remembering our No Skanking pledge, I fought the urge to think lascivious thoughts about what exactly well-trained young men might do with suntan oil and overheated young women. I made do with haphazardly squirting factor 10 over my shoulders while surreptitiously grinding myself into the baked hard earth. Don't know why I bothered cos Shell immediately ordered Damien to get her sun-protected too.

We hung around the tent till the sun went down and the boys lit us a campfire. It was all getting way too cosy, but they had a bottle of brandy and the Michelles were making puppy-dog-please noises so eventually I had to relent and let them play Truth or Dare. Which is fine when you're interested in copping off but not when you've got a definite agreement that this would be a girly holiday. No lads, that was the deal. Didn't seem to bother the Michelles though.

The evening turned into a predictable pairing-off prefuck flirt fest with me the gooseberry fool in the middle. I was bored (the lads were definitely not my type) but, as we'd arrived early to get a good pitch and the festival hadn't officially got going yet, there was nowhere I could go to escape from them. I turned in early, stuffed my glowstick under a rucksack and crawled gratefully into my sleeping bag.

Sometime later, the rip of velcro woke me as the Michelles came crashing into the tent, nearly dismantling it in the process. I was pissed off with them for reneging on our deal so early, so I played dead as they bumped around getting undressed and mumbling and giggling at each other. It took some time before I realised that one of the voices was definitely a lower register than either of the girls'. Shell had dragged Damien back with her, on the first night too. What had happened to Riot Grrrl? And the no-boys agreement? I made my feelings plain by doing a big production of tossing and turning before trying to get back to sleep.

Needless to say, to no effect. After a period of subdued muttering and murmuring and general rustling, I became aware of the static crackle caused when manmade fibres are rubbed vigorously against each other. Something was kicking and churning around by my face. Whatever it was had managed to knock my sack and the six-hour glowstick I'd snapped five hours earlier was partially exposed. A sulphurous, crepuscular glow dimly lit the tent. A few feet from my nose, Damien's bare buttocks were rising and falling, framed by Shell's ankles dangling midair. Somehow, they'd managed to reverse their alignment in the tent; their heads by my feet, and vice versa. And they were, to quote a phrase, bang at it.

I was about to give it my best, 'Oi, copulation? No!' when the thought struck me that I could have a bit of fun and not compromise my own morally superior kept-the-pledge status. Shell and Damien were probably way too pissed and/or stoned to realise that they were illuminated, albeit faintly. They could be my personal floorshow for the evening. Now, I'm no innocent, but

I'd never actually watched people fucking before, certainly not from such close quarters. I have to admit that, aggrieved as I was at their selfish behaviour, the spectacle was interesting.

So, I relaxed and watched as Damien's rather scrawny cock slithered and bashed inexpertly around Shell's fluffy-haired, spreadeagled crotch, while Shell issued a continuous stream of instructions and comments, largely concerned with the rigidity of Damien's performance. It was not all that it should be. Maybe it was the brandy, maybe the occasion, but Damien was increasingly wilting, while Shell was getting increasingly pissed off. I could see this going on all night. Someone needed to take the matter in hand.

I had an idea. I quietly squirmed deeper into my sleeping bag, surreptitiously pulling my zip down with me so that I could maintain eye contact. After I'd slithered down about a foot, I was level with the action, or lack of it. Tentatively, I reached out and took hold of Damien's semi-flaccid penis by the base and applied pressure. Gradually, the member increased in girth and length till it was at least semi-respectable. Then, I aligned it with Shell's slippery hole and, plop, it was sucked straight in. Now, the performers, who seemed oblivious of my assistance, were able to get down to it properly. Damien spread his knees and started ramming Shell with a degree of vigour that surprised me. I watched, fascinated, as the bulging prick slapped and pushed against Shell's crack which, maintaining full-on receptiveness when the cock was withdrawn, remained hungrily, urgently gaping for its return. Sometimes Damien's aim was true and he slipped straight in, sometimes he missed and slithered up Shell's gleaming slit or down into the crevice between her buttocks.

Much as I didn't really fancy him, I couldn't help picturing Damien's cock slithering in and out of my own hole. I was so slick with juice, I knew I'd just engulf it whole in seconds. I knew, because I'd just swallowed three of my fingers with ease. Soon, I was rocking them in and out of my own orifice while my thumb worked against my anxious clit. The problem was, I was far more expert than Damien and got myself sorted while he was still thrashing at an increasingly noisy Shell. I wanted sleep now, so I snaked a hand beneath Damien once again and managed to cup his balls with it. Then I squeezed gently. Immediately, his cock stiffened and lurched. With a moan, he forced himself deep into Shell's pussy, trapping my wrist between their bodies as he did. Automatically, Shell curved her spine to receive him and I could feel her tighten round his pumping cock.

Honestly, I'd never touched a cunt other than my own before and I don't know if my brain got confused or what, but my fingers sort of circled the slippy entrance to her hole and, as my own clit began to spasm again, I automatically slipped a finger in. Then I got annoyed that I'd allowed myself to get so turned on. I yanked my hand away quickly, not caring if they realised I'd been there, and sealed myself back inside my sleeping bag for the rest of the night.

Next day, I was tired and irritable. I tried guilt-tripping the Michelles, reminding them of our agreement. They laughed at me and Meesh said, 'You're just sulking cos you didn't cop.' I played my morally superior card and said I didn't give a toss who they wanted to shag as long as I didn't have to spend the night listening to them trying to do it. They laughed harder and called me a prude. I was seething, partly cos I did feel a prude. Then Shell said, 'Maybe you could swap tents with the boys?' I was in such a nark that I snapped back, 'Fine, it's every girl for herself, then, is it?' and moved my stuff into the boys' tent there and then. So, for the next 48 hours, I sulked around on my own while the Michelles and the Gallaghers played at being engaged or something like that. I could have hung round with them or copped off myself if I'd wanted to, but I'd gone right off the idea of boys.

On the Sunday, there was a dance act I wanted to see, Hyperhyper. I was determined that the entire weekend was not going to be a complete blow-out and insisted that the Michelles accompany me. They must have been feeling guilty and maybe they were wearying of the Gallaghers' attentions, cos they agreed. I insisted on going down early to get a good spec even though Hyperhyper wouldn't be on for hours. We hung out by the dance tent but the temperature was too suicidal to venture in. It was only mid-afternoon but the ravers were dropping like flies, completely cabbaged. I made do with dancing outside, enjoying the attention I was getting cos I am a fucking good dancer.

Then a big flatbed truck, full of security, came thundering through. They weren't coming to assist the whacked-out punters or anything as useful as that. They were doing it simply to show that they weren't punters. See, festivals operate within their own universe, with their own hierarchies. Punters at the bottom. Stallholders and crew and performers have their allotted places. Security are a breed apart. As few vehicles have access on to the main site, those that do flaunt it as showily as possible. The flatbed was no exception. It hurtled past, air horns blasting, scattering assorted ravers and hippies, then wheeled round in a huge cloud of dust.

The security guys were sat all over the cab roof and crammed into the back, bursting the seams of the wagon like Keystone Kops. The truck passed right by us and, as it passed, two guys leaned out and scooped up little Meesh into the back. Shell ran alongside, yelling

and screaming at the occupants to release her friend.
Next thing, she too was hauled on to the wagon. My
heart zinged. At last, some excitement. I hollered, 'What
about me?' The wagon did a loop, came back and a
giant of a man reached down and hauled me on board.

I sat on the roof of the cab with the big bloke who'd
lifted me in holding me tight round my waist. I waved
at Damien and Jeremy, who looked distinctly non-
plussed at the hijacking of their girlfriends. The Michelles themselves were shocked into silence as the
wagon took off once more through the crowd.

Floyd, who had lifted me into the wagon, was like
the captain. He told me he was a boxer. A heavyweight,
natch. I thought, right, I'm with Floyd. I wasn't scared
because, though Floyd was massive, he was quite sweet
and polite. He'd just grabbed us for a laugh. He was
going to drop us off but the sight of Damien and Jeremy
doing their concerned boyfriends routine had sparked a
revolt inside me. Weren't we supposed to be having
some girlfun, not pairing off? These guys looked like
they knew how to give a girl a good time.

'Keep on truckin',' I said to Floyd.

'Anything you say,' he said.

The wagon bounced off and into Bouncertown. This
was the place where the security guys camped out.
They'd been there a fortnight. Without women. When
we arrived, it felt like the stagecoach bearing whores
arriving in the Klondike. Three girls and about a hundred, decidedly non-boyish, men. The Michelles were
visibly panicking, but not me. Bouncertown sounded a
decidedly civilised place. Floyd had told me it had its
own shower block and everything. Seeing as the Michelles had decided it was an every-girl-for-herself weekend, I couldn't see a reason to change now. I called out
cheerily, 'Enjoy yourselves,' before turning to Floyd and

adding, 'That ride's left me so dirty. Howzabout you show me those showers?'

Now, I was expecting to have to fight Floyd off but he just handed me some shower gel and said to yell if I needed anything else. Well, I did, and I thought Floyd was just the man to provide it (as I said, boys aren't really my style). 'Wanna scrub my back?' I asked matily.

He suddenly looked all bashful and said, 'It's not that you're not a very attractive girl or anything but I'm engaged.' I was lost for words. Oh fuck, I thought. Haven't I been here once already this weekend?

So I stood under the jet, alone, and indulged in hot water heaven. After a couple of minutes I realised that the place was filling out with guys coming off shift and piling into the other cubicles. They were moaning about the job and about being stuck with all the other guys. One even said it was worse than being inside, cos at least inside, you weren't confronted with thousands of half-naked babes prancing around in front of you day after day. They all agreed that it was a bummer and I could see their point.

I waited until they had gone and was about to leave when I realised that there was still somebody in the next shower. The stalls were only divided by makeshift partitions with a gap next to the wall. It dawned on me that whoever was there could have spied on my cubicle from his. I was worried about what might happen if he knew that a naked babe was only inches away from him, alone. I decided the situation needed checking out. I squinted through the gap and was rather surprised to discover he was far too preoccupied to be thinking about me.

He was leaning, braced one handed against the back wall of the shower. A big man – not as big as Floyd maybe, but big enough – with a really muscular body and dark, silky skin. He had a broad chest, with tight little whorls of hair, and an arse like a Grand National winner. And a cock to match. About the biggest I'd seen in my life. It was big because his other hand was wrapped firmly round it, lazily pulling along its length.

I held my breath. I knew I shouldn't watch but I was riveted. I had never seen a man really do this. Sure, I'd had boyfriends wank themselves in front of me, but I always felt they were acting. This man wasn't. He obviously needed what he was doing and it obviously felt good. Soon, he was leaning back against the partition opposite me. His right hand was stroking his cock from base to tip, deliberately teasing it, while his left fondled his balls. His head was thrown back and his eyes were closed in concentration. I had to watch now. I knew he'd want me to, if he'd known I was there. (Well, if he'd known I was there, I think he'd have probably come right through that flimsy partition, but you know what I mean.) What he was doing was sorta private but it was better shared. He had his hand cupped under his balls, which didn't look like they needed much supporting, and he was really getting into it now, running his hand all over his cock, squeezing it, feeling the shape, enjoying the swollen plumpness, unashamedly fondling himself. He was completely gone. Suddenly, he looked down. His cock bulged and a spurt of white shot out the end, then another and another, as his come cascaded on to the shower floor.

I pulled back from the gap, trying to control my breathing so I wouldn't give the game away. I had a desperate urge to indulge myself, to do to myself exactly what that guy had done to himself, while I pictured him jerking furiously at his handsome, heavy member. More than anything, I wanted some cock, but I was scared. Then his shower was turned off and I heard him moving outside my door. He banged on it and shouted, 'Come on, wanker. I know what you're doing!' I held my breath in terror. Then I realised that, of course, he assumed I was another bloke. So that's what guys get up to in the showers!

When I was sure he was gone, I yelled for Floyd and asked him if he had a clean T I could borrow. 'Sure thing,' he growled and padded off, returning to toss a T-shirt over the door. It had 'Behave' emblazoned across its front and was big enough to wear as a dress. I pulled it over my head and fished my thong from inside my shorts. Floyd discreetly turned away while I hoicked it up my legs, which was a disappointment. The T-shirt came down lower than my crotch (just), so I decided to abandon my disgustingly crusty cut-offs. I stood up on tiptoe and tapped Floyd on the shoulder.

'It's OK, I'm ready now.'

Floyd said, 'Not quite.' I thought he was implying I wasn't properly decent but he merely fished something out of his pocket and clamped it around my wrist. At festivals, everyone is issued with a plastic bracelet, like in hospital. Different status, different colours, for instance, red for punters, blue for press. My new one was gold. The Holy Grail; an Access All Areas wristband. 'You're female security now. Right?' Floyd said.

'Cool,' I said. 'A bounceress.'

'Ms Bounce!' he corrected me.

Floyd led me through the campervans of Bouncertown into Showbiztown, where the trailers were beautiful aluminium Winnebagos and the tents were marquees kitted out with real furniture. One was all minimalist silver inflatables and white flowers and giant bubble lights. Another was a Bedouin tent with carpets and cushions and tables laden with fruit and big hubbly-bubbly pipes. Rock and roll, heh? They even had proper toilets.

Floyd said he'd make sure I got back to my tent when

I wanted, then got off, saying that he had work to do. I wandered round a bit but the initial excitement of seeing musos in the flesh soon wore off. All they were doing was moaning about the catering and asking each other where they were staying. I was contemplating going back to the girls when I saw Todd disappearing into the Bedouin tent. Todd is one half of the famous Hyperhyper. I, of course, attached myself to the rear of the entourage and followed on in.

A harassed young woman clutching a clipboard and a walkie-talkie came panting in behind me. She hissed at a tall, languid black girl flopped on a cushion next to me, 'Gina, Chloe's ankle is fucked. Definitely broken. She won't be doing any dancing tonight.'

Gina rolled her eyes and said, 'So who've we got instead?' Harassed Girl shrugged her shoulders. Gina popped the gum she was chewing. 'Are you gonna tell him or am I?' Todd was turning out to be a total fuckwit. He was like a sulky little boy, ordering people to fetch things for him then, when they produced what he wanted, tossing things aside, saying they were the wrong colour, shape, size. The guy was a prick. I could see the girls' problem.

Then Gina noticed me. She looked me up and down, scrutinising my T-shirt especially, then asked, 'Girl-friend, who are you?'

I smiled my biggest, dippiest smile. 'Ms Bounce!'

'And do you?' she asked.

'Definitely,' I replied. I didn't have to expand further because Todd noticed there was something going on that did not revolve around him.

'Oi, Sophie, where the fuck's that silly bitch Chloe?'

Gina and Sophie looked at each other, then Gina said, 'Change of plan, Todd. This is, err, Ms Bounce.'

Todd looked me up and down before saying in a bored voice, 'She'll do.'

Well, I'm not a dancer, really. But I look like one. And I can keep a mean rhythm and can wiggle my arse to any danceable beat. And, truth was, at that point I was up for just about anything. I'd been revving up ever since I climbed on that wagon and I was all set for take-off. I'd seen Hyperhyper more than a few times and I knew what the girl dancers had to do. Not much, really, apart from look good. Let's face it, two nerdy boys behind a bank of keyboards and computers isn't the most visually challenging experience you're gonna get, is it? So, a couple of females wiggling arse downstage makes all the difference.

Gina considered me through narrowed lids then drawled, 'All right, sister, if you're gonna dance with me, I wanna see what you can do.' She led me off to a little area between a herd of grazing Winnebagos and said, 'First thing first. Let's see your body.'

Now, I'm not shy about getting my kit off, as you know, but I wasn't sure I liked Gina's tone. 'Why?' I demanded.

Gina clicked her tongue. 'Because, girlfriend, if you can't shake your arse at me, how're you gonna shake it at our adoring public?'

I pulled a face at her and hauled Floyd's T-shirt over my head. I could see her appraising my body quite openly. Good job I was fit. After the Michelles had pissed me off, I'd traded a good wedge of our food kitty for whizz, figuring, with nothing to go to bed for, I could stay up and lose weight too. I knew I looked good.

'OK, turn round,' she said eventually. I did a neat pirouette and smirked at her. 'Fine for ballet school, but it ain't hip hop,' she drawled.

'Well, put some fucking music on, OK?' I snapped.

Gina raised her eyebrows and clambered up the steps into one of the trailers, reappearing with a portable CD player. She sat down on the step and hit play. A solidly phat beat boomed out. I grinned and went for it. As a finale, I slipped my string so I was completely naked then turned my back on her, arched my spine and shook my arse so it bounced and shimmied. I thought I'd let Gina know I could live up to my new name.

I heard her laughing hysterically. 'For a skinny bitch, that's a fine bootie! OK, hon, you'll do.'

So that was it; I was in. Gina played Hyperhyper's set and we worked up an act. She'd do a move, then I'd add something to it and throw it back and so on. Like a competition. Gina, who was built like me, except a tad more African in the bootie department, found me something more clubby to wear on stage than an outsized T-shirt. Then we had a few smokes and hung out together for the rest of the day. She was cool; I liked her.

I started off in ultra-baggy combats and a waistee over bikini top and batty riders. Gina was wearing a sarong and loose-fitting cotton top over same. The idea was that, as we danced and got hotter, and our dancing got hotter, and as we started competing with each other, we'd strip down to a tiny bra and shorts. It didn't quite work out like that. We got into some pretty dirty moves, holding on to each other and sliding around in each other's arms, and my bikini just sort of rode up my tits. The crowd loved that, so I hauled it off and flung it at them. Not to be outdone, Gina unfastened hers. Lovely tits, impressively pert nipples. Back to me now, so I unzipped my shorts and I left it so they were resting on my hips. I turned my back on Gina and shook my bootie at her, like I did back at camp.

Next thing, she'd spooned in behind me and held me tight with her arms round my tummy so we were dancing coupled together. Her satiny skin was sliding over mine, our sweat acting like a lubricant. I could feel her breasts in my back and her hard nipples against my skin. It all really happened at once from that point.

Gina yanked down my batty riders and I was completely bare-arsed naked in front of two thousand people. Just as that happened, down below me, I saw two familiar faces. Two mop-headed Gallagher faces staring up at me, agog. It was brilliant. I dived on Gina and wrestled off her satin boxers to reveal her gleaming, dusky arse. We finished the set *au naturelle*, to massive applause.

Immediately afterwards, we fled to the Hyperhyper Winnebago and got stuck into Todd's supply of charlie before any of the liggers could come piling in. As we'd just been shaking our respective booties in front of thousands, it seemed pointless to go all bashful on each other now, so Gina and me barricaded the door and flopped naked on the cushions.

'Girlfriend, you are fun.' She grinned at me. 'Wanna do that again sometime?'

I giggled and was about to say, 'Like when?' when there was a knock at the door and a familiar Brummy voice enquired, 'Everything OK?'

'It's Floyd,' I said, unlocking the door and letting him in. Gina looked quizzical. 'We're safe with Floyd – he's engaged,' I added sarcastically as he stepped into the trailer, visibly startled at so much naked female flesh.

Gina considered him appraisingly. 'Is he now,' she purred before carefully relocking the door.

Poor Floyd didn't stand a chance. We sat him between us and Gina asked him to tell us all about his fiancée. He started mumbling away, while Gina selected a huge strawberry from the obligatory platter of fruit on the table and began sucking it thoughtfully. When she leaned across him and pushed it into my mouth with her tongue, he started to stammer.

'Floyd!' Gina teased wickedly. 'You're supposed to be telling us about your fiancée!'

Floyd swallowed. 'What about her?'

Gina smiled mischievously. 'Well, for instance, what does she like you to do to her?' Floyd didn't reply. 'Jo,' she said, 'pass me a strawberry.' I did as I was told. Gina drawled, 'Floyd, you've gone quiet!'

She swivelled to face him on the cushioned seat, exposing her pussy to his gaze. Then she rubbed the strawberry at the entrance to her cunt before mashing the glistening fruit between her pink pussy lips and rubbing the pulp around her clit. The juicy gash looked shocking and violent against her chocolatey skin. Then she lifted the squished mess up to Floyd's lips and smeared it over his mouth. Leaning against Floyd as I was, I could feel his heart pounding against his rib cage almost as hard as my own. 'Perhaps she likes that?' Gina smirked. Floyd was beginning to sweat.

'Well, would you like it if she did it to you?' asked Gina, and deftly unfastened his fly. 'Jo, get another,' she instructed, 'and rub it along his cock.' Floyd let out a great gasp of air. I tentatively pushed the strawberry through the gap so it squashed against Floyd's taut, trapped cock while I stared at Gina with a big silly grin all over my face. She smiled coolly back. 'Girlfriend, we're safe with Floyd. He's engaged!'

I fumbled around and eventually uncoiled Floyd's erection so it sprang free from his flies. I said he was a heavyweight. There were absolutely no surprises in the cock department. I rubbed and squished the fruit along the underside of his handsome prick till the strawberry turned to mush in my hands and as much juice was coating his cock as was flowing down my fanny.

'Floyd, honey, I think you'd better take your clothes off now, before you get in any more of a mess,' Gina suggested. Floyd stripped and stood naked before us, his swollen cock sticky and gorgeously rigid. 'Now,' Gina said to him, 'you get a strawberry – and rub it into Jo's cunt.'

Floyd looked at her for a second, then, kneeling between my legs, he inserted its tip tenderly between my pussy lips. I held my breath. 'Relax, Jo,' encouraged Gina, moving to kneel beside me. She lifted my thigh out so my own pink pussy was open and exposed and said, 'Come on, Floyd, she's waiting.' Floyd put the fruit against my hole and I yielded so easily that I almost swallowed it. 'Not there, Floyd,' said Gina. 'Higher up. Watch.' Then she took the strawberry out of Floyd's hand and mashed the fruit into my pussy, pulping it against my clit until the juices ran in a sweet sticky mess all over my inner thighs and seeped down the cleft between my buttocks.

'Oh, Floyd, we've made a mess of this girl,' Gina tutted. 'Better start cleaning her up.' She pushed me over on my back and began licking the inside of my thighs, her own gorgeous arse high in the air. I looked down at her and up at Floyd, his cock bulging urgently. Gina's darting tongue reached the skin between my pussy and my arse. I'd never been licked by a girl before and my brain was spinning with 'Do I, don't I?' thoughts. But, when she suddenly stopped, I could have screamed. Floyd stood panting and shaking, on the edge of self-control. He was staring at my exposed cunt like he wanted to take me there and then. I would not have objected.

'Now what,' said Gina smoothly, 'is the most practical way of doing this?' Floyd and me were staring at each other hungrily. 'Floyd, do you want to fuck Jo?' asked Gina. Floyd winced, but his cock tightened in assent. 'I think you do,' she said. 'But what about me? I'm filthy. Look!' she added, and, kneeling in front of us, she parted her pussy lips before squishing another luscious fruit on to her exposed clit. Then she began to finger herself. We both watched, hypnotised, as Gina shamelessly rubbed herself, her eyes closed like the man in the shower stall, till she was trembling with excitement too. I expected her to come but she stopped and, in a voice hoarse with sex, asked, 'Floyd, what would your fiancée say about you getting two girls so dirty? You're a bad, baaad boy. I think you've got to clean your act up *now*!'

Then Gina told me to lick Floyd's cock clean. I kneeled before him and tried to take the swollen, plum-like end in my mouth, while Gina pushed me over to my side and finished cleaning me. Her long, slender tongue began retrieving the strawberry from inside me. Then, while I slurped on Floyd, she moved up to my clit. So this was what it was like with a girl; I remember thinking, I like this. But when she suddenly stopped and gently pulled me away from eating Floyd, I groaned, cos my cunt was aching to be finished off.

'I can't help thinking this isn't fair on Floyd's fiancée,' she said teasingly. 'I mean, what's in it for her? Floyd, you're getting all the fun. It's payback time now. Lie on the floor.'

Floyd stared at Gina intently for maybe a couple of seconds, then did as he was bid, his cock raised like a flagpole. I kneeled beside him and began sucking again while I cupped his balls, just as the man had done in the shower stall. Gina straddled his other end, lowering herself on to Floyd's mouth and working against him urgently. 'Go ahead, sugar, if you want,' Gina groaned, nodding at his erection. I manoeuvred his penis up to my swollen, juicy entrance. The head was so fat, I could hardly work it in, but, with help from Gina's agile fingers, we eventually eased it up my lubricated sheath and I immediately began riding it vigorously. At last! Three days of watching cocks and finally I'd got one inside me, and a fine one too.

Gina and me were face to face now; rocking, grinning, panting pretty much in unison. I threw my arms round her and kissed her joyfully. I said 'Thank you,' though I didn't know why, but I meant it. She returned my kiss and soon we were snogging and stroking each other's backs and caressing each other's tits while we both hammered down on poor old Floyd, prone and trapped beneath us. 'What about his fiancée?' I panted in her ear.

'She'll be OK,' she murmured, slipping a finger down to feel Floyd's flesh tightly filling my cunt mouth.

'She's one horny bitch. She'll do anything to get her man to eat her out.'

It was three hours before knobhead Todd got his trailer back. By then, there wasn't much left in the fruit bowl. Both Gina and me had given Floyd an extended seminar in the art of eating fruit, while alternately having our respective pussies thoroughly attended to by his heavyweight cock. That man had stamina.

When we'd done, Floyd was as good as his word and returned me to my tent. I was received with stupefied acclaim by the Gallaghers and sheepish grins by the Michelles, who, incidentally, seemed to have lost all interest in nice boys.

I keep the gold pass above my bed as a little reminder of my best fest ever. Oh yes, and I'm going up to Brum next week, dancing with Gina. Ms Bounce and Gina G. We're staying with Floyd and his fiancée. Or should that be Gina and her fiancé? Either way, it'll be healthy. They eat loads of fruit, apparently.

Wytchfinder Lois Phoenix

Rosa-May holds tight to her sister's hand as the small band of girls race across the clearing. Her chest is so tight with fear and excitement she can hardly breathe. Once under the giant oak the girls droop against the trunk, weak with the thrill of escaping the village.

Rosa-May's face looks small and pale in the moonlight. 'I'm not sure I want to come now, Clara,' she whispers.

'Too late now,' Clara hisses back. 'You should have been asleep like you were supposed to be.'

'But this is wrong, isn't it?' the youngster asks, unsure whether to be delighted or terrified.

'If the elders won't allow us any fun, we shall have to make our own. I'm tired of being put to bed like a baby every night. I'm old enough for a walk in the woods, unchaperoned.'

Sarah giggles and clutches her nightgown closer around her bare legs. 'Aunt Rachel told me that greenwood marriages were still allowed when she was young.'

The girls gather around, clutching her arms and suppressing the urge to screech with excitement.

'Tell us again, Sarah!'

'Well, boys and girls of a certain age were allowed to spend the whole night together in the woods at Beltane.' Sarah's eyebrows rise dramatically. 'The whole night!'

'Can you believe it?' Clara whispers. 'Now we aren't allowed to show our hair or even think about boys.' She shakes her dark hair vigorously. 'But tonight we claim our lost rites. Have you brought the branches?'

Every girl holds up a small bough, one from each of the nine sacred trees, each collected and hidden in utmost secrecy.

'Excellent. Then we shall make a Bel-fire and conjure ourselves a lover.'

'A lover!' Rosa-May is giggling fit to bust.

'Not in your case. Stop screeching, Rosa-May, or you'll have the entire village out here. Now, while the moon is high we'll gather flowers in the bottom meadow for our garlands. And when we enter the woods I don't want anyone screaming.'

Deftly the girls gather armfuls of mugwort, mint and rosehip before passing through the veil of trees along the meadow edge and slipping into the wood. They walk in silence, feeling their way with bare feet over damp, springy moss.

'Here,' Clara whispers. 'This is the copse I was telling you about.'

A ring of flowering hawthorn shines like embroidered beads around them in the moonlight. At once the spring night feels milder and safer.

Stamping down a patch of fern Sarah sits down, clutching her flowers. Her toes curl into the fronds beneath her. How wonderful to be free of the constraints of Puritan dress. Her body feels curiously alive, as though a small bird were fluttering low down in her belly.

Clara is eager to begin. 'Pass the boughs into the middle, here. Helena, you help me light the fire. The rest of you, start to weave your flower crowns.'

They do not take long. Their fingers, used to embroidery and weaving, soon entwine the fragrant blossoms and leaves around fern stems.

'Yours is better.'

'No, yours.'

The girls giggle and weave until a small tongue of golden fire flickers amongst the kindling. Their laughter sinks into sighs as they are drawn towards it.

Clara's face reflects the flickering light as the flames consume her small bunches of dried lavender and heather. The scent is sublime. The girls stand transfixed and watch as the flames lick over the boughs of alder, maple, elm and birch.

'Rosa-May, pass me the rowan sprig,' commands Clara. Twisting it into a loop, she holds it aloft. 'Through this loop I shall see the man who loves me.' She takes a deep excited breath. 'Let us begin.'

Slowly, Clara slips her nightshift from her shoulders and turns for Helena to place a garland on her head.

'Do we have to go sky-clad too?' Rosa-May asks.

'Better than explaining burnt nightclothes,' Sarah whispers.

With hushed laughter, the girls step out of their cotton shifts and place a flower crown on each other's heads. Their eyes are full of dancing flames.

'Now let's show the church elders that they cannot stop us from conjuring up handsome young men!'

Whooping and laughing the girls follow Clara around the fire, elegantly dancing towards the warm flames, then pulling back towards the dark whispering woods – around and around until their skin glistens. When the flames start to die and the embers glow deep red, they take it in turns to jump over them. Clara first, of course, her long pale limbs easily clearing the fire.

'Queen of the May,' she calls out, 'bring me a lover to . . .'

A cracking of branches brings the girls to a halt. Their breath beats hot and fast but their flesh is suddenly doused with chill fear. They have not been alone in the forest; someone else has been here with them.

Clara's eyes strain to make out a fleeting shape in the darkness. Not a deer. She catches a glimpse of white shift and dark hair. A girl, then, but who from the village would dare to join them?

Then her heart leaps to her throat. Through the leaves, she can just make out two hats of the church elders pushing their way through the laurel bushes. Clara drops like a felled partridge and her friends fall too. They scurry into the bushes and clutch each other in the darkness, bare skin against bare skin, flower crowns crushed as they press together in terror. Rosa-May bites her fist to stop herself from crying.

Through the fern fronds, Clara can just make out two pairs of boots as the elders step into the clearing.

'Did you see her?' Church Elder Smithson booms. 'Fleeing through the wood like a familiar?'

Clara's mouth feels dry with fear. Surely they have seen them also?

'I didn't recognise her. This seems like trickery to me. It will be a matter for the Wytchfinder General,' the other elder snaps. 'My cow in the top field lost her calf today.'

Clara's head swivels to glance at Sarah's white face. She recognises the girl's uncle.

'Woe betide any one who is foolish enough to be caught up in this witchery.' Two pairs of boots kick earth into the flames and the girls are left in darkness.

When they have left, Sarah chokes back a sob. 'What am I going to do, Clara? My father will turn me out.'

'No he won't. They haven't seen us. Anyway, it would be a disgrace on your uncle also, and he wouldn't give up his position as church elder for anything.' Clara scrambles out of the ferns. 'Come on, get dressed. We'll be back in our own beds by sunrise and no one will know where we've been.'

Nine garlands are dropped reluctantly into the ashes

of the Bel-fire. They smoulder and the scent of freesias is overwhelming.

Clara looks down at her sister's face, still transfixed by the dying flames. 'No one, Rosa-May, I mean it.' She turns away to gaze at the last of the burning petals. 'You don't want to find out what they do to wytches.'

I have found the perfect cottage, a small step away from the village, secluded and solitary. The soil is heavy with clay but I manage to plant a small herb garden. The brambles and overgrown roses at the gate I leave; it gives the impression that no one lives here. All is peaceful. The cats doze on the porch and the stream tinkles over fat brown stones at the bottom of the garden. Warm May days drift by, and I wonder how long it will take for them to find me.

It takes longer than I thought. Springtime has already begun to bring the valley alive with fresh green, and young ferns are unfurling in the bright sunshine when the first villager comes. I am collecting water from the well, lost in the images shimmering on the black surface, when I hear the hooves and brace myself. A large grey mare rounds the corner and whinnies, jolting her rider. I look up and see a young man watching me. I bite my lip and take in his shape, thick thighs spread across the horse's back, thin shirt stretched across his broad chest. His voice is low and stern as he commands the mare to stand, but she is unhappy and turns in circles before he allows her to walk on.

It only last a few seconds but I see how he sees me.

Alone in the cottage these last weeks I have lost the trappings of polite dress. My bodice is low and tatty, my breasts blushed by the spring sunshine. My hair is loose and blows about my face, catching small leaves and burrs in its dark curls. My lips are sore and red from the outdoors. I feel the burn of his arousal in my own belly. Drops of water splash onto the porch steps as I re-enter the cottage. I ladle the water into my cooking pot and stir; my hand shakes with the knowledge that others will soon follow.

I am not wrong. Two young girls from the village arrive later in the week. They stand on the front step, all smiles and scrubbed cheeks, bearing a pie wrapped in muslin and a pot of preserve. Despite their starched white caps, I recognise them from the fire-jumping but I am careful not to show it. Their cheeriness soon wavers as they follow me in and notice my slatternly housekeeping: saucers of milk on the rugs and potato peeling in the grate. I offer them camomile tea from greasy pewter mugs and they perch, nervous as birds, on the settle, as the cats weave between their slender, stockinged ankles. My calmness makes them chatter with embarrassment and I sense their eagerness to get away and gossip about me in the village.

Then the elders pay me a visit. I see them coming in the flames and I am ready. I clean the cottage, my hair is combed, my dress buttoned. The questions are polite but suspicion glitters behind their eyes. Where is my husband? My children? How do I support myself? Among them is the man who rides the grey mare. He rotates his cup between his big rough hands and glances at me when he thinks I am not looking. His jaw is clean-shaven and he smells of Lyle soap. I sense he is a good man. He shouldn't come here.

But come he does, later – offering to chop wood and repair the front step. I have been sitting by the fire, watching deep in the flames, looking for tomorrow, when he knocks on the door. He looks startled at my appearance; my hair is loose and my bodice undone. My face is warm from the fire. I call him in. The day is cloudy and dull, I have no wish to see it.

He stands looking and saying nothing until I notice

the drops of blood staining his boot. He has caught his fingers with his axe. The cut is deep. I seat him by the fire and fetch a bowl of water and some clean rags. I mix a poultice to prevent poisoning of the blood. He is starting to sweat and I tell him to remove his coat while I brew some tea. He is broad, dwarfing my settle. I kneel between his thighs. He tries not to stare at my nipples grazing the lace at the opening of my bodice. His discomfort excites me and I stand close as I clean the cut. Bending to dip my rag into the bowl, I feel his breath warm against my hair.

The gash is deep across three fingers and, as I wash it, he winces in pain. I clean deeper than is strictly necessary, feeling a pulse begin to quicken deep in my gut. The flesh is tender. I press myself close to his legs, aware of my nipples hardening. His face has paled, and a thin layer of perspiration forms on his upper lip. My fingers wander to the wiry hair on his wrist. He is perfectly still, his eyes lowered, waiting.

I think of his rough, hairy thighs between mine. I can see the sheets of my bed tangled around him, the warmth of his huge body on me, the wetness of his tongue inside me ...

The cat spits and hisses. He jumps and pulls his hand away, wincing at the pain. The fire has fallen and the room feels chill. I tell him to go and he does.

That night I lie in bed surrounded by flickering candles and think of him. My nipples tighten and chafe against my nightdress. My hand dips between my legs and I imagine him there but the satisfaction will not come.

In the morning I prowl, aroused and restless. I brew tea laced with woodruff, watch the flames and gather some berries, but all day the feeling churns inside me. When he comes in the late afternoon, it is to tell me there is talk of wytchcraft in the village. Some of the silly young women have been playing games in the woods at night. Arousing each other, and afraid of being found out, they are pointing the finger away from themselves. Away from the village – a small step away.

Silly girls and their girlish urges.

I'm burning applewood in the grate, and the room is full of smoke. He leans towards me but I sense the Wytchfinder coming, hooves thundering and black mane flying. My throat is dry and my hands shake. The village will turn against me and the good man shouldn't be here.

I am collecting logs when the Wytchfinder comes. His black eyes brood with menace under the brim of his hat. His stallion snorts at the gate, its breath clouding the sharp morning air. I barely have time to throw on my cloak before I am dragged down the steps of the cottage. The villagers have gathered to gloat over my fate, thankful it isn't them. I see the village girls watching from a safe distance. They look small under the canopy of the ancient rowan, their faces pale like mistletoe berries. My faithful cats defend me by howling and spitting on the porch. I hope they have the sense to disappear into the forest.

The Wytchfinder towers over me then takes a length of rope from his well-polished saddle and fastens it around my wrists. His eyes hold mine for a moment as his cruel mouth twitches into a half-smile. Holding the other end of the rope he pulls himself effortlessly back into the saddle. I am jerked forwards as he rides towards the village. Arms outstretched, I struggle to keep up, and my feet are soon aching and raw. My flesh is chill under my thin cloak.

At the meeting hall, the stallion is tethered and my wrists released, then a strong hand pushes me up the wooden steps. The Wytchfinder throws me through the doors and I struggle to catch my breath, hiding behind my curtain of hair. The villagers crowd into the warmth of the meeting hall. The elders have a table at the back of the hall. Perched like vultures, their beady eyes glitter when they see that it is a young woman they are testing and not some dried-up old crone.

The Wytchfinder has a good sense of the dramatic. His voice rolls across the hall like the threat of a summer storm, condemning the evil that has gripped the young girls in the village. He tells of the spells that have been cast to bring out carnal lusts in their young, budding bodies. The girls of the village squirm in their seats, craving his hard mouth, his dark eyes, his long legs as he strides to and fro, his broad hands as he grips the table in his anger.

'Harlot!' he hisses and the girls cringe, blushing with shame.

'Here she is!' He grabs my long, thick hair and pulls me forwards to where all can see.

My face is smeared with dirt, my hair wild and my dress torn. I must confess that I have the true look of a wytch about me, wanton and wild.

'This is the wytch who stirs up trouble in her well. Casting spells to ignite us all to join her filthy lusts.' He rips away my cloak and I feel vulnerable and exposed in my thin cotton bodice and skirt. Pulling back my head, he reveals a bruise on my neck, dark blue. 'See the mark of her coupling with the devil.'

A murmur ripples through the crowd. Standing behind me, the Wytchfinder pulls the bodice low over my shoulders to reveal another bruise below the collar-bone. He is standing close enough for me to feel his excitement at my humiliation. The eyes of the whole village are on me. I should be terrified, begging for mercy, but my skin is hot and tight. The Wytchfinder has my head pulled back and my bodice low and tight, so that my hard, excited nipples are pushing towards the crowd. From under my lowered lashes I can see the young girls chewing their lips till they are sore and surreptitiously grinding themselves onto the hard wooden seats.

'The marks of the devil,' the Wytchfinder rumbles, his big hands burning through the cotton of my bodice. 'Were we to strip this wytch naked I am sure we would find more.'

My heart hammers and my breathing quickens. The atmosphere in the room has changed. The men are gloating, leaning forwards in their eagerness to see more of the dirty whore in front of them; to see more evidence of her lusts. The Wytchfinder's fingers are toying with the laces of my bodice. From behind them the elders clear their throats. The Wytchfinder turns her slowly to face them.

'What say you gentlemen? Shall we see the marks?'

Their lust is evident – their faces florid, their eyes bright. Years of frustration and puritanical living are being brought simmering to the surface in this village and it is all being blamed on me.

One of the elders is cleverer than I thought. Clearing his throat, he takes charge. 'Wytchfinder. I think I speak for the other elders when I say that these marks are evidence indeed. The village has been gripped by strange and ungodly happenings since this woman has appeared on the edge of our village. Judging by the effect that this woman has had on the younger females in our midst, I think that this meeting hall should be cleared and the matter of judgment now be taken up by the elders.'

An audible groan from the men of the village runs around the room. My heart beats faster and I feel slippery between my thighs with anticipation and fear. Clever, very clever. The elders will be free to inspect the wytch in detail without the whole village looking on.

No risk of criticism later. Better that the elders have me all to themselves.

The Wytchfinder pulls me up tight to him and his rod digs hard against my buttocks.

'I think you are right to say so,' he agrees. 'Her powers are potent. I think it best we shield the others from them.'

The men of the village don't want to be shielded at all. There is much grumbling and black looks as they leave. But they are careful not to dissent too much. After all, this is a wytch trial and all are aware how quickly the tide can turn. There is always someone ready to point the finger and condemn. So they shuffle out, aroused and frustrated.

Eventually the meeting hall has emptied except for the long table of elders, one of whom bolts the heavy wooden door and shuffles back.

'Bring her forwards,' the chief elder barks. 'Let us see those marks.'

The Wytchfinder releases his grip on my hair and pushes me towards the table. My neck aches and I shake my head to soothe it so that my hair tumbles over my shoulders.

'A pretty little wytch indeed, but your charms are wasted on me. Step up to the table where I can see you.'

I step up and eye him defiantly. He lies about my charms. I know I excite him. He leans across the table and prods at my bruises as if I were a heifer at market.

'I'm not convinced. It's not much to condemn such a pretty young thing on.' The others murmur their assent; more proof would probably be prudent.

'Oh, I am sure that there are more marks of devilry, gentlemen.' The Wytchfinder's fingers are in my hair, scooping it back to reveal the proud arch of my throat. They drop to the fastening of my bodice and a pulse hammers in my groin. I can hardly breathe. He seems to take a lifetime to release my breasts. They are sore from the chafing of the bodice and it is sweet release when they are bared. The Wytchfinder pulls the cotton down to my ribcage, allowing his rough fingers to snag my nipples. 'See the nubs, gentleman? The wytch has no shame. Even now she revels in her power as lust-maker.'

I can feel the breath of the elders panting on my bare flesh. My nipples pucker even more. The Wytchfinder's hard finger digs a line down my spine and I arch my back, pushing my breasts even closer to the elders.

'And here, gentlemen, is the third nipple, where the devil sucks.' His finger rotates the dark-brown mole on my ribcage. Any fool can see it isn't a nipple, but the elders shift excitedly in their seats.

'Not convinced? Here, feel its likeness to the other two.'

I swallow a gasp as the Wytchfinder pushes me hard against the table. The chief elder licks his thin dry lips and squeezes the mole between forefinger and thumb.

The Wytchfinder's breath is hot on my ear. 'Compare,' he urges.

And he does, squeezing each aroused nipple in turn so that my chest becomes so tight I start to whimper. My eyes slide shut as I am moved down the table and one by one the elders fondle first my mole and then my nipples till they are sore with handling and burning with arousal. Tweaked and pulled and rotated between hard fingers, over and over as the elders of the village convince themselves that the wytch has a nipple to suckle the devil.

One elder takes forever to decide, mumbling under his breath as he traces my puckered areolæ and finds the mole wanting. My knees are weak. I would collapse if I weren't lodged between Wytchfinder and table.

'I am not convinced, Wytchfinder. Not convinced that

this is a wytch's third teat. I have heard tell that a wytch's nipples taste of sulphur. I see no evidence of it here.'

'Surely a wytch has the sense to disguise the smell with rosewater?' the chief elder asks.

'Still,' the elder ponders, flicking a thin tongue over my nipples. 'I'm not convinced.'

I am glad that I am pressed up against the table. I swallow another whimper. I fear I will faint from arousal before this examination is over. The elders are panting with lust, eager for the next degradation.

'If you are still not convinced, gentlemen, then I must show you the wytch's most secret place, where it has been penetrated by the devil.'

The elders gasp and murmur, afraid to move out of their seats lest their own lust becomes evident. The Wytchfinder releases me and moves to find a chair. He pulls me from the table and turns me round before bending me over the back of it. I am weak and compliant with arousal. I bend from the waist and surreptitiously rub my tortured nubs on the rough wood. The Wytchfinder is rolling up my skirt, exposing my bare legs to the elders and finally pushing the cotton up over my waist so that my backside is exposed. His fingers trace the cleft of my buttocks before his strong, warm hands push my legs apart, wider, until my wet secret place is in plain view. The elders' silence speaks volumes. Their desire is heavy and potent in the air.

'Witness the pink, aroused sex, gentlemen. What woman save a wytch would be aroused by the humiliation she has received at our hands today?' His fingers are fluttering over the sex lips, separating them and dipping into the lushness there. I stifle a moan and push myself back onto his fingers. He allows me a brief moment of fulfilment before withdrawing them from my moist sex.

The sound of shifting and buttons popping fills the silence. I glance around and upside down I can make out several of the elders undoing their trousers under the table and fumbling for their overexcited genitals.

'Look, gentlemen. There can be no further proof. This wytch has allowed the devil inside her most private entrance and still she writhes and drips with lust. There is no end to this woman's lewdness. I will put her in gaol overnight and tomorrow she takes the ducking stool. What say you?'

A few murmured assents but the elders of the village are masturbating as one, slack-jawed, eyes locked on the wytch's splayed legs.

'Up, wytch, and prepare for your punishment.'

My skirt drops and I am stood upright. The Wytchfinder pulls my bodice up and roughly tightens the laces. We leave silently through the back door as the elders of the village jerk themselves to guilty climaxes. The air is cold on my hot, fevered flesh.

The horse again, and my swollen sex rubs greedily on the saddle. The hooves spark on the village streets as they pick up speed. We are out of sight before the dazed villagers realise that their lustful wytch has been stolen from under their noses.

The Wytchfinder puts a good distance between ourselves and the village before he reins the stallion in. We are on the edge of the woods. A river gushes nearby and the floor is soft with pine needles. He pulls me into the quiet darkness, where the sunlight doesn't penetrate the canopy and throws me to the ground. His eyes are dark and menacing under the brim of his hat.

'I thought you were never coming,' I murmur.

The hat is removed and thrown to the ground. 'How could you think I wouldn't find my wytch?' he grins and drops to his knees. 'I always do, my sweet. Although come the morning she could be gone.' He leaves the inevitable unsaid and I know our ultimate pleasure will be for just this once more. Tomorrow I will make for the west – where the old faith, I've heard, is safer from the interrogations of the pious.

I spread my legs like the whore he wants me to be and he pushes up my skirt. 'You have the charm of the devil himself,' I groan.

'It's my golden tongue,' he whispers back and buries it deep inside me.

Visit the Black Lace website at
www.blacklace-books.co.uk

LOOK OUT FOR THE ALL-NEW BLACK LACE BOOKS – AVAILABLE NOW!

All books priced £6.99 in the UK. Please note publication dates apply to the UK only. For other territories, please contact your retailer.

MIXED SIGNALS
Anna Clare
ISBN 0 352 33889 X

Adele Western knows what it's like to be an outsider. As a teenager she was teased mercilessly by the sixth-form girls for the size of her lips. Now twenty-six, we follow the ups and downs of her life and loves. There's the cultured restaurateur Paul, whose relationship with his working-class boyfriend raises eyebrows, not least because he is still having sex with his ex-wife. There's former chart-topper Suki, whose career has nosedived and who is venturing on a lesbian affair. Underlying everyone's story is a tale of ambiguous sexuality, and Adele is caught up in some very saucy antics. **The sexy *tour de force* of wild, colourful characters makes this a hugely enjoyable novel of modern sexual dilemmas.**

Coming in August

SWITCHING HANDS
Alaine Hood
ISBN 0 352 33896 2

When Melanie Paxton takes over as manager of a vintage clothing shop, she makes the bold decision to add a selection of sex toys and fetish merchandise to her inventory. Sales skyrocket, and so does Mel's popularity, as she teases sexy secrets out of the town's residents. It seems she can do no wrong, until the gossip starts – about her wild past and her experimental sexuality. However, she finds an unlikely – and very hunky – ally called Nathan who works in the history museum next door. **This characterful story about a sassy sexpert and an antiquities scholar is bound to get pulses racing!**

PACKING HEAT
Karina Moore
ISBN 0 352 33356 1

When spoilt and pretty Californian Nadine has her allowance stopped by her rich Uncle Willem, she becomes desperate to maintain her expensive lifestyle. She joins forces with her lover, Mark, and together they conspire to steal a vast sum of cash from a flashy businessman and pin the blame on their target's girlfriend. The deed done, the sexual stakes rise as they make their escape. Naturally, their getaway doesn't go entirely to plan, and they are pursued across the desert and into the casinos of Las Vegas, where a showdown is inevitable. The clock is ticking for Nadine, Mark and the guys who are chasing them – but a Ferrari-driving blonde temptress is about to play them all for suckers. **Fast cars and even faster women in this modern pulp fiction classic.**

Also available

THE BLACK LACE SEXY QUIZ BOOK
Maddie Saxon
ISBN 0 352 33884 9
£6.99

- What sexual personality type are you?
- Have you ever faked it because that was easier than explaining what you wanted?
- What kind of fantasy figures turn you on – and does your partner know?
- What sexual signals are you giving out right now?

Today's image-conscious dating scene is a tough call. Our sexual expectations are cranked up to the max, and the sexes seem to have become highly critical of each other in terms of appearance and performance in the bedroom. But even though guys have ditched their nasty Y-fronts and girls are more babe-licious than ever, a huge number of us are still being let down sexually. Sex therapist Maddie Saxon thinks this is because we are finding it harder to relax and let our true sexual selves shine through.

The Black Lace Sexy Quiz Book will help you negotiate the minefield of modern relationships. Through a series of fun, revealing quizzes, you will be able to rate your sexual needs honestly and get what you really want from your partner. The quizzes will get you thinking about and discussing your desires in ways you haven't previously considered. Unlock the mysteries of your sexual psyche in this fun, revealing quiz book designed with today's sex-savvy girl in mind.

Black Lace Booklist

Information is correct at time of printing. To avoid disappointment check availability before ordering. Go to www.blacklace-books.co.uk. All books are priced £6.99 unless another price is given.

BLACK LACE BOOKS WITH A CONTEMPORARY SETTING

☐ SHAMELESS Stella Black	ISBN 0 352 33485 1	£5.99
☐ INTENSE BLUE Lyn Wood	ISBN 0 352 33496 7	£5.99
☐ A SPORTING CHANCE Susie Raymond	ISBN 0 352 33501 7	£5.99
☐ TAKING LIBERTIES Susie Raymond	ISBN 0 352 33357 X	£5.99
☐ A SCANDALOUS AFFAIR Holly Graham	ISBN 0 352 33523 8	£5.99
☐ THE NAKED FLAME Crystalle Valentino	ISBN 0 352 33528 9	£5.99
☐ ON THE EDGE Laura Hamilton	ISBN 0 352 33534 3	£5.99
☐ LURED BY LUST Tania Picarda	ISBN 0 352 33533 5	£5.99
☐ THE HOTTEST PLACE Tabitha Flyte	ISBN 0 352 33536 X	£5.99
☐ THE NINETY DAYS OF GENEVIEVE Lucinda Carrington	ISBN 0 352 33070 8	£5.99
☐ DREAMING SPIRES Juliet Hastings	ISBN 0 352 33584 X	
☐ THE TRANSFORMATION Natasha Rostova	ISBN 0 352 33311 1	
☐ SIN.NET Helena Ravenscroft	ISBN 0 352 33598 X	
☐ TWO WEEKS IN TANGIER Annabel Lee	ISBN 0 352 33599 8	
☐ HIGHLAND FLING Jane Justine	ISBN 0 352 33616 1	
☐ PLAYING HARD Tina Troy	ISBN 0 352 33617 X	
☐ SYMPHONY X Jasmine Stone	ISBN 0 352 33629 3	
☐ SUMMER FEVER Anna Ricci	ISBN 0 352 33625 0	
☐ CONTINUUM Portia Da Costa	ISBN 0 352 33120 8	
☐ OPENING ACTS Suki Cunningham	ISBN 0 352 33630 7	
☐ FULL STEAM AHEAD Tabitha Flyte	ISBN 0 352 33637 4	
☐ A SECRET PLACE Ella Broussard	ISBN 0 352 33307 3	
☐ GAME FOR ANYTHING Lyn Wood	ISBN 0 352 33639 0	
☐ CHEAP TRICK Astrid Fox	ISBN 0 352 33640 4	
☐ THE GIFT OF SHAME Sara Hope-Walker	ISBN 0 352 32935 1	
☐ COMING UP ROSES Crystalle Valentino	ISBN 0 352 33658 7	
☐ GOING TOO FAR Laura Hamilton	ISBN 0 352 33657 9	

BLACK LACE BOOKS WITH AN HISTORICAL SETTING

BLACK LACE ANTHOLOGIES

BLACK LACE NON-FICTION

To find out the latest information about Black Lace titles, check out the website: www.blacklace-books.co.uk or send for a booklist with complete synopses by writing to:

Black Lace Booklist, Virgin Books Ltd
Thames Wharf Studios
Rainville Road
London W6 9HA

Please include an SAE of decent size. Please note only British stamps are valid.

Our privacy policy
We will not disclose information you supply us to any other parties. We will not disclose any information which identifies you personally to any person without your express consent.

From time to time we may send out information about Black Lace books and special offers. Please tick here if you do <u>not</u> wish to receive Black Lace information. ❑

Please send me the books I have ticked above.

Name ....

Address ....

....

....

....

Post Code ....

Send to: Virgin Books Cash Sales, Thames Wharf Studios, Rainville Road, London W6 9HA.

US customers: for prices and details of how to order books for delivery by mail, call 1-800-343-4499.

Please enclose a cheque or postal order, made payable to Virgin Books Ltd, to the value of the books you have ordered plus postage and packing costs as follows:

UK and BFPO – £1.00 for the first book, 50p for each subsequent book.

Overseas (including Republic of Ireland) – £2.00 for the first book, £1.00 for each subsequent book.

If you would prefer to pay by VISA, ACCESS/MASTERCARD, DINERS CLUB, AMEX or SWITCH, please write your card number and expiry date here:

....

Signature ....

Please allow up to 28 days for delivery.